November
Blues

For my children,
Wendy, Damon, Cory, and Crystal

ALSO BY SHARON M. DRAPER

Copper Sun
The Battle of Jericho
Double Dutch
Romiette & Julio

The Hazelwood High Trilogy:
Tears of a Tiger
Forged by Fire
Darkness Before Dawn

November
Blues

SHARON M. DRAPER

Atheneum Books for Young Readers
NEW YORK   LONDON   TORONTO   SYDNEY

Atheneum Books for Young Readers • An imprint of Simon & Schuster Children's Publishing Division • 1230 Avenue of the Americas, New York, New York 10020 • This book is a work of fiction. Any references to historical events, real people, or real locales are used fictitiously. Other names, characters, places, and incidents are products of the author's imagination, and any resemblance to actual events or locales or persons, living or dead, is entirely coincidental. • Copyright © 2007 by Sharon M. Draper • All rights reserved, including the right of reproduction in whole or in part in any form. • Book design by O'Lanso Gabbidon • The text for this book is set in Trade Gothic. • Manufactured in the United States of America • 10 9 8
Library of Congress Cataloging-in-Publication Data • Draper, Sharon M. (Sharon Mills) • November blues / Sharon Draper. — 1st ed. • p.   cm. • Summary: A teenaged boy's death in a hazing accident has lasting effects on his pregnant girlfriend and his guilt-ridden cousin, who gives up a promising music career to play football during his senior year in high school. • ISBN-13: 978-1-4169-0698-8 • ISBN-10: 1-4169-0698-3 • [1. Pregnancy—Fiction. 2. High schools—Fiction. 3. Schools—Fiction. 4. African Americans—Fiction.] I. Title. • PZ7.D78325No 2007 • [Fic]—dc22 • 2006101343 • "You Are My Sunshine" by Jimmie Davis © 1940 by Peer International Corporation. Copyright Renewed. Used by Permission. All Rights Reserved.

CHAPTER 1
NOVEMBER NELSON
TUESDAY, MARCH 30

NOVEMBER NELSON LURCHED TO THE BATH- room, feeling faint and not quite in control of her suddenly unsteady legs. She touched her forehead and found it warm and glazed with sweat. Sinking down on the soft blue rug in front of the toilet, she was grateful for the momentary stability of the floor. But her head continued to spin, and her stomach churned. She lifted the toilet lid, gazed into the water, and wished she could disappear into its depths. Her breath became more shallow, and her nausea more intense. Finally, uncontrollably, and forcefully, all her distress erupted and she lost her lunch in heaves and waves of vomiting. Pepperoni pizza.

She flushed the toilet several times as she sat on the floor waiting to feel normal again. Finally she stood up shakily, gargled with peppermint mouthwash, and peered at herself in the mirror.

"You look like a hot mess," she whispered to her reflection.

Her skin, instead of its usual coppery brown, looked gray and mottled. She hadn't combed her hair all day, so it was a halo of tangles.

November knew her mother would be home soon and would be angry to find out she'd skipped school. She didn't care. Her thoughts were focused on the package in her backpack. Even though she knew the house was empty, she made sure the bathroom door was locked. She dug the little purple and pink box out of her book bag and placed it on the sink. It seemed out of place in her mother's perfectly coordinated powder blue bathroom.

With trembling hands she unwrapped the plastic and opened the box. She read the directions carefully. She looked out of the small bathroom window and watched the last of the early spring snow melting on the grass. Everything looked the same, but she knew in her heart that it was all different now.

November finally turned back to the little white tube in the box and followed the instructions, which were written, she noticed, in Spanish and French as well. Three minutes later the indicator silently screamed the news that she already suspected. She was pregnant.

"I BROUGHT YOUR HOMEWORK, GIRL,"
Dana announced as she bounded through
the front door. "Whew! It's cold out there.
Calendar says spring, but the weather doesn't
seem to know that." She shivered and tossed
her coat on the sofa.

"Thanks," said November quietly. "Did I
miss much?"

"Same old junk. Busywork. The chemistry
might kick your butt, but everything else is pretty
easy. You got anything to eat? I just left the library
and I'm starved."

The thought of food made November instantly
queasy, but she heated up a bowl of her mother's
spaghetti in the microwave for Dana. "Dig in," November said as she fished for a spoon in the silverware
drawer and slid the bowl across the table.

"Aren't you gonna eat?" asked Dana. "Your mom makes
the best pasta in the world!"

"I already ate," November lied. She picked at a crumb on the table.

"What's wrong, November?" her friend asked, cocking her head.

"Nothing. Just thinking about Josh, I guess."

"Still hurts deep, doesn't it?" Dana said, reaching for November's arm.

"You don't know the half of it," replied November.

"Well, let's see what we can do to make you feel better. You ever heard of a brush and comb?" Dana teased.

November chuckled and ran her hands through her hair. "I didn't feel like messing with it today. I stayed in bed and watched game shows and soap operas. Talk about depressing!"

Dana finished her spaghetti, put her bowl in the sink, and said, "Let me braid your hair for you. That'll make you feel better."

November grinned, went to get her hair stuff from her bedroom, and returned to sit on a pillow in front of the sofa. "You're gonna need magic fingers," she said, handing Dana a comb.

Dana turned on the CD player, and the two girls sat in silence in the living room, while Dana deftly combed November's hair. November could feel some of the tension leave her back and neck as her friend worked.

"Josh used to like your hair braided, remember? He'd call you his African queen," Dana said softly.

"Yeah, he was always makin' up stuff like that." November sighed. She shifted her weight on the cushion.

"It's gotta be hard to lose somebody you love," said Dana.

"I don't know how you deal with it, girlfriend. I'd go crazy if anything ever happened to Kofi."

Despite the music, silence filled the room. "I never really loved Josh," November whispered to the floor.

Dana stopped in mid-braid. "What did you say, girl?"

"I never really loved Josh," November repeated, her voice full of regret. "I know I *said* I loved him. Isn't that what you're supposed to say when you're going out with somebody?" And then she started to cry.

"Girl, you trippin'," Dana said as she put the comb and brush on the table. Fine strands of dark brown fuzzy hair laced the teeth of the comb. She sat down next to November and put her arm around her friend's shaking shoulders.

November pulled a tissue out of her pocket and blew her nose. "I'm for real. I never told anybody this before."

"But . . . but you two always seemed to be so happy together," Dana exclaimed. "Lots of kids at school envied the two of you because it seemed so deep, so real."

"Josh made me laugh. He was so much fun to be with—always cracking jokes and acting silly. But I don't know if that's enough to be called love."

"He was the most lovable, craziest kid I ever met, that's for sure," Dana said with a smile. "Remember when he rode on all the kiddie rides at Kings Island? His legs were sticking way up over the edge, and he kept telling the ride operator that he never wanted to forget what it felt like to be six."

"That's what I mean," November said, her face a frown of confusion. "I'm all about helping disabled kids learn to walk, or teaching a second grader how to read. Josh was always just looking for the next joke, the next laugh. He didn't have a serious bone in his body."

Dana looked November in the eye. "So why did you stay with him?"

"Be for real! Josh was fine and he was fun. But I'm sixteen years old! I just wanted to have a good time—I didn't want to marry him or anything." She sighed. "Isn't having a boyfriend just what happens in high school—like doing math homework or going to dances or buying new shoes?"

"I don't know. I never really thought about it. Kofi makes me tingle when he touches me. I guess that's love."

November tried again to explain herself. "The girls at school say they love somebody until he makes them mad, or they find somebody better to love, and then they move on. You don't plan to marry the dudes or have them in your life forever. You just say 'I love you,' enjoy the juicy feelings while they last, then you go your separate ways. Sometimes it hurts, and sometimes you're just glad it's over."

"This is heavy, November," Dana said quietly. "Maybe you're just overreacting to all that's happened. Maybe you miss him so much that you're just saying this to help you get over all the hurt—you know—'cause he's gone." She looked at her friend with concern.

"No, it's more than that." November picked up the comb and began slapping it in her hand. "Don't get me wrong—for a while I really did think I loved him. I figured that love meant going out on dates and getting dressed up and making out in the backseat of somebody's car."

"That's what me and Kofi do," Dana admitted.

"I loved being with him. But I didn't love him—not deep down inside where those feelings are supposed to be."

"But that's okay, November. That's no reason for you to feel guilty."

"Josh died exactly two months ago today," said November sadly.

"I know. It seems like his funeral was just yesterday. I miss him so much."

"I do too. But everybody treats me like the broken-hearted girlfriend. I feel like . . . a fake."

"You two had been together for a couple of years, right?"

November nodded. "But now that he's gone, everybody seems to be expecting me to feel something that just isn't there—at least the ones who still talk to me."

"What're you sayin'?"

"Kids treat me funny—like they don't know what to say or something. It's like death is a bad word, so they pretend like they're in a hurry and book out of there instead of talkin' to me."

"Don't let them stress you, November. Soon enough, when more time's gone by, people will start to treat you like before, and let you get on with your life."

"Somehow I have a feeling that's not going to happen." November began pulling hairs from the comb, tears spilling down her cheeks.

"Girl, what's wrong with you? What do you care about what people think about you and Josh? It's none of their business, anyway!"

"My life is a mess, Dana," November said deliberately.

"You flunk that chemistry test that O'Brian gave us last week?"

"No. I'm pretty sure I got most of the questions right."

"Your mother sweatin' you about your clothes?"

"No. Actually, she gave me some money to buy clothes just last week. Mama deals with stress—my problems and hers, too—by spending money."

"I'll switch mothers with you any day!" Dana said with a grin. "So what's wrong? You look like you just found out they're gonna quit making chocolate chip ice cream."

November took a deep breath and looked directly at her friend. "I'm pregnant."

CHAPTER 3
TUESDAY, MARCH 30

DANA GASPED. "SHUT UP!" THEN SHE whispered, "Are you *sure*?"

November nodded, her eyes welling again. "I bought one of those home pregnancy tests, and it came out positive. I didn't want to believe it, but there's no mistake."

Neither girl spoke for a moment. The CD played in the background—pounding bass rhythms and a soulful singer wailing about hot love. Finally Dana asked quietly, "Josh?"

November stared at her. "Dana! Who else?"

"Oh, girl, this is so messed up. You wanna talk about it?" Dana hugged November tightly.

November began slowly. "I'm pretty sure it happened the night before he died. It had been a while since we had, like, you know, fooled around." She kept her head down. "Josh was so excited about finally getting into the Warriors of Distinction. We decided to celebrate that Thursday night, even though the formal induction wasn't until Friday."

"You must have really partied hard," Dana said carefully.

"Not really. We talked and laughed and ate pizza and chicken wings until three in the morning—right there in his basement—in the rec room of his house. Then we stopped talking and started kissing, and . . . well, usually we're better prepared, but this time things just got out of hand. It wasn't anything either of us planned. Everything just started feeling really mellow and we just rode the wave."

"Did you think about . . . ," Dana began.

"I didn't think at all. It was like everything was swirled with color and I was, like, seeing all these different shades dazzling around me."

"You make it sound like it was pretty cool that night."

November shrugged. "You know what?"

"What, girl?"

November looked away from her friend. "I think it's overrated," she admitted quietly. "When the colors faded and reality came back, I felt, I don't know, like, disappointed or something, like it didn't really mean anything."

"What do you mean?" Dana asked gently.

November frowned, trying to make sense of her jumbled thoughts. "You know when you're a kid and you put together those jigsaw puzzles?"

"Yeah."

"Well, I always felt like a piece was missing—that big crooked one in the front that all the others connect to. You feel me?"

Dana nodded.

"When you look at movies, it seems like the actors feel some kind of magic when they make love—with violins and pretty music playing. All I ever heard was creaking springs. It was really pretty pathetic."

"What does 'make love' mean, anyway?" Dana asked, frowning. "Seems to me love is something you ought to feel, not make."

"Would loving him have made a difference?" November asked bleakly.

Dana had no answer.

November put her hands to her face and wept again. "What am I supposed to do with a baby?"

Dana let her cry for a few minutes. Then, when November seemed to have calmed down a little, Dana began brushing her friend's hair again in the uncomfortable silence that followed.

"Have you told your mother?" she asked finally.

"No. Just you."

"What will she say?"

"She scheduled me to go on the Black College Tour in a couple of months. That's all she talks about these days— college and majors and tuition and stuff. This is gonna kill her. And then she's gonna kill me!"

"That didn't make any sense, but I'm not gonna argue with a pregnant woman!" Dana said in a teasing tone.

But the words seemed to sober November. "I'm no woman, Dana. I'm just a kid. I don't know how to raise a child. I don't think I can!"

"So you think you're going to keep the baby?"

November looked up. "I guess. What else can I do?"

"There are lots of options, you know," Dana said tentatively.

"No. I can't go there. But the kid deserves better than me," November replied.

"What do you think Josh's parents will say when they find out?" Dana suddenly asked.

November looked startled. "I never even thought about them! What would they care?"

"November, Josh was their only child! I have a feeling they would be real interested in a potential grandchild."

"It's none of their business," November said, her jaw set. "This is my problem. I'll figure it out somehow." But she knew she was just spouting words. She had no idea what that meant.

That night November shivered as she curled up in bed with her Big Bird stuffed toy that she'd gotten when she was five. She would never let her friends know she still slept with a stuffed animal, but Josh had known. He'd even bought her a little green Kermit the Frog for her birthday last year. When she'd asked him why Kermit, Josh had said, "The frog can keep the bird company while you're at school, and besides, it will drive Miss Piggy crazy with jealousy!"

They'd giggled and pretended and figured they'd have forever to laugh together. But they didn't. Kermit was still around to keep Big Bird company, but November knew *she* was now on her own. She cuddled the well-worn toy and cried herself to sleep.

AS SHE RODE THE SCHOOL BUS THE NEXT morning, which she hated because she figured she ought to be driving to school by now, November looked out the grimy window and recalled how the local papers and television stations had covered the story of Josh's death. Even CNN had broadcast it, the reporters shaking their heads at teenage foolishness.

"The death of sixteen-year-old Joshua Prescott has rocked Frederick Douglass High School to its core," a reporter had cried that Saturday from his post in front of the school, she remembered. They were filming the informal student memorial assembly for Josh. "Young Prescott had been pledging for a school club called the Warriors of Distinction, a highly reputable, long-established organization known for its good deeds in the community. The dark, deadly secrets of the club, however, have become horribly apparent." November knew she'd never forget how oddly excited the journalists looked, like scavengers after a kill.

One particularly pushy reporter, with her hair so heavily sprayed it didn't budge in those January winds, had spotted November and jammed her microphone into November's face while signaling to her cameraman to record.

November had tried to avoid her, hurrying to the corner to catch a bus home, praying it would come soon. Her eyes were swollen from crying, and she had tried to keep her back to the camera, but the reporter had been determined. "Aren't you Joshua Prescott's girlfriend? We're very sorry for your loss, but—"

"You're not sorry for my loss," November had interrupted. "People say that all the time. It doesn't mean anything."

The reporter, undaunted, had continued, "You're right, young lady. So, let me ask you—are you angry that the club made him perform that deadly stunt?"

"No, I'm angry that you're asking me dumb questions!" November had responded, thinking back to how she and her girlfriends had been thrilled that their dudes were going to be in such a hot club, with hookups to parties every weekend and cool privileges like keys to the teachers' workroom at school.

"Did Joshua share with you any of the dangerous activities the Warriors of Distinction were involved in? Why didn't you try to stop him?"

November stared at her, incredulous. "How was I supposed to know? It was just supposed to be stupid high school fun," she had replied, trying again to walk away. But the reporter, and her cameraman, had followed her.

The reporter continued speaking to the camera. "Only club members and pledges knew of the secrets the Warriors of Distinction hid. Not until Prescott's untimely death did the community find out what really went on." Excitement rose in her voice. "New members had been made to undergo a series of hazing rituals that included having their heads flushed in a toilet, being dragged around on leashes like dogs, and, on the final night, jumping from a second-story window."

"Please, leave me alone!" November had begged. The close-up of her crying had appeared on every major news outlet the next morning.

The reporter turned back to the camera. "Fourteen of the fifteen pledges survived Friday night's 'Leap of Faith,' as it was called. Eleventh-grader Joshua Prescott did not." The reporter kept talking. November had run back into the school and had called her mother to pick her up.

The Warriors of Distinction had been abolished by the school board shortly after Josh's death, as November knew it probably would be; the club's faculty adviser had been fired; and at least one of the members, Eddie Mahoney, had received some jail time. Everybody at school felt that Eddie got what was coming to him. He was a nasty piece of work. His cruel comments had made more than a few students miserable. None of this had changed the outcome of that horrible night, as far as November was concerned, but it seemed to put a little salve on the deeply felt wounds of the school.

November hurried off the bus and into the school building. The fumes from the school bus made her feel ill. Even though it was almost April, the air was crisp and chilly, and she shivered as she walked into the main hall. A picture of Josh, the frame trimmed in black, still hung prominently near the main office. She automatically turned her head away so she wouldn't have to see that infectious smile, those eyes that crinkled mischievously. Josh was the only person she knew whose school picture had actually captured his personality.

She went to her locker, got her books out for the morning, and tried to get her thoughts together. She regretted the blueberry yogurt granola bar she'd eaten on the school bus; her stomach was churning. Just as she closed her locker, she felt her stomach heave. She covered her mouth, rushed across the hall to the girls' bathroom, and made it to a stall just in time to throw up seemingly everything she had eaten since the third grade.

"You okay in there?" she heard a voice ask.

"Yeah, I'm fine," November managed to reply. "I got the flu. That's all." November wiped her mouth with toilet paper and leaned her head against the cool surface of the bathroom stall. The smell was horrible, even after she flushed.

"Stinks," the voice stated flatly.

"Why don't you mind your own business?" November replied angrily.

"I got breath mints if you need 'em," offered the voice.

"Just leave me alone," November pleaded. She heaved once more and gagged on nothing.

"You want me to call the nurse?"

"No, please don't. I'll be okay." November took a couple

of deep breaths and felt a little less queasy. "But thanks anyway." She glanced under the stall door and saw the ugliest pair of shoes she'd ever laid eyes on. They were scuffed gray leather with rounded toes and faded blue laces. She waited until she heard the girl's footsteps leave the bathroom, then opened the stall door. She looked in the mirror. She'd lost quite a bit of weight after Josh's death, and she looked thin, unhealthy, and weak.

"School mirrors always make you look bad, anyway." It was that voice again.

November whirled around, surprised that the girl had returned. The girl's large brown face, pulled taut by tightly braided cornrows, was peppered with acne. "Aren't you supposed to be in class?" November asked her.

"Aren't you?" the girl tossed back.

"I'm sick. I'm going home. What's your excuse?"

"I was worried about you."

November didn't know what to say to that. She looked at the girl suspiciously. Finally she asked, "Me? Why?"

"You sounded pretty bad in there. I wouldn't have slept tonight if you had dropped dead or something and I hadn't come back and tried to help you." The girl shrugged and tossed her book bag onto the floor.

November smiled thinly. "That's pretty cool of you. But I'll be okay."

"Whatever." The girl shrugged.

"You're, uh, Olivia, right?" November made a face, trying to remember the girl's last name. "I'm November Nelson."

"I know who you are. I'm in your first-bell American history class. Sergeant Fox, the king of worksheets and quizzes."

Embarrassed, November looked at the girl closely. "Uh, I'm sorry. I usually use that class to finish my morning nap."

"You should sit in the back like me. Easier to catch those z's." She smiled. "I'm Olivia Thigpen. An unfortunate name, I must admit, since I've had to endure stupid boys saying 'Oh-liv-in-a pigpen' as they made oinking sounds."

Olivia was noticeably overweight, but compact, as if her clothes had been neatly stuffed with extra substance. She wore a massive boy's football jersey that came down to her knees and a well-packed pair of blue jeans. And then there were those unfortunate-looking shoes. She wore no makeup on her cocoa brown face, and her very high cheekbones and dimples were things November could only wish for. She grinned at November warmly.

"Oh, yeah, I know you," November said weakly. But Olivia was one of those girls who sat in the back of every classroom, never joined in hallway conversations, never caused a scene or did anything to bring attention to herself, the type easily ignored by girls like November and Dana. "Aren't you in the band?" November asked. She vaguely remembered a concert her friend Jericho had once played in. She knew that Jericho, Josh's cousin and very best friend, grieved deeply for him as well. The two had been as close as brothers.

Olivia brightened. "Yeah! I play the tuba in concert band, but the sousaphone in marching band. Tubas aren't good for marching," she explained.

"I don't think I could handle either one," November

said frankly. "They're awfully big suckers to lug around."

"Yeah, but I do my best to keep a low profile. Well, as low as I can, seeing how I'm the biggest thing in the eleventh grade!" Changing tones, she added, "Everybody and their sister knows you, November. You the bomb, girl. You got millions of friends, and you used to go with Josh Prescott."

"The only thing you're right about is the Josh part," November replied. "It's hard to get over the fact that he's never coming back." She felt like she might cry.

"He was always nice to me, you know. In fifth grade, he knocked a boy down who was making fun of me, then he did a little jig on the boy's backpack. I'll never forget that."

"Yeah, that was Josh—making the world go 'round." November felt another wave of nausea and rushed back into the stall. The flushing toilet echoed loudly, to November's further embarrassment.

But Olivia said nothing when November reemerged from the stall. "You sure you don't need the nurse?" she finally asked.

"That little old lady can't help me," November replied sullenly. "By law all she's allowed to give out to kids are bandages and tissues and candy. She can't even slide anybody a cough drop, let alone an aspirin." She rinsed her face with cold water, while Olivia watched her silently.

"You're pregnant, aren't you?" Olivia finally asked bluntly.

November looked at Olivia in the mirror, astonished. "I don't know what you're talking about."

Olivia shrugged. "Forget I asked. It's none of my business, anyway." She picked up her bag to leave.

November suddenly felt the need to talk to someone, even an almost stranger like Olivia, and before she could stop herself, she put her hand out and touched the other girl. She glanced around the small bathroom, making sure no one else was in there with them. "You've got to promise not to tell anybody," she said, her voice low.

"Who's gonna listen to me, anyway?" Olivia replied with a shrug. Her look then turned serious. "But for real, girl, you know that this is the kind of secret you can only keep for a little while."

"I keep feeling like if I don't think about it, it won't be true, and everything will go back to like it used to be."

"Not gonna happen. You've got to deal with this. Have you seen a doctor?"

November blinked. "Oh, I couldn't. Not yet."

It was Olivia's turn to look astonished. "Well, that's stupid. You have to get yourself checked as early as possible. Don't you have a brother who's disabled or retarded or something?"

"How do you know that, and what business is it of yours, anyway?" November retorted, her voice hard with resentment.

"I couldn't care less. You gave a report in English class last year—remember? You talked about how you volunteered at Stepping Stones every summer, working with the handicapped kids, and how your brother's disability got you involved in the program."

"You remember that report?" November looked amazed.

"I can't help it, I never forget anything—it's a blessing and a curse. I can tell you what I had for dinner two months ago, and the lyrics to every single rap song ever produced—and that's a mouthful, I can tell you! I remember that report because you were, like, straight up—you know what I'm sayin'? Lots of folks don't like to talk about people in their family with mental or physical screwups."

November told her quietly, "His name is Augustus. We call him Gus."

"Born in August?"

November nodded.

"Your mama got issues with names, girlfriend."

November laughed. She took out her lipstick and tried to add a bit of color to her sallow face. "You got that right."

Olivia picked up her backpack again and slung it over one shoulder. "Well, I better get to class. If you need to talk, I'm here. I've been around the block more than you might expect. Here's my cell number."

November took the number and leaned against the bathroom wall. As she watched Olivia saunter out, she entered the number into her cell phone. She thought about the girl's unexpected kindness; then, for no reason she could explain, she started to cry. She slid down to the cold concrete floor and sat there sobbing until the bell rang.

"HOW'S IT GOING, JERICHO?" JERICHO looked up from digging for a book in his locker. It was Mr. Tambori, his music teacher.

"I'm hangin'," Jericho mumbled, turning back around. He dug in his locker again, pulled out his history book, and avoided the music teacher's eyes.

"It's been a couple of months since you've come for your trumpet lesson. Are you ready to start up again? I still have every Wednesday at three o'clock free just for you if you'd like to try loosening up the keys a little."

"I don't even know where my trumpet is, man."

"The trumpet you named 'Zora' and carried around with you twenty-four/seven? I have a feeling you know exactly where it is."

Jericho sighed. "I tossed it under my bed a couple of weeks after Josh's funeral. I guess it's still there. When I look at it, all I can think about is Josh and how he's never gonna hear music again. And I just can't put it to my lips. I'm too big to be cryin'."

Mr. Tambori put his hand gently on Jericho's shoulder. "I understand, son. I really do."

Jericho twisted away from the teacher's touch. "No, you don't. Don't nobody know how I feel!"

"You can't blame yourself, Jericho," Mr. Tambori said, kindness and patience in his voice. But Jericho didn't want kindness.

"Then who, Mr. T?" demanded Jericho. "I told him to jump. I cheered him on, then stood there like a fool and watched him die. I will *never* forgive myself."

"Music will help you work this out, Jericho. Let your trumpet speak for you. Give Zora a chance."

"I know what you tryin' to say, Mr. T, and I appreciate it. For real I do," Jericho said. "But right now every day I feel like I got rocks in my gut. I need more than music. I need Josh back."

Mr. Tambori nodded. "The music will be there when you're ready, Jericho. I know jazz is your specialty, but you know your place in the marching band next year is always there for you." He hesitated a moment, then added, "Maybe the necessary precision and strict rules will add a bit of order to your life. We need your talent, Jericho."

"I'll think about it, Mr. T," Jericho said as he hoisted his book bag on his back. "But the football coach has been talking to me about coming out for the team. Maybe I need a change. All I'd have to do is sweat and run and tackle."

"Football?" Mr. Tambori asked, sounding shocked. "Have you ever played before?"

"I played all through middle school—defensive end. Actually, I was pretty good, but I got lazy. Coach has been after me since I got here in ninth grade, but I always blew him off. But I'm six-three and I weigh two-sixty, man. All the dudes on the team tell me they could use me on the line."

"Make sure you're making your decisions for the right reasons, Jericho," the teacher warned.

"Ain't nothin' right these days, man. Nothin' at all," Jericho said sadly as he walked away.

JERICHO PUSHED THROUGH THE CROWDED
hallway, head down, a scowl on his face.
He went to school because it was required,
because it kept him busy, because it was a
break from sitting at home every day feeling
sorry for himself. But he rarely smiled, said as
little as possible to teachers and friends, and
kept his grief bottled up inside him. Some days
he felt like he would implode.

Then, as he stormed down the corridor, he
heard a familiar lilting laugh, and, in spite of himself, his heart did a flip-flop and he looked up
hopefully. Arielle Gresham, dressed in bright green
leggings and a matching top that flowed as she
walked, was heading in his direction. She held hands
with Logan Holbrook, giggling as he whispered something in her ear.

Logan was not only captain of the basketball team, but
also had his own singing group, which, rumor had it, might

be offered a recording contract. He had an after-school job during the off season, and he always seemed to have a pocket full of money. When the Warriors of Distinction had had their toy drive last year, Logan had donated a hundred dollars to the club to buy gifts for the poor. He walked with a confident athleticism that Jericho could only envy.

Arielle, who'd been Jericho's girlfriend until the horrible events of two months ago, looked directly at him but acted as if he were one of the dull brown lockers that lined the wall. She then purposely gazed up at Logan and whispered something while pointing at Jericho, and they both exploded with gales of laughter. Jericho could still hear them laughing as they disappeared down the hall.

With his mood even blacker than before, he pulled his hoodie over his head and trudged down the hall to his class. He didn't notice the girl coming the opposite way until he had collided with her. Her books flew out of her arms. "Watch where you goin'!" he yelled at her, trying to regain his balance.

"You're the one who's walking like an armed bulldozer!" she replied. "I was trying to get out of your way. What war are you fighting?" She rubbed her shoulder.

Jericho looked at her sharply. "Oh, hey, Olivia. I'm sorry. I didn't mean to hurt nobody. I just got a lotta stuff on my mind." He helped her pick up her books.

"Like Arielle and Logan?"

Jericho gave her a look. "You don't miss much, do you?"

"I saw them a few minutes ago, headed this way, stuck together like waffles and syrup. She dis you?"

"Every chance she gets," Jericho admitted, allowing himself a rueful smile.

"Give it up, my man. Girls like Arielle are like champagne bubbles—light, sparkly, and full of nothing!" She smiled at her own joke. "And dudes like Logan . . ." She paused and frowned. "Nothin' but caramel-covered vomit."

"Hey, remind me never to get on your bad side. But you're right. How you know so much, Olivia?"

"I just see stuff. When we have our class reunion in ten years, I'll be the one who'll be able to remember everybody's secrets from high school."

"If they realize that, you might not be invited," Jericho said.

"Hah! They probably won't invite me anyway! I'll be the one they forget about, the one whose address gets lost, the one nobody cares didn't show up."

"Talk about dissin' somebody—why you always comin' down on yourself?"

"It's easier if I do it first," she replied quietly.

"You gonna do marching band again next year?" Jericho asked, to change the subject.

"Probably. Tambori is cool, and I love my sousaphone. Walking around with that big old thing strapped on makes me feel powerful!"

"And tired?"

Olivia laughed. "Wimps like you play the trumpet. You gotta be tough to handle a tuba or a sousaphone! What about you? You know Tambori be drooling over somebody who's actually got skills with an instrument. Most kids show up in the band with just a horn, a big grin, and no idea how hot those uniforms can get when you're marching."

"Yeah, I know," Jericho replied. He suddenly felt he couldn't meet her eyes. "But I may go out for football this year instead," he finally admitted.

"Talk about wimping out! You want to join the crew of the giant sloths?"

"Hey, don't be talkin' 'bout my boys, now," Jericho told her with a laugh. "They eat rocks for breakfast and rip their pillows to shreds before they go to bed at night."

"Sounds like a bunch of Neanderthals to me! You sure you want to be a part of that?"

"I need a change. I need to hurt something, hit something—you feel me?"

"Yeah, actually, I do. Hang in there, Jericho. I better get to class." She started down the hall.

"Hey, Olivia!" Jericho called.

"Yeah?" she replied, turning.

"Thanks."

"For what?"

"Knocking some sense into me. I needed that."

"If I remember correctly, you were the one who knocked *me* down," she replied, grinning.

"Maybe I should do that more often!"

"Don't even think about it!" Olivia disappeared into the thinning throng of students.

"HI, SWEETIE, I'M GLAD YOU'RE HOME already. Did you have a good day at school today?" November's mother, an eighth-grade art teacher, breezed into the living room carrying the day's mail. Her hair, which she wore softly blow-dried, fluffy, and long, seemed to float along with her orange-and-red-hued African caftan in one fluid movement. She tossed the stack of envelopes on the telephone table and reached over to turn on her satellite radio. Soft blues music filled the room.

November sat curled on the sofa, sipping on a diet cola. She held the TV remote in her other hand, mindlessly flipping through the stations. She barely looked at her mother. "Yeah," she mumbled.

"Don't you do tutoring at the YMCA on Friday afternoons?" asked her mother.

"I didn't feel like going."

"That's not like you. What's that kid's name—Neelie—

who you're so fond of? You spend so much time down there that little girl must think you're her other mama!" Mrs. Nelson teased. "Won't she miss you this week?"

"I guess," November said as she stared at a woman selling pearls on the home shopping channel.

"What's wrong, November? Are you coming down with something?" Her mother looked concerned.

"I'm fine. Just a little tired. I think I'll go take a nap." November clicked off the television.

"You know, I just read in the paper that there's a big sale at Macy's. Why don't you and I go shopping tomorrow? We could take a look at a pair of those new slim jeans you've been wanting."

November looked at her mother as if she had suggested a brain transplant, and, even though she hadn't really meant to, she exploded. "You are so shallow, Mom! Why is it whenever something isn't quite right you have to fix it with something trifling like shopping? Maybe I don't want any skinny jeans!"

"What on earth has come over you?" her mother replied, looking both hurt and angry—a combination look that only mothers know how to do, November thought glumly. "I'll not have you talking to me like that. If you don't want to go, just say so."

November looked down at the pale blue carpet. "I'm sorry," she mumbled, her anger disappearing like an extinguished flame. "I just don't feel good today."

"It's always fun shopping with you, November," her mother said. "You know it's not what we buy, but the walking through the mall together, talking about some of the outrageous outfits people show up in, eating cheesecake in the food court. Maybe we need a day like that real soon."

"Yeah, you're right." November brightened a little. "I'll never forget how you used to surprise me by coming and getting me out of middle school at lunchtime to take in a movie matinee and a shopping trip."

"Highly improper and loads of fun!" Her mother laughed. "I'd tell my school secretary, and then the secretary at your school, that you had a doctor's appointment—and we'd blow the day on each other!"

"I hope I can be as good a mom as you are," November said quietly. "I don't think I could have survived what you did, Mom—all the bad stuff—I'm not strong like you."

Her mother reached over and gave her daughter a hug. "Years from now, when you finish college and get married and are ready to think about starting a family, you will be an outstanding mother. I'm sure of it."

November twisted out of her mother's embrace. "Maybe not."

Mrs. Nelson touched her daughter's forehead. "You do feel a little clammy. Are you sure you aren't getting sick?"

"I might be. Those kids at the YMCA are always wiping their runny noses around me. Maybe I picked up a bug or something." November stood up. "I'm going to bed early, okay?"

"I think that's a good idea." Mrs. Nelson picked up the mail then and sifted through it carelessly, tossing sales catalogs directly into the trash. She stopped abruptly and inhaled as she read the return address on the business-size white envelope. "November! The letter from Cornell is here!" she said, her voice sounding a little shaky.

November, instead of jumping up with excitement as she knew her mother expected, simply shrugged. "It's no big deal—it's just the information about the Cornell program."

"Of course it is!" her mother insisted, holding the letter as if she was dancing with it to the beat of the music on the radio. "You've been so excited about this! Open it! Open it!"

November took the letter and looked at it without smiling, without comment. She ripped the edge of the envelope, tapped it on the coffee table, and the single sheet of folded paper inside fell out. Her mother, still dancing with excitement, hovered closely. November picked up the letter, unfolded it, and read it out loud in an expressionless voice. "We are pleased to announce," she began, "that you have been accepted in the Cornell University Summer College. Welcome to what could be the most personally rewarding, academically enriching, and socially exciting summer of your life." November stopped, then let the letter fall to the floor.

Her mother whooped with joy. She picked up the letter, and did another little dance in the middle of the living room, her face aglow with pride. "I knew you'd get this, baby girl. This is going to get you into an Ivy League school! I'm so proud of you I could just pop! Wait till I call all my friends! Now for sure we're going shopping. This is the best news in the world!"

November, still oddly quiet, nodded her head in agreement. "Yeah, it is." She paused, then added, "There's nothing in the letter about a scholarship, Mom. How are we gonna pay for it? This program is almost five thousand dollars for just three weeks. Maybe I better not go."

"I'll get a summer job! We'll apply for a loan! We'll figure it out and make it happen, baby girl!" her mother said happily. "You're on your way." She waltzed over to November and pulled her up to join her silly dance, but November pulled away.

"What's wrong, November?" Her mother asked. "Did you change your mind about Cornell? You can still go to Howard or Hampton, you know. You can do anything you want—that's what's so cool about being the smartest kid in high school."

"I know, Mom. It's really good news." November forced her face to smile. "I know it doesn't seem like it, but I really am excited. Honest. I just don't feel good today."

"You run upstairs and get a nap, sweetie, and I'll go down to the drugstore and make a million copies of this letter! I'm sending one to everybody we know."

"It's just Cornell, Mom, not the Pearly Gates. Get a grip." Her mother's cheerfulness was starting to get on November's nerves.

"Well, who put salt in your cornflakes today?" her mother replied, an edge to her voice.

"Nobody. I'm sorry, Mom. It really is cool." As she headed up the stairs to her room, November turned and asked her mother, "Why do you think so many bad things have happened to us, Mom? Gus is all messed up. Daddy's gone. My boyfriend dies on me. Why us, Mom?"

"You just got accepted to an elite Ivy League college

summer program, November! Your future is full of wonderful possibilities. Focus on the good stuff instead of the bad," her mother suggested as she adjusted the volume on the radio. "Maybe that's why I play the blues every day. All that bad stuff is in the past, and I put all that pain in a box on a very high shelf. Maybe the blues can help you, too."

"Doubt it," November mumbled.

"All I know to do is focus on you and what a great kid you are. I'm really proud of you, baby girl," her mother told her. "You are my heart and my joy, November. You make me happy to get up each morning."

"Shut up with all that crap, Mom! Just quit!" cried November, unable to bear it. "You sound like one of those drugstore greeting cards!" She ran to her room and slammed the door, leaving her mother stunned and silent.

AFTER A NIGHT OF TOSSING AND TURNING, November got up early and told her mother she'd be gone all day, working at the YMCA book fair. Her mother gave her some spending money and promised roast beef for dinner when she got home. November hugged her mom, apologized for her outburst the night before, and hurried out of the house.

After talking to Olivia, November had made an appointment at the office of a lady doctor she had never visited before. She had picked the name out of the phone book. November walked down to the corner and got on the bus that would take her downtown. She felt queasy and hoped she could manage the bus ride without being sick. Fortunately, the bus was almost empty. She felt completely alone. She tried not to think about anything—not about what the doctor might say, not about tomorrow, not about the next few months.

When November got to the office, she was asked to fill out lots of paperwork full of questions about her general health, her family's health background—*pretty awful*, she thought to herself—and information about medical insurance. She had copied the number off the card in her mom's wallet. She wondered how long it would take for her mother to get the bill and figure out what was going on.

Finally she was taken to a small room and given a paper gown to put on. On the end of the examining table were funny-looking footrests. She'd seem them in movies, and she shuddered when she realized their purpose. Tuneless music played from somewhere in the ceiling, and a photo of a mother duck and her ducklings crossing the street decorated one wall. Otherwise the room was white and sterile and very cold.

A woman walked briskly into the room. "Good morning. I'm Dr. Holland," she announced. She had long, gray-black braids tucked under a scarf, and the smoothest taffy-colored skin November had ever seen. The doctor had a warmth about her that made November instantly relax—she seemed motherly and professional all in one package.

"Hi. I'm November."

"That's an unusual name. I like that. I think a name ought to stand out and be bold. My first name is Obioma. It's a Nigerian name that means 'kind and caring.'"

"Well, I hope you are—kind and caring, that is. I'm in big trouble," November said quietly.

"You want to tell me about it?" asked the doctor gently.

November looked up at the woman and began. "Looks like I got myself pregnant."

"All by yourself?" The doctor smiled kindly.

November felt stupid. She couldn't even talk straight, let alone think. "No, of course not. My boyfriend was . . ." She didn't know what else to say.

"He's not around anymore?" the doctor asked.

"No." November didn't go into details. She bowed her head.

Dr. Holland scribbled something on the chart, then took November's blood pressure and listened to her heart. "Have you talked to your mother?" the doctor asked.

"No, ma'am."

"Will she be understanding?" The doctor motioned for November to lie down on the paper-covered table.

"Not a chance. She'll roll over and die." The ceiling was cracked, November noticed.

"She might surprise you. And you're going to have to tell her eventually," Dr. Holland said.

"That's what my friends tell me," November replied glumly.

"When was your last period?" the doctor asked as she adjusted the lights at the end of the table.

Instead of answering, November said, "I know when it happened."

The doctor looked mildly surprised. "You're absolutely sure of the date?"

"Yes, ma'am. It was January twenty-ninth."

"You're sure about that?"

"It was the night before my boyfriend died."

Dr. Holland inhaled sharply. "How did he lose his life, child?"

"Stupidity. He jumped out of a window." Fury coursed through November, and she balled her hands into fists.

"Say what? You poor child. What was his name?"

"Joshua Prescott."

"Hmm. Was that the young man who died over at Douglass High School in that school club accident? I saw it on the news."

"Yes, ma'am. That was Josh."

"Such a shame." She shook her head and gently placed her warm hand over November's cold and trembling one.

November, trying not to cry, nodded in thanks for that small gesture of understanding.

"Well, let's examine you and we'll take our time and discuss all your options," Dr. Holland said then. "You have nothing to be afraid of. I'm going to take good care of you, okay?"

November nodded and let herself be examined. She was glad she had chosen a woman doctor. She figured having this exam done by a male gynecologist would be a little like getting a car checked by somebody who had never owned a car.

The whole examination was incredibly embarrassing. She had to put her feet into those footrest things—the doctor called them stirrups. *Isn't that what you use when you ride a horse?* November thought. The effect was the same—her legs were spread wide apart. The doctor began inserting a cold metal examining tool into the most private part of her body. Even though she was covered by a paper sheet, November felt nasty as the doctor palpated her belly and checked her rectum.

"Sit up, dear, put your clothes on so you'll be warm and comfortable—I know it's like a refrigerator in here—and let's talk. I'll see you in my office in five minutes."

November, terrified of what the woman would say, hurriedly got dressed and found her way down the hall to Dr. Holland's office, which was decorated with dozens of pictures of laughing, smiling babies. She relaxed a little as the doctor sat down.

"You're almost three months pregnant, November," Dr. Holland said without preamble.

November inhaled quickly, even though she already knew. This was the official confirmation. "Is my baby okay?" she whispered.

"As far as I can tell right now, yes, of course. But a healthy baby needs good prenatal care. You shouldn't have waited so long to see me, and you must promise me you will return every month for checkups."

"I promise." November felt like a preschooler being scolded by her teacher. How could she feel like such a child when her body was acting like an adult? "How big is it?" she finally asked.

The doctor smiled. "About the size and weight of four quarters in your hand."

"That small?" November exclaimed.

The doctor nodded. "Would you like me to walk you through the story of your child's life to this point?" she offered.

"Yes, please. I thought I knew all this stuff from health class, but . . . it didn't seem like info I'd need for . . ."

"I hear you. Okay, so, according to what you told me,

somewhere around January twenty-ninth, a ripened egg burst out of your ovary. Several hundred million of Josh's sperm headed for that egg. A couple hundred survived the trip. But just one of those bad boys got through."

November tried to suppress a giggle. Somehow the doctor's description sounded just like something Josh would say.

Dr. Holland continued, "As soon as the winner sperm broke through your egg's membrane, the rest of them gave up and went home. And in that instant, your baby's sex and skin color and hair color was determined."

"For real? Just like that? It's already a boy or a girl?"

"Yes. And it's already destined to have sandy brown hair or copper-colored skin, or whatever coloring it will end up with."

"I had no idea," November said in amazement. "Then what happened?"

"By the end of February, that fertilized egg had divided lots of times. Then it connected itself to the wall of your uterus—a safe, soft resting place."

"So why do I feel sick all the time?"

"Your body is adjusting to its new visitor. It takes a little time to make all the systems work together. You should start to feel better next month."

"Does it look like a baby, or just a glob of cells and stuff?" November asked, not sure how to word the questions swirling in her head.

"At this stage it's called an embryo, but it looks like a teeny, incomplete person. It's got little feet already."

"Wow," said November. "Feet!"

"It's about a half inch long, and most of that is taken up by the head," the doctor continued.

"Josh had a big head," November said in a soft voice.

Dr. Holland smiled. "The baby's eyes are forming now, as well as its ears, nose, and mouth. When you come for your visit next month, you will be able to hear its heartbeat."

"Really?" November glanced down at her belly, afraid to touch it.

"Yes, indeed. Loud and clear. All your baby's internal parts are present, but they are tiny and immature."

"When will I start to show?"

"You already have a little swelling around your waist." Dr. Holland looked directly into November's eyes. "You're not going to be able to keep this a secret much longer," she said gently.

"Are you going to tell my mother?"

"No. It's not my place to tell her. But *you* should confide in her as soon as possible. You're going to need your mother's help."

November suddenly felt claustrophobic. She couldn't tell her mother—she just couldn't! She covered her face with her hands.

"Are you okay?" Dr. Holland asked when November didn't respond.

"I can't tell my mom," November blurted out. "She'll be so disappointed."

"Does your mother love you?"

"Yeah. I'm like her dream child—the one who makes it. I can't do this to her."

The doctor nodded slowly. "Yes, you can. Trust her. I

have confidence that she has enough love for you to handle this."

November shook her head, then asked, "When will this happen? I mean, when am I due?"

"Since we are pretty positive about the date of conception, I'd say around November second."

November looked up with a small smile. "Hmm. A November baby. How ironic."

"There's nothing ironic about it, my dear. Everything is very physiological from now on."

"Thanks for being straight with me. There's so much I don't know—I'm not even sure what questions to ask," November admitted.

"You can call me any time of the day or night. I promise to get back to you within a day if it's a general question, and right away if it's an emergency. I'm here for you and your baby. Understand?"

November felt herself getting teary-eyed. Her emotions changed as quickly as she blinked, it seemed. She sniffed and thanked the doctor once more.

"Here are some pamphlets that describe every single month in bright juicy detail, as well as some vitamins I want you to take every day."

November opened the jar and looked at the large red capsules inside. "How am I supposed to swallow these things? They're huge!" November sniffed the bottle and made a face. "And they stink. Why do I have to take them?"

"To keep your baby healthy. Don't worry—you'll get used to them," the doctor said. "You'll be surprised what you're going to get used to in the next few months."

"Like what?" November asked. All this information was making her dizzy.

"Your body is making room for a very demanding passenger. The baby rides first class. You're just the transport system. So take good care of both of you. You don't smoke or drink, do you?"

November shook her head emphatically.

"Good. Don't start now. You'll do just fine. Drink lots of water and juice. Eat lots of fruits and vegetables. No fatty foods like french fries and fried chicken."

"That's all the good stuff," November muttered.

"Here's a list of foods you should concentrate on, and some menus as well," Dr. Holland said, reaching for a booklet.

November flipped through it. "Broccoli soup? Roasted asparagus? Yuck!"

"And oranges and apples and pears and plums," the doctor added briskly. "Surely you'll find something you like that's good for you and that baby. And see my secretary about scheduling another appointment. If you don't, I'll hunt you down and show up in your third-bell class!"

"Oh, please do. I hate that class. Any excuse to get out is welcome," November replied, glad for a chance to laugh.

"And November?"

"Yes, ma'am?"

"Talk to your mother."

"I will." November sighed and walked out of the doctor's office into the overcast Saturday afternoon.

WHEN NOVEMBER GOT HOME, HER MOTHER was sitting at the kitchen table, working a crossword puzzle. "Hi, honey. Glad you're home early. How was the book fair?"

"It was okay." November flopped down in the kitchen chair across from her mother.

"What's a six-letter word that means 'worn down'? I think it starts with an *e*."

"Eroded," November answered.

"Thanks," said her mother as she scribbled the answer. "Okay, here's another one. Who was Cleopatra's lover? Oh, it's a long one."

"Marc Antony. It could also be Julius Caesar. Cleo got around." November chuckled mirthlessly.

"Hey, you're good. Which reminds me, your registration for the Black College Tour came in the mail today," her mother said as she frowned over another clue. "You're all set to leave when school gets out in June. Then, as soon as you get back, you're off to Cornell! I think checking out the Black colleges is a good idea, in spite of the Cornell program, just to make sure you end up at the college that's right for you."

November didn't answer. She shifted nervously in her seat. "Did you already pay for it?"

"Of course. Dana's mother has signed her up for the same tour, so the two of you can share a room at the various stops. We've got lots of time to work out the details."

"Maybe I shouldn't go, Mom," November said softly.

"Not go? Why not? The tour ought to be fun, even if you're just window shopping!"

November couldn't believe how hard this was. Her mother, blissfully unaware, chattered on about colleges and crossword clues without even noticing November's mood. "Maybe I should look into other options, Mom," she said, her voice flat.

Mrs. Nelson looked up. "What's wrong, November? Did something happen at the book fair?"

"No." November offered no explanation. She just couldn't get the words out. She knew that as soon as she said them out loud, nothing would ever be the same.

Her mother frowned. "Come to think of it, you've had the blues for the past few weeks. What's up, baby girl? You know you can tell me anything."

Mothers say that kind of stuff, November thought, *but they don't* really *want to know everything.* "Everything is a mess, Mom," November began, her voice a whisper.

"Is it Josh?" her mother asked gently. "You know, when your daddy died, I felt cold all the time, like I'd never get warm or feel right again. So I really do know how you must hurt about losing Josh." She reached over and touched her daughter's cheek.

"You don't get it, Mom. It's worse than you think," November mumbled, pulling away.

"What is it, baby?" November's mother asked again, even more gently.

November tried not to cry, but she couldn't help it. "What's an eight-letter word that means I've screwed up my life forever?"

Mrs. Nelson looked at her daughter sharply. "What are you talking about, November?"

"I didn't go to the book fair today. I went to a doctor." She paused and studied the pattern on the kitchen floor. "I'm . . . I'm pregnant, Mom."

Her mother said nothing for a full minute. Her mouth opened. Then closed. Then opened again as if she was trying to speak, but no words came out. Finally she said simply, "Oh my." Her voice was a squeak.

"Are you mad at me?" November stared at her wild-eyed mother.

"Oh, my Lord." Mrs. Nelson stood up, sat down, then stood up again. "You can't be—you better not be!" Her voice was gravelly and threatening. She walked around the kitchen, then returned to her chair and put her head on the table. Then she sat up and raked her hands through her hair. "I can't deal with this! Not you. Not *you*, November!"

"Please don't be angry, Mom. Please . . ." November cringed.

"Angry? I'm not sure if that's the right word. Astonished,

maybe. Outraged, perhaps. Maybe even just plain pissed. The thought of you . . . my baby girl . . . oh my."

"I'm sorry," November whispered.

"How *could* you?" Her mother's face was the palest November had ever seen it.

November was sure her mother didn't really want the answer to that one. "I know you're disappointed," November said to the floor.

"Right now what I'm feeling is disgust, I think."

November sniffled. "I feel so bad, Mom. I feel like I just beat you in the head with a hammer."

"I've got to be honest. I do too." Her mother's hair was a mess as she kept massaging her temple with her fingers.

"Please don't hate me," November begged.

Her mother said nothing for a minute or so. Finally she breathed deeply. "I hate that this has happened to us, November." Then her eyes went wild once more and she moaned deeply, then began to sob.

All November could see was the heaving of her mother's shoulders. Afraid to even touch her, November stared at her parents' faded wedding photo on the mantel and wished she were on another continent, another planet. Any place but this small kitchen full of grief and disappointment. "Please stop crying, Mommy," she whispered.

"How long have you known?" asked her mother, when she finally sat up. Her mascara had smeared.

"A month or so."

"And you didn't tell me?" Her mother got up and blew her nose on a paper towel. "I need some coffee," she said absently. She turned to make a cup of coffee but seemed to have trouble finding her favorite red cup, which was sitting right on the counter, or locating a spoon in the drawer full of silverware.

"I was afraid to tell you. And ashamed," November admitted, looking back down at the floor. It was easier to watch the floor than her mother's jerky, uncomfortable movements.

Mrs. Nelson scooped three tablespoons of instant coffee into a cup, added water, and popped it into the microwave. "I'm confused," she said to November. "When did this happen? None of this makes sense."

"Just before Josh died," November whispered.

"I guess most parents are the last to know about what their children are doing, but I know that you and I have had lots of open and honest conversations about sexual stuff since you were a little girl." The microwave bell dinged and she removed the coffee.

"Yeah," November said, shrugging. "I know."

"You always came to me with any questions, and I've always tried to be straight up with you." Mrs. Nelson poured skim milk into her coffee.

"I always thought that was really cool you talked to me like that. None of the other girls' moms would even say the word 'sex,'" November said, almost afraid to look at her mother.

"I guess that's why this hits me so hard. I thought we were kinda close and able to discuss everything. I didn't even know you were, uh, you know, sexually active."

"It's not like we did it a lot," November tried to explain.

Her mother looked as if she had been slapped. "It's like I don't even know you!"

November wanted to sink through the floor. "I'm so sorry, Mommy."

Mrs. Nelson had returned to the table. She put seven spoons of sugar in her coffee before she noticed what she was doing. "Go on," she said, trying, it seemed to November, to sound a little more encouraging.

"I'm scared, Mom. I didn't mean for any of this to happen. Me and Josh just got carried away—it's amazing how easily it happened." November put her head in her hands.

"You didn't use any kind of, uh, you know, protection?"

"We never even thought about it."

"How dumb can you be?" her mother almost screamed.

"There's a big difference between those movies they show at school in health class and the real deal," November told her. "You don't even think about thinking, you know what I'm saying?"

"Not really. You're an intelligent girl. Where was your brain?"

November shrugged. "Stuff just happens. By the time your brain comes back, it's over."

"I should have warned you better. Watched you better." Her mother stirred the coffee. "It's my fault."

"It's not your fault, Mom. I did this, not you."

"Yes, I guess you did." Her mother sighed and gave the coffee another furious stir. Then she looked up sharply. "Oh, my Lord!" she said with dismay.

"What?" November couldn't imagine anything worse coming from this conversation. She was wrong.

"The Cornell program," her mother said, her voice thick. "There's no sense in going now. This was your stepping stone to get into one of the best schools in the country next year. There goes that dream." She gave November a hard stare.

"What am I gonna do, Mom?" November asked quietly.

Her mother didn't answer right away. She blew her nose and finally took a sip of her coffee. "Good Lord!" she said. "That's the worst coffee I've ever had in my life!" She got up and poured it down the sink. Then she said, looking directly at November, "I've got to be straight with you, honey. I'm *real* disappointed, and I'm so angry I could bite something."

"Please don't be mad at me," November said again.

Her mother rinsed out her coffee cup and said in a measured tone, "I'm not mad at you, November, just at the mess you've gotten yourself into. This is certainly not what I pictured for your future. You're so young, and you've got so much potential. What a damn waste." She wiped away another tear.

"I'm so scared."

"It's going to take a while to absorb all this. We've been through a lot together, me and you. I don't know how, but we'll get through this." She looked at her daughter. "Oh, my Lord, I wish we didn't have to."

November ran to her mother's open arms.

LATER THAT NIGHT, AFTER HER MOTHER had gone to bed, November was suddenly, unexpectedly famished. She got up and fixed herself a grilled cheese sandwich and a glass of milk. Then she took one of the vitamins the doctor had given her. "It's like swallowing a watermelon," she grumbled as she managed to choke it down.

She took out another vitamin capsule and stared at its enormous size. *Good grief! Why don't they just make them half the size and have us take two?* she thought. *Instead I gotta gag on this horse pill every day.*

As she ate her sandwich, she couldn't stop thinking about her mother. She was glad she no longer had to carry the secret alone, but it had truly cut her heart to see how deeply her mother had been hurt. Her mom had suffered so much already—it seemed to November that the least she could have done was to be the dream child her mom needed. *I am such a screwup!*

She picked up the phone to call Dana, but then remembered that her friend was out of town visiting her dad. Feeling edgy, she scrolled through the numbers of her friends and found there was no one to whom she could talk or unload her feelings. Finally she noticed a number that took a moment to recognize. It was the number Olivia had given her that day in the bathroom. On a whim, November dialed.

Olivia picked up right away. "Hello," she said tentatively.

"Hi. This is November. Were you asleep?"

"No, just sitting here looking at the home shopping channel."

"You watch that too? You ever buy anything?"

"No, I'm too cheap. I think it's funny how hard they try to convince you that if you don't buy that stuff—in the next three minutes—your life will come to a complete stop!" She had a warm, reassuring laugh. "How you been feeling?"

"Better, thanks." November paused. "I finally went to the doctor."

"Well, that's good. What did he say?"

"I went to a lady doctor. She said the first week of November."

"Heavy stuff. Will you come back to school in the fall?"

"Oh, snap! I hadn't even thought about it. I'll be as big as a house! Everybody will be laughing at me and making fun of me and talking about me behind my back."

"Join the club," said Olivia quietly. "You tell your mama yet?"

"Yeah, I finally did."

"Did she freak out?"

"Well, she didn't get out the chain saw, but she was real hurt. I hate making her feel so bad."

"It's not your mother who has to go through this," Olivia observed. "She's not the one who's gonna swell up like a blimp."

"Thanks for reminding me." November groaned. "That's one part I try not to think about." Then she paused. "Can I ask you something, Olivia?"

"Sure."

"When we were in the bathroom that day, why did you come back? I mean, for real now, if I knew somebody was throwing up, I'd lace up my kicks and jet out of there as far away as possible!"

Olivia was silent for a long time. Finally she said, "Well, I envy you a little. I never had anybody cool like Josh who really cared about me. Hold on a second."

November could hear the rattle of a candy wrapper. "I needed a chocolate fix," Olivia said finally, her words suddenly thick-sounding.

"I feel you. I never used to like chocolate that much, but now I wake up in the morning needing a Hershey bar," November admitted.

"I can't even use pregnancy as an excuse. I just crave chocolate. It's my favorite food group!" Both girls laughed.

"So finish what you were telling me."

Olivia's end of the line grew quiet again. "Well, two years ago I went out with one of those morons on the basketball team."

November made a slight sound.

"You think girls like me can't get dates?" Olivia asked sharply.

"I didn't say anything," November protested.

"Well, usually, we can't. At least I can't. I was really flattered when Logan asked me out. But I thought he liked me for my mind, my wit, my ability to quote long passages of Shakespeare!"

"Let me guess. He wasn't after your intelligence," November suggested.

"You got that right." Olivia laughed harshly. "When he first asked me out, I couldn't believe it. I was so excited. I went and got my hair and my nails done, bought a new dress. I even went on a diet. How stupid is that?"

"You were just a kid—ninth-grade girls aren't the sharpest pencils in the box when it comes to figuring out dudes."

"Yeah, maybe. Anyway, he took me out a couple of times, he let me think he cared about me. He bought me stuff and took me out to dinner at nice restaurants. It was like one of those made-for-television movies—not quite realistic, but a nice way to pass the time. I was so happy." She paused, and November braced herself for what she figured was coming next.

"Bottom line, he got way too friendly way too soon. But I didn't want to lose him. I was so excited that a fine dude like Logan was interested in me that I let him talk me into something I really didn't want to do. When he got what he wanted, he dumped me that very night. I'm half dressed and shivering in his car, and he told me as he was driving me home, with a look of disgust on his face that I will never, ever forget, 'I guess it's true what they say about fat girls being easy!'"

November gasped.

"I started to cry, and he told me, 'Hey, you ought to be grateful!' Then he laughed, made me get out on the corner of my street, and drove away." Olivia's voice broke, then she added, "I cried all night."

"Oh, Olivia. I'm so sorry."

"The next morning at school he told all his friends how successful he had been." She paused. "He had my panties, November. When I got to school about ten of his friends were in the front hall tossing them around, making jokes about how big they were."

November gasped again and shook her head in acknowledgment. "Oh, man! I remember that day now. You started crying, and you ran past me into the bathroom."

"And you followed me, and gave me some tissues and a peppermint."

"You remembered that?"

"I told you I never forget anything. You were talking to Dana and Arielle, giggling about whatever it is that fly girls laugh about, and you took the time to leave them, check on me, put your hand on my shoulder, and ask if I was okay. You don't know how much that meant."

"I don't know what to say," November admitted.

"So that's why I came back. I had seen you run in there, heard you get sick, and I figured maybe I could return the favor."

"Now that you tell me about it, I wish I'd done more."

"It was enough."

"What a dirty rotten piece of scum he is!"

"It was worse than that. Each of them had picked what they called 'an ugly girl' to go out with. They had money bets on how long it would take to get each girl in bed. I fell right into their trap." She took a deep breath. "They laughed about it every time I passed them in the hall for weeks after that. I almost died of shame."

"It wasn't your fault," November said gently.

"I know that now. But at the time I felt like I needed to be pretty and popular and that would be an easy way to do it."

"Well, at least you didn't get pregnant."

"You've got a point there."

"Are you okay with it now?"

"Well, I try to take one day at a time, but sometimes several days attack me at once!" She laughed at her own joke. "Seriously, I no longer let gutter trash like those dudes make me feel bad. I'm cool with who I am. I got high hopes and great expectations. I'm gonna be a doctor."

"You know, you really are pretty cool, Olivia," November said. "You're so easy to talk to."

"I'm the best-kept secret at Douglass High School!" Olivia chuckled. "Call me anytime you need to talk. Hang in there, November."

JERICHO SAT IN HIS LAST-PERIOD CLASS, trying not to fall asleep, praying the bell would ring soon. The math teacher droned on in the front of the room—something about polynomials and negative numbers. *How can a number be less than nothing? I don't get it. If I don't get out of here, my head is gonna explode!* It was all Jericho could do to stop himself from screaming, "Shut up, man! I really don't care! Just let me out of here!" at the top of his lungs. Josh had always been good in math classes and had helped Jericho endure the calculations and details of geometry and algebra by cracking jokes and drawing cartoons of the teacher on his homework. Now it was all one giant lump of meaningless information without Josh there to help him make sense of it all.

Spring had finally decided to show up, and the warm sun reached Jericho through the closed classroom windows. He raised his hand. "May I be excused, please?"

Mr. Bormingham, who all the kids called Boring Man, looked over his glasses at Jericho and rolled his eyes. "Please hurry, Jericho. We will truly miss all your stimulating input into our classroom conversation."

Nothing worse than a sarcastic teacher, Jericho thought as he hurried out of the room. No one else was out of class, and he breathed in the silence and the glorious emptiness of the moment. He didn't really have to go to the bathroom, so he took his time as he walked down the hall, baggy jeans dragging on the floor. He listened to bits of laughter from one classroom, a video playing in another, and a teacher having a lively conversation with her class in another. He felt himself relax.

Coming at him down the hall he could see Luis Morales, one of the guys who had pledged with him for the Warriors of Distinction. Luis had lettered in both track and football, and he walked with an easy stride. Jericho had watched how the girls hovered around Luis like he was hot caramel fudge in a muscle shirt.

"What's crackin', dude?" Jericho asked as Luis approached him.

"Ain't nothin' to it, man. I'm aight. Track's keeping me pretty busy. Makes these last days of the school year go faster. Then I go right into football."

"I hear you. Man, I'm so ready for school to be out. I feel like I got fire ants in my veins. I had to get out that class for a hot minute."

"I feel ya. You got Boring Man?"

"How'd you guess?"

"Had him last year." Luis glanced down the empty hall,

then back at Jericho. "You handlin' this—you know, the stuff about Josh?"

"Just barely. But I ain't got no choice but to keep on steppin'."

"It sucks, don't it?"

"Even the halls feel different with Josh not in 'em. Every morning me and Josh and Kofi would sit right here in the main hall, just waiting for Arielle, Dana, and November to walk by."

"I hear you, man—the Delicious Divas," said Luis. He slapped palms with Jericho. "And they knew it too. The three of them walked in together every morning, soaking it up like sunshine."

"Like fine wine, my man!" Jericho looked at his watch and wondered how much longer he could stall before going back to class.

"Miss Arielle had you runnin' around like one of those hamsters in a wheel!" Luis reminded Jericho with a laugh.

"What can I say—I was dumb," Jericho admitted. "Not that it matters now that she's hooked up with Logan."

"Well, since it looks like you're gonna have some time on your hands this summer, why don't you come on out for football? Conditioning starts in a couple of weeks."

Jericho looked thoughtful. "I heard you got the quarterback spot for next season, man. That's tight."

"I've been working for that position since ninth grade. It's good to be a senior," Luis told him with a grin. "We could use you, Jericho."

"I don't know if I can be goin' back to football as a senior."

"It's not like you never played before. I remember back in middle school—you were one tough little hard-nosed lineman. And didn't you play on the freshman team for part of the year?"

"Yeah, but I quit so I could concentrate on my trumpet. Music is smooth and easy. Football meant sweat. You feel me?"

"You could get back in shape pretty easily," said Luis earnestly.

"Maybe. It's been a while," Jericho said doubtfully.

"As big as you are, all you have to do is stand there and block!" Luis laughed, slapping Jericho on the back. "Seriously, man, you ought to come out for the team. We've got a pretty good backfield—Roscoe is a good little scatback, but we need some beef on the line."

"Truth? I've actually been thinkin' about it. 'Specially since I'm not doing marching band this year."

"Just let Coach Barnes know. He'll do backflips."

"Now *that's* something I don't want to see!" Jericho grinned, then wondered how long he'd been in the hall. He'd better be getting back to class.

But then Luis asked, "Hey, have you talked to Josh's parents recently?"

Jericho paused. "I guess it's been a couple of weeks. His mother, my aunt Marlene, is seriously depressed—won't get out of bed at all some days—and my uncle Brock has taken up karate, spends hours at it. Kinda off the deep end, if you know what I mean."

"I guess you gotta do something to fill up that hole in your life," Luis said. "When my grandfather died, my father knocked out walls and built a new room on our house. From scratch. He hardly ever slept. When the room was done, it seemed like he got closer to normal. At least whatever passes for normal for a man who thinks nylon shirts and bell-bottom jeans are still in style."

Jericho grew pensive. "It's kinda weird to talk to Josh's folks. I don't know what to say, anyway. I know they blame me for what happened."

"No, they don't. Parents always blame themselves. When I was ten, I totaled my bicycle and almost busted my stupid head, doing wheelies on a ramp I made out of garbage cans and a refrigerator box. Instead of yelling at me for being dumb, my parents blamed themselves for not watching me better. Trust me—Josh's folks think that somehow it's their fault."

"You might be right," Jericho said, but without conviction.

"Yo, the bell is about to ring. You better get back to class before Boring Man sends out the troops for you! I'll catch you on the field, man." Luis disappeared down the hall and Jericho reluctantly returned to class.

JERICHO WALKED INTO HIS HOUSE, FEELING glum. His stepmother, Geneva, was busy with dinner, stirring the potatoes and adding sauce to the green beans. She smiled at him. "Did you have a good day?" she asked.

Jericho shrugged. "Same as usual, I guess. Dinner smells good."

"Roast beef," she said as she opened the refrigerator door. Then she added, "Brock called today."

"From the karate dojo again?"

"I know he's gone a little overboard with that karate stuff. I guess everyone has their own way of dealing with tragedy. I don't know how I would cope if something ever happened to you or Rory or Todd," she told Jericho. She took out two onions and began to chop them furiously.

Jericho was surprised and pleased that she'd mentioned him with her two sons, but he only said, "Yeah. Deep. What did Uncle Brock say?"

"He wanted to talk to your dad. It seems your aunt is not doing well. She needs something to get her back into the world. She's dug herself into a hole and she either won't or can't get out."

"I wish I could help her," Jericho replied hopelessly.

"We all do. She's seeing a doctor, and I think he's put her on some kind of medication, but nothing seems to make a difference. She's not functioning well without her boy."

"Neither am I," Jericho said quietly.

"I know, Jericho. Really, I do."

"Thanks, Geneva," Jericho said earnestly. He opened the refrigerator and got out a gallon of milk.

"Mr. Tambori called also. He's concerned about you—not just about your music, but about your spirit, I think," Geneva added.

"Tambori is cool, and he thinks he knows me, but he doesn't. I'm through with the trumpet. Forever."

"That's a very long time," Geneva told him gently.

"That's how long Josh will be gone."

Geneva didn't reply all at once. Finally she sighed and told Jericho, "Call the boys down and tell them dinner is ready. Your father called and said he'd be late. They're short a couple of cops down at the precinct and he took an extra shift."

After dinner, Jericho trudged upstairs to do his homework—a couple of hours of math, he knew for sure. Ordinarily he would have begun the evening with his trumpet, letting the music carry him away from the stresses of the day. Then he'd call Arielle and let her soothe him in ways the trumpet never could.

But Arielle spent her time these days soothing Logan, and the trumpet lay under Jericho's bed collecting dust. The back door slammed downstairs. He flopped down on his bed and balled up his pillow under his head. He stared at the ceiling, thinking of dark window ledges, boy-birds in flight, and muddy, bloody landings.

GENEVA KNOCKED ON JERICHO'S DOOR A few minutes later, startling him. He was surprised to realize that he'd dozed off, and as he turned over on his pillow he mumbled, "I'm sleepy, Geneva. Can it wait?"

"November is here. She says you've got her class notes for the chemistry project."

Jericho sat up immediately. He knew there was no such project. "Yeah, that's right, I do. Tell her to come on up." He looked around his room, which was a disaster, and moved some dirty clothes off his desk chair so she could at least sit down.

"What's up, Jericho?" November said as she walked in. She wore a Douglass sweatshirt and baggy sweatpants to match.

"Nothin' happenin'. What's up with you? I know I'm dim sometimes, but I would have remembered a chemistry project." He waited. He hadn't seen November much, except at school. They used to hang together every weekend, but since

Josh had been gone, and Arielle had dumped him, there seemed to be less and less to talk about.

November glanced at the mess on Jericho's desk—several empty CD cases, soda cans, lots of wrinkled food wrappers, scribbled-on school notebooks, a few books, and several copies of *Sports Illustrated*, including the swimsuit issue. "You need one of those extreme makeover shows to come in here with a bulldozer," she declared.

"I tried. They turned me down," he told her, and they both laughed.

November was quiet for a moment, then moved aside two empty boxes of cornflakes, revealing a framed photo of Josh that was sitting on Jericho's desk. It had been taken at last year's school picnic, at the end of the junior-senior footrace. Josh's face glowed with sweat, and his feet barely touched the ground as he lunged for the finish line. Arms upraised and waving, wide grin signaling victory, the photo captured him so completely that it seemed he might burst out of the frame. She picked it up, almost expecting it to feel warm. "He looks so . . . alive in this picture," she said softly.

"Yeah, I know. It's hard to look at." Jericho glanced away.

"I want him back, jumping on the bed like Todd and Rory, acting a fool and making me laugh," she said.

"I can't believe all the little molecules that made up Josh have simply disappeared, like . . ." He paused, searching for an analogy. "Like kids' soap bubbles when they pop. Just gone. I never did like science," he added, suddenly kicking his pillow with fury. They both watched it sail through the air and land on a pile of dirty clothes.

Then November said quietly, "Not all of Josh's atoms are gone, Jericho."

"Huh?"

"Maybe a little piece of Josh will stick around for a while."

"You talkin' crazy," Jericho said.

She leaned forward. "I got something to tell you."

"About chemistry class?"

"More about biology."

"I'm not followin'. We don't even take biology this year."

November took a deep breath. "I'm going to have a baby, Jericho. Josh's baby."

Jericho inhaled sharply, as if he'd been punched in the gut, then fell back on the bed. "Are you sure?"

"How come every movie I see, that's always the first question dudes ask? Like I'd come over here and tell you this unless I was absolutely, positively sure."

"I'm sorry. It's just . . . that's the last thing I'd expect you to say." He paused, his head swimming. "I would have been less surprised if you had said you were running away to join the circus!"

"I still might have to do that," she said ruefully, "if my mother doesn't stop crying herself to sleep at night."

"I guess she didn't take it so good, huh?"

"Well, I was my mom's perfect princess, and I screwed that up big-time."

"Does Aunt Marlene know?"

"No! Only my mom, the doctor, and a couple of girls from school."

"News like that's gonna travel fast. You told Dana and Arielle?"

"Dana, yes. Arielle, no way. I hate the way she dumped you," November said with feeling.

"Thanks for lookin' out," said Jericho, avoiding her eyes. Needing to move, he got up and began to toss the cereal boxes and food wrappers into the trash can. *November's pregnant?* he thought, trying to get his head around the idea. Then his heart lurched. *Josh will never know!*

"I told a girl I didn't know very well," November continued. "I needed to talk and she had a good ear. Her name is Olivia. She won't tell anyone."

"Olivia from band?"

"Yeah."

"I like her. She's solid."

"What do you mean by that?" November asked, bristling a little.

"Nothing. Look, as big as I am, I have no right to talk about anybody but myself. Olivia is cool with me." He looked at November closely. "So what are you gonna do?"

"Swell up. Get huge. Miss the prom. Buy flip-flops. I don't really know."

"I wonder what the kid will look like," Jericho mused as he sat back down on the bed. "Josh had that odd straw-colored hair."

"And crooked teeth," November added.

"Don't forget his skinny legs and his stick-out ears!"

"And his bushy eyebrows!" November laughed a little.

"Sounds like a really ugly baby, November!" Jericho looked at her closely to make sure he hadn't hurt her feelings, but she was gazing at Josh's picture, her hand on her stomach.

"It'll also have Josh's smile—that stupid grin of his was so bright you needed shades," she said softly. She inhaled deeply and closed her eyes. "Yeah, it will be a beautiful baby. But it's stuck with a stupid mother," she added.

"How you figure?"

"I don't know anything about kids. I don't even *like* babies that much. They poop all the time and they cry all night and how am I gonna go to school like everybody else if I have a baby in my backpack?" Tears of frustration ran down her face.

Jericho got up and walked over to where she sat. For the first time in months, he felt he knew exactly what he needed to do. He put his hand on her shoulder. "I'll help you, November. I'm the uncle—sort of. I'll be like the stand-in daddy. Whatever you need me to do, I'm here for you."

She wiped her eyes on a napkin from Pizza Hut. "That's sweet of you, Jericho. But there's no need for you to mess up your senior year because of me."

"No, for real. I want to do this. Honest. I want to help."

November stood up suddenly and ran out of Jericho's room to the bathroom across the hall. She didn't have time to close the door, and her vomiting echoed in the hallway. Jericho headed for the door in alarm.

When she walked out of the bathroom a few minutes later, she looked pale and unsteady. "Are you sure you want to help?" she asked, a wan grin on her face.

"I'm with you all the way," he answered, and wondered what that really meant.

NOVEMBER AND DANA SAT TOGETHER IN the back of the cafeteria, each sipping a box of the fruit juice that the school had installed in the vending machines to replace the sodas the kids preferred.

Dana rummaged through her large leather Louis Vuitton knockoff bag she'd bought on eBay and pulled out her lip gloss. November glanced at her friend's lavender leather vest with matching boots. She felt like a cow in her University of Kentucky sweatshirt and faded jeans.

"You talk to Arielle lately?" Dana asked.

November shook her head. "Not much. Seems like she's changed since she broke up with Jericho. She started hanging with Logan, and all of a sudden she's got this major attitude."

"Logan makes me itch. He comes across as slimy or something."

"I hear ya." November nibbled on a carrot stick and

thought about what Olivia had told her about Logan. "It was fun last fall when me and you and Arielle would sit together every day at lunch and just dominate."

"Sharing shoes!"

"And clothes!"

"And gossip!"

"But never boyfriends!" November added. Both girls laughed.

"Dudes trippin' all over their shoelaces just to talk to us," Dana said with a smirk. "And the rest of the girls be hatin' because of it!"

"Well, they don't have to worry about me anymore. I can't believe how fast I'm gaining weight. I feel like a whale."

"You're still skinny. Wait a couple of months, then I'll listen to your whale tales," Dana said.

November sighed. "I gotta remember not to stand too close to Miss Size Two Arielle. Not that she stops to give me the time of day anymore. It's like she changed the station and moved to a different TV channel."

"Tell me about it. When I pass her in the hall, she acts like she doesn't know me. You know, to be perfectly honest, I don't think her elevator went too deep underground anyway. You know what I'm sayin'?" said Dana as she sucked down the rest of her drink.

"That's my girl Arielle. Fluttering around like a little butterfly to whatever makes her look good," November said decidedly.

"She hurt Jericho real bad." Dana squashed her juice box.

"Yeah, I know I felt bad enough when Josh died. But

Jericho and Josh were tight like brothers. He needed his girl to be there for him."

"And she dissed him. Like somebody steppin' on a roach."

November nodded. "She'll get what's coming to her one day."

"Maybe not. Girls like Arielle always get over," Dana said with a shrug. "So, have you thought any more about what you're going to do?"

It was November's turn to shrug. "I don't know. Get fat. Get talked about. Get a job, I guess. I just hope I can graduate next year with the rest of you." She scraped at the red fingernail polish on her thumb.

"You seem to have a handle on things, sort of."

"Not hardly! My life is one huge, red-glowing question mark sitting in front of me like a neon sign. What am I supposed to do with a *baby*?"

"I feel for you, girl. I've got your back, but I gotta tell you—I'm glad it's not me."

"You know, it's like I've lost control of my whole body. One minute I'm laughing like a crazy bird, not even aware I'm peeing in my pants, and the next minute I'm on my knees in tears. So is my mother, and she's not even pregnant!"

Dana hesitated. "Can I ask you something?"

"Sure."

"Did you ever think about, you know, like, getting rid of the baby?"

November scraped the polish off another nail before she answered. "When I first figured out I'd got myself knocked up, I gotta admit, the thought crossed my mind. I was stupid scared, and I'd never felt so alone in my life. I got to thinking maybe I could just delete this mess-up in my life like I delete a computer file. It sure woulda made everything easier."

"So why didn't you?"

"Well, I was terrified of going to one of those places where protesters picket out front with pictures of dead babies on posters. And the thought of somebody digging inside my body to scrape a human being out scared me even more. I just couldn't do it." She blew the fragments of red polish onto the floor.

Dana started to answer, but the rattle of a food tray crashing to the floor, a huge thud, and someone screaming, "Quit it!" caught her attention. Sudden silence followed in the noisy lunchroom.

Only one teacher was monitoring the cafeteria—a short, thin, first-year teacher named Mr. Price, who seemed to be scared of the kids. Once they'd all figured that out, it was over. Kofi and Jericho used to run up behind him and shout, "Hey, Mr. Price! Hey, Mr. Price!" The little man would jump every single time. They all predicted he wouldn't be back next year.

November watched Mr. Price scurry out of the lunchroom, and then she and Dana rushed to the far side of the cafeteria. Arielle and Logan were there, laughing and pointing at Olivia Thigpen, who sat in the middle of the floor. The school lunch special, which today had been spaghetti and meatballs, decorated her hair. A few students started to join in the laughter but stopped when they saw Dana stomping toward them, and the fire in November's eyes.

November marched over to where Olivia sat and reached out to help her up, but Olivia shook her off.

"I got this under control," she said, her voice tight.

"You ought to try to keep that waistline under control," Arielle snipped, hands on hips.

"What are you doing, Arielle?" Dana asked her furiously. "Are you crazy? Leave her alone!"

"Logan told me all about her—the tramp!" Arielle replied angrily.

November glanced over at Arielle with amazement. Could Arielle actually be *jealous* of Olivia?

Finally Olivia stood up with amazing dignity, even though chocolate milk ran down her arms and spaghetti sauce dripped down the back of her red-striped T-shirt. "I can fight my own battles, Dana," she said with quiet menace.

Arielle scooted over to Logan. "I'm not scared of a pig-pen like you," she told Olivia. "If you weren't so big and clumsy, you wouldn't have spilled your food."

Olivia took a deep breath and stepped toward Arielle, who seemed to shrink as Olivia got closer. Olivia was like an approaching electrical storm—thunder and lightning and extreme danger. November figured she had a hundred pounds on Arielle. No one spoke.

Olivia stopped only when her face was inches away from Arielle's. As her face grew darker with fury, Arielle's grew paler. Then she spoke, loudly and clearly. "I'm here to warn you. I *never* forget anything! Never. For now, just run, little salt shaker, run! Because if I hit you, I swear I will hurt you."

Arielle ran. She grabbed Logan's hand and darted out a side door.

Everybody in the cafeteria cheered as they left. November looked at Olivia with new respect. "Are you okay?" she asked.

Olivia gathered her belongings and answered, "Just leave me alone." She stormed out the cafeteria door and onto the sidewalk.

"Should we go after her?" Dana asked.

"No. Leave her some dignity."

"I can't believe Arielle did that," said Dana with disbelief.

"She was dizzy before, but not mean. Logan sure brings out the worst in her."

By that time Mr. Price, who had first peeked in the door to make sure all was quiet, walked over to the area where bits of brown milk and red sauce remained on the floor. "Anybody see what happened?" he asked.

"Yeah, I saw it," a boy replied. "One of the little ninth-grade boys spilled his lunch."

"That's right, man. Clumsy little kids," another girl added.

Mr. Price looked down at the food, then directed his question to November and Dana. "Was there a problem here, girls?"

"No, sir," they answered together.

"I think the boy ran into the bathroom over there," November told the teacher.

Mr. Price seemed to be relieved that he didn't have to deal with a major altercation. He thanked November and hurried out into the hall to find the boy who would not be there.

INSTEAD OF ATTACKING THE PROBLEM head-on, November and her mother seemed to have developed a system of dealing with each other, and with November's pregnancy, by talking in circles. November thought it was almost funny.

"Would you like some extra eggs?" her mother would ask at breakfast. She would never suggest that November should eat more or eat healthier for the baby—only that November might be hungry.

Or November would say, "I think I'll wear my blue warm-up suit to school this morning." She never mentioned that her jeans were getting too tight in the waist, and the warm-ups felt much more comfortable. November wondered how long they would continue to tiptoe around the situation.

As far as November knew, her mother had told no one, not even her best friends. Probably especially not her best friends, November thought ruefully. Much too embarrassing to admit that the daughter you had boasted about to everyone had gotten herself knocked up.

When her mother came home from work that day, she turned on her satellite radio to the blues station and cranked up the volume as high as she could. It was her daily relaxer. "Healthier than a glass of wine!" she'd always tell her daughter.

November used to hate the guitar-belting, sorrow-singing blues wailers when she was younger, but lately she found herself sometimes moving to the deep rhythms or tapping her feet to the heartache spoken by the gravel-voiced singers. Actually, sometimes she found the gut-busting sorrow that exploded from the blues music oddly comforting, especially considering the mess she was now in.

As a sultry-sounding woman sang, "My man is gone for good!" November helped her mother fix dinner—chock-full of healthy foods neither of them had bothered with a month ago. Enough lettuce to choke a rabbit. Fresh carrots, green beans with almonds, and baked chicken—never fried these days. November sighed. "I *really* miss junk food, Mom."

Her mother looked at her with her head tilted a bit. "You're going to miss a lot more, you know," she began.

"Yeah, I know. I know." November didn't want to hear any speeches.

"I've been thinking, November," her mother said, "that you don't have a clue about what you've gotten yourself into."

"It's not like I planned it," November retorted as she poured low-fat dressing on her salad.

"Do you have any idea how much baby stuff costs?" her mother asked.

"You mean like little T-shirts and stuff? Don't people give you those at a shower?" November had never really thought that far into the future.

"Oh, come on, honey. Don't be so naive. Assuming you have a shower, what happens when those three or four pieces you receive as gifts get dirty, or the baby outgrows them?"

"I don't know. I guess I'd have to buy some more." November wished her mother would get off her back. This was getting annoying.

"And what will you use for money? Your American Express Gold Card?" Mrs. Nelson wore a faint smile.

November scowled. "I guess I'll have to use my allowance money."

"Allowance money is for teenagers who go to school and need notebook paper or lunch money or a candy bar. It's not for baby clothes and diapers. You've kinda moved from the world of a kid who really has nothing to worry about except doing homework and washing the dinner dishes, to the other side of the street—to the domain of a young mother who has to take care of her own kid." She waited for this to sink in.

"So what am I supposed to do?" November finally replied, a little fear in her voice. "You're not gonna help me?"

Instead of answering, her mother asked, "How much does a box of diapers cost, November? And how many diapers does a baby use in a day? Or a week?"

"I don't know. Can't we just figure out all that stuff as

we get to it?" November felt like she was choking on her salad.

"What about baby food? Formula? Bottles? Spoons? Blankets? Clothes? Do you have any idea how much any of this costs? What about day care? Who is going to watch the baby when you go back to school? I certainly can't—I have to go to work."

"Why are you sweatin' me like this?" November said, becoming frightened as well as annoyed.

"I don't sleep at night, November, wondering about the answers to all those questions," her mother said honestly. "I think it's time you figured some of this out yourself."

"I guess I'll get a job," November said weakly. "Babies are little. It couldn't cost *that* much to feed one. Right?"

"Babies grow up, and become children, and then young adults like you," her mother reminded her. "Have you given any thought at all to how you'll take care of this baby, how you'll pay for what it needs?"

"You're scaring me, Mom," November said, putting down her fork.

"Good."

When November's cell phone rang, she grabbed it thankfully.

"Hey, Jericho," she said when she checked the caller ID. "Nothing. Just finishing dinner. Hey, you want to take me to the store? It will save my mom a trip. Cool. See you in half an hour." She snapped the phone shut, relieved to escape the lecturing. "That's okay, isn't it?" she asked her mother.

"Sure, that's fine. I have some papers to grade anyway."

Mrs. Nelson stood up and took her plate to the sink. "Uh, does Jericho know?"

"Yeah, I told him."

"I figured you had. Well, I have a job for you while you're at the store."

November sagged. "More health food?"

"No. Take a notebook and pen with you, and I want you to write down the prices of all those things we talked about. Diapers. A baby gets changed at least six times in twenty-four hours—maybe more. Find out the cost of a week's worth. Milk. How much is a can of baby formula? A baby probably drinks eight bottles a day—small ones at first. How much will you need to feed it for a week, and how much will that cost?"

"It sounds like a lot," November said slowly.

"You'll be surprised," Mrs. Nelson told her. "While you're there, get the cost of bottles to put the milk in, nipples for the bottles, bibs, wipes, pacifiers, and anything else you think a baby might need for a week."

"What if I breast-feed?" November asked hopefully. "Won't that save money?"

"You're going to breast-feed a naked baby?" her mother asked with a smile. "The child will still need clothes and a crib and blankets and a car seat. . . . The list is endless."

November looked at her mother and blinked hard. "Oh, Mom. This is such a mess."

"Yes, it truly is." In the awkward silence that followed, they cleared the dinner dishes.

November's cell phone rang again just as she closed the silverware drawer.

"Hey there," a voice said quietly.

"Oh, hi, Olivia," November said. "Are you okay?"

"If you mean am I still covered in spaghetti, the answer is I took a shower. If you mean am I still upset and angry, the answer is yes, and yes, I do plan to kick her butt."

"I'm so sorry, Olivia."

"Why? You didn't do anything."

"I mean, I'm just sorry that something so awful had to happen to a friend of mine."

"You sayin' you consider me a friend?"

"Well, sure."

"Cool."

"You know, I didn't actually see it happen. How did Arielle manage to get one over on you like that?"

"That skank. I was heading to my table, planning to eat by myself to work on SAT prep stuff."

"I got that SAT prep book too, but I think it's in the bottom of my book bag," November replied with a laugh.

"You better get to it, girlfriend. That exam will kick your butt. Anyway, I was minding my own business, thinking about big fat vocabulary words, and before I even knew what had happened, they'd double-teamed me. Logan bumped me from behind, and as I fell forward, Arielle snatched my tray and dumped it on me." November could hear Olivia breathing hard. "I should have taken a fingernail to her face."

"No, you did the right thing. She would have screamed like she was bleeding to death, pleaded innocent to ever touching you, and you would have gotten suspended. She's not worth getting in trouble for."

"Maybe." Olivia paused. "I really appreciate what you and Dana did, though. I know I didn't thank you then—I was a little . . . preoccupied." She laughed.

"I'm glad we were there, but you didn't really need us. Did you see the look in Arielle's eyes?"

Olivia hooted. "I think she wet her pants!"

"I hope she did. Hey, I gotta go. Jericho's at the door. He's taking me to the store. I'm going to turn orange if I eat one more carrot stick, so I'm gonna stock up on chocolate and eat it when my mom's not looking!"

"Save some for me!"

"Bet."

"And November?"

"Yeah."

"That was really cool what you did today."

"Forget about it. Talk to you tomorrow."

WHEN JERICHO RANG THE DOORBELL, November already had her jacket on and hurried out the door before he had the chance to say two words. "Bye, Mom!" she called. "I'll be back in an hour or so!"

"Get those prices!" her mother called out.

"Yeah, okay. Whatever. I'm outta here."

Jericho looked at her with raised eyebrows. "Your mom sweatin' you?"

"Smothering me is more like it. She's killing me—one vegetable at a time!"

"I suppose there're worse ways to go."

November climbed into Jericho's ancient Grand Am, slammed the door, and fastened her seat belt. "I was so glad you called. I had to get out of that house. I think my mother is crazy!"

"What makes you say that?"

"I catch her weeping and sniffling, or just blowing her nose after a crying spell, every single day. She doesn't sleep. She spends hours on the computer looking up stuff about pregnancy. And now she's making me figure out the cost of everything. She's driving me nuts!"

"I guess this must be hard on her," Jericho reasoned.

"She's not the one who's got a baby stuck in her gut! Why should it be hard on her?"

"Have you ever noticed parents are not always as grown-up as they're supposed to be? And they hardly ever act like we think they ought to," Jericho said as he drove them to the large supermarket near the mall. "Look at Eddie's dad. He wanted to sue the school for sending his dirt-devil son to jail. And Madison's dad, instead of punishing Madison for what he did with the Warriors, went to the principal's house and punched him in the nose. What a wack job!"

"Yeah, I heard about that. But this is me and my mom. I can't make it another six months without her, and I don't think I can survive the next six months with her!"

"You always got me to depend on," Jericho said quietly.

"How many babies have *you* had?" she asked glumly. "You gonna hold my hand during contractions?"

"All I know is what I've seen on TV. The girl is always sweaty and screaming and the man with her acts all stupid and then faints. Are you gonna scream?"

"Yep—they'll probably hear me in Jamaica! You gonna faint?"

"Nah. I'm tough. But your mama's gonna be there to hold your other hand, November. That's her grandbaby we're talkin' about—she'll be there for both of you!"

"Getting in the way and getting on my nerves, probably," said November.

"Straight up!" he agreed, laughing.

But November was quiet. "I don't think she can forgive me, Jericho."

"Maybe it's you who can't forgive yourself, November. Ever thought about that?" He pulled into a parking space.

"It's just that . . . that . . . she used to be so proud of me," November mumbled as they got out of the car. She twisted her nose, trying hard not to cry. "Look at me. I talk about my mother being all stupid and weepy, and I'm no better."

"I know how to cure that," Jericho said as they entered the fluorescently bright Wal-Mart Supercenter. "Let's go find where they keep the chocolate doughnuts!"

November wiped her eyes and dashed after Jericho. They each grabbed a cart and began to race each other down the aisles of the store. He grabbed a package of brownies and tossed it into his cart. "Ooh, double chocolate!" he crooned.

She then found a container of whipped cream and a can of presweetened strawberries, crying, "And yummy goodies to go on top!"

He piled ice cream, cookies, and candy into his cart, while she grabbed potato chips, pretzels, and nachos. Laughing wildly, they pushed their carts full speed, gleefully piling in packages of forbidden foods.

"Mom would have a heart attack if she saw all this!" November said as they turned a corner, almost knocking down a display of dish detergent.

"If she ate all this high-calorie crap, she'd explode anyway!" Jericho said as they slowed down. "Are you really gonna buy all this stuff?"

85

"I doubt it," November admitted. "I think I'll get some ice cream and maybe some of these bran muffins. This was fun, but I don't want to do anything to hurt the baby."

Jericho looked at her for a moment. "You'll be a good mother, November," he said.

"I don't see how. I haven't got the slightest idea what to do." She took the chips out of the cart and placed them on a shelf.

"I don't guess anybody does at first—they just figure it out as they go along." When November turned her head, Jericho slid the chips back into his cart. "But what do I know about pregnant girls? I'm clueless."

"Let's go over to the baby aisle," November suggested. "Mom insisted that I find out how much all this is gonna cost."

"Couldn't be that much," he said breezily as they steered their carts to aisle seven.

November couldn't believe the vast array of baby items that seemed to explode from the shelves. Baby bottles in curved shapes, with pastel and brightly colored nipple holders; five different brands of disposable diapers in sizes from newborn to toddler; rows and rows of baby fruits and vegetables; and even more shelves filled with formula. "Good Lord!" she exclaimed. "Look at all this stuff!"

"How do you know which of these a baby needs?" Jericho asked. "You need a college degree just to figure it out." He gingerly picked up a package of bright green baby bibs. "Package of six. Seven ninety-nine. For something a kid spits on? Gimme a break!" He put it back on the shelf.

November took out a small notebook from her purse and started to jot down prices. "Looks like baby formula runs about eight ninety-nine for a quart of ready-to-serve milk, and a little less if you mix it yourself," she said as she read the labels.

Jericho looked at the vast array of items and shook his head. "Why do stores put 'ninety-nine' at the end of all the prices? Why don't they just say it's nine dollars?"

"I think it's so people think they're getting something cheaper than they really are. It's all one big mind game," she said as she picked up jars of baby juice and packages of infant oatmeal. She frowned as she wrote down the cost of everything. "I hate it when Mama is right," she told Jericho.

"You need to win the lottery to buy all this stuff!" he said in amazement.

She checked the packages of strained fruits and vegetables, which came in tiny little plastic tubs, as well as the bibs and gowns on display. "Most of these little baby clothes are, like, seven and ten dollars each!" she croaked as she read the tags.

"Baby shoes?" Jericho asked. He held a pair of size zero infant shoes in his hand. The shoes looked lost in Jericho's huge palm. "Can you imagine the size of the teeny little feet that go into these suckers? Why does a baby even *need* shoes?" he asked. "It's not like it's gonna run track or something."

November smiled and said, "To keep the kid's feet warm, I guess. But it seems like socks make more sense when the baby is really young."

"See, you're sounding like a mom already," Jericho said encouragingly, but she just shook her head. "Look, November," he said then. "They even have car seats here!" Jericho reached for the price tag. "The cheapest one they have is eighty dollars! And look at this one. It's two hundred dollars! Babies can make you go broke quick!"

November sighed deeply. "Yeah." She took out her calculator and typed in the numbers. "The way I figure, it's gonna cost about fifty or maybe even sixty dollars a month for diapers, almost eighty dollars for formula, and that's not counting bottles and clothes and one of those Cadillac-priced car seats. I don't have that kind of money, Jericho. What am I gonna do?"

He took the chips out of the cart and placed them back on the shelf. "I got a little money saved, November. I'll help you."

She looked up at him in surprise. Then she gently touched his broad shoulder. "Thanks, but I couldn't let you do that, Jericho. I'll figure this out. But I *will* let you buy the kid a pair of those little shoes one day, deal?"

"You got it," he said. They continued to push their carts, but slowly this time. They paused at the fruits and vegetables. Jericho looked directly at November and asked, "Would it have been easier for you if Josh was here with you instead of me?"

"No, if Josh were here, he'd be riding in the cart instead of pushing it," she replied with a small smile.

"Sticking green beans up his nose and wearing lettuce leaves as a hat!" Jericho added. "I miss him so much, November. It has to be even harder for you."

"Yeah," she said vaguely. "I guess." She concentrated on the five different types of apples on display, wondering when a baby could eat something like an apple, when she bumped into another cart.

"Oh, excuse me," a middle-aged man in a crisp beige trench coat cried out. "I wasn't paying attention."

"Uncle Brock! Aunt Marlene! Great to see you," Jericho cried out. "You remember November, right?"

November's stomach immediately clenched. She wasn't ready to deal with Josh's parents! She darted a glance at Josh's mother. She seemed to look right through her. Her eyes were focused on a place that was clearly not in that store. Her hair, which November remembered as being reddish bronze and always freshly styled, was uncombed and almost completely gray. She had lost weight—her jacket looked as if it were hanging from a coat hanger. She wore bunny-rabbit house slippers on her feet. November didn't know what to say.

Josh's dad, who used to carry an extra ten pounds around his waistline, looked lean and angular—like a pencil that had been sharpened too much. His face was chiseled with deep angles, and his body moved with nervous intensity. Even though their shopping cart had stopped, he continued to pace in small circles.

"Hello, Mr. and Mrs. Prescott," November forced herself to say. "It's, uh, good to see you again." They looked so different from when she had seen them at the funeral that she was stunned. Had it really been just four months ago?

"We miss seeing you, November, as well as those chocolate chip cookies you baked that Josh loved so much," Mr.

Prescott said. "Please stop by the house when you feel like it. We could use a nice smile like yours." His mouth said the right words, but his voice was not inviting. It was as if he was reading from a script.

"Yes, sir," she mumbled.

Josh's mother, still not focusing very clearly on November or Jericho, said in an equally toneless voice, "Yes, cookies. That would be nice." She leaned heavily on the shopping cart.

Jericho frowned. "Aunt Marlene! It's me, Jericho! You're a great cook. Could you make some cookies for me?" he almost shouted at her.

She blinked and looked at him. "I don't have that much energy these days, Jericho." She looked down at her house slippers.

"Uncle Brock?" Jericho's voice asked a thousand questions.

Jericho's uncle lowered his voice. "Deep depression, the doctors tell me. She needs to exercise, but she won't go to the gym with me." He lowered his voice still more. "She barely gets out of bed." He was still pacing nervously.

November looked more closely at Josh's mother as Jericho nodded. "You look like you've been working out like a pro. Seems like you're in great shape," Jericho told his uncle.

Brock's eyes blinked rapidly. "I'm almost a black belt," he said proudly. "The sweat, the activity—keeps my mind and body alert."

"And stops you from thinkin' about Josh," Jericho said quietly, a funny look on his face as if something were clicking.

Brock raised his eyebrows, then quickly said, "We better go. I wanted Marlene to get some fresh air before I head to the gym. Stop by the house any time, Jericho. You too, November," he added. He grabbed the front of the shopping cart and gave it a gentle tug. His wife pushed slowly on the other end. They disappeared behind a display of cashews and almonds.

Jericho and November stared at each other. "Now that was a freaky, sad scene," Jericho finally said.

"For real now. I feel sorry for them—Josh's mom is a mess."

"Yeah, she's in a bad way. But I don't think there's anything we can do."

"Except bring Josh back," November said.

"What if . . . what if they knew about Josh's baby?" Jericho asked her carefully.

A thousand thoughts immediately came to mind, and there was an uneasy silence as they paid for the groceries and headed back to November's house.

JERICHO DIDN'T SLEEP WELL THAT NIGHT. Dream images of a baby grinning at him with Josh's face, of a baby with tiny wings on its tennis shoes, jumping from a second-story window, darted through his mind as he tossed uncomfortably, praying for morning. Finally, just before his alarm clock was set to chime at six a.m., he gave up and lay there, his head smashed against his pillow, hints of dawn peeking through the vertical blinds.

His father tapped lightly on Jericho's bedroom door. "You up, son?"

"Yeah, Dad. I never really got to sleep."

"Still having bad dreams?"

"Every night."

His father sat down on the side of the bed next to Jericho and put his hand on his shoulder. "I really do understand, son. I do. But maybe it's time to start getting back to your regular routine. Hanging around the house moping isn't going to help."

"My regular routine was hangin' with Josh," Jericho muttered.

His father ignored that and said, "Geneva says she's seen more of you in the past four months than in the past four years. And you know Josh would smack you upside the head if he saw you like this. Come to think of it, I haven't heard you play your trumpet in months."

Jericho groaned. "I can't, Dad. I just can't. Besides, there's more goin' on than you know."

"You want to talk about it?"

Jericho sat up. "What would you say if I got a girl pregnant, Dad?"

Mr. Prescott gulped, then asked carefully, "Have you?"

"You didn't answer my question, Dad. What if I told you I was going to be a father?"

"I'd 'smack you all the way to Saturday,' as my grandfather used to say."

"No, seriously, Dad."

His father thought for a moment. "Well, I'd be deep-down disappointed, Jericho. And pissed. Truly pissed at you." He paused. "Then I guess I'd make sure you took care of the child—because I sure wouldn't."

"Is that all? You wouldn't yell and scream and call me all kinds of stupid?"

"Should I start collecting bad names to call you?" his father asked warily.

Jericho avoided the question. "Is it different for dudes, Dad? Do guys get off easier?"

"Ask the boys who are paying child support for being the 'baby-daddy,'" his father said. "They don't think about eighteen years of taking care of something they produced one night in a motel room or the backseat of a car. Sometimes these boys have lots of babies to pay for. With different girls. I see it down at the precinct all the time."

"But girls have to raise those kids."

"I don't think it's fair or right, but yeah, I think it's harder on pregnant girls than the boys who get them pregnant. Girls get the bad reps, go through all that mama trauma, sometimes have to leave school to take care of the kid—yeah, it's rough for them."

"I'm glad I'm not a girl," Jericho said decisively.

"In my day people used to look down on girls who had babies before they got married. I guess that makes me old."

"Nothing is like it was back in the day, Dad. To lots of kids, sex doesn't mean anything at all. It's just something to do, like going to the mall."

"That's sad," his father said with a shake of his head. Then he looked carefully at his son. "I'm an old-fashioned kind of guy, Jericho."

"I know, Dad."

"I still believe a girl ought to be treated like a jewel to be treasured instead of a rock to be tossed away when you're done with it."

"I get what you're saying."

"But even when I was in school, boys were sometimes congratulated for proving that the plumbing worked—that they were man enough to reproduce."

"That hasn't changed. You'd faint if I told you what the dudes in the locker rooms say when they make it with a girl." Jericho looked uncomfortable.

"Jericho, in my line of work, I've heard it all and seen worse. You can't shock me."

"I guess you're right." Jericho began kneading his pillow.

"So, are you going to tell me? Is it Arielle the airhead? I thought you broke up with her."

"She dumped *me*, Dad. But it's not Arielle. These days she's letting Logan Holbrook be her plumber, not me."

"Then who?" Jericho's dad tensed.

"You have to promise not to tell anybody yet."

"News of a pregnancy gets out within nine months, I've heard," said his father dryly.

"It's November," Jericho said finally.

His father jumped to his feet. "November? Josh's girl-friend? She's having *your* baby? Jericho—what a mess!"

"No! No! You've got it all wrong!"

"I'm not following you, son."

"Be for real, Dad. You make me sound like some kind of lowlife. Yeah, November's pregnant. But she was Josh's girl. It's Josh's baby."

His father sat back down on the bed and exhaled. "Okay. I get it now." He ran his fingers through his thinning hair. "It's still a mess."

"Yeah. November is way confused and scared. And her mother is a basket case. And Josh . . ." The grandfather clock in the downstairs hall chimed loudly.

"Oh, that poor kid. What is she going to do?"

"Have the baby, I guess. I told her I'd be there for her—

whatever that means—I guess to hold her hand and stuff. There's not much else I can do."

"Do Brock and Marlene know yet?"

"No. We saw them at the store last night. It was like watching two cartoon characters—one moving at hyper-speed, and one in slow motion."

"Maybe this news will cheer them up," his father mused.

"I suggested that to November, but she got all prickly about it, so I didn't say anything else. And you can't either." He gave his father a steady stare. "You can't tell them," he said again. Then he asked, "How do you think Josh would have taken this news—about being a father?"

Mr. Prescott smiled softly. "Josh could be pretty silly, but he wasn't irresponsible. He would have done all he could to support November."

"What must it be like, Dad, to know you're carrying the child of somebody who will never see it, never even know it existed?"

"I'm sure a lot of women whose husbands are killed in military service can answer that, son. Women have been dealing with that tragedy for centuries."

"Do you think any less of November now that you know she's pregnant?"

"Of course not."

"Is it because Josh was your nephew, and this baby will be related to you?"

Jericho's father started to answer, but the phone rang and interrupted their conversation. "I've got to get to the station," he told Jericho after he hung up. "A semi has turned over on I-71, and the whole interstate is shut down." He hurried down the stairs.

Jericho thought about November as he got dressed—how her world was just about as messed up as that semi.

"GIRL, YOU PICKED THE WRONG DAY TO skip school," Dana said excitedly the instant November answered her cell phone.

"I didn't skip. I just didn't feel good. My body said go back to bed, so I did."

"When my body tells me stuff like that, my mother makes me get up anyway," Dana said with a chuckle.

"My mom is still in the guilty phase—like me being pregnant is somehow her fault. So she let me stay home."

"I've been trying to call you since lunchtime."

"I just turned my phone back on. What happened?"

"Are you ready for this? Logan Holbrook got arrested!"

"Shut up!"

"Prime time, girlfriend. Right in the middle of lunch. In front of everybody in the cafeteria!"

"And I missed it? No way! What did they get him for?" November made herself comfortable on the living-room sofa.

"Drugs!"

"Using or selling?"

"Probably both, but they found out he's been selling drugs to little kids at the elementary and middle school."

"Logan? I can't believe it." November's thoughts reeled. Logan, the captain of the basketball team. Logan, the National Merit Finalist. He was one of those kids who had a path of gold already paved for him. It didn't make any sense. Why would he get caught up in that stuff?

"I feel you. One of the teachers actually *fainted*. But most of them looked either shocked or kinda teary-eyed."

"No way! Who passed out?"

"Miss Veneterri—teaches computer math."

"Oh, she's so fake. She tried to act like she was gonna faint at Josh's funeral, but nobody paid her much mind, so she pulled herself together. But you still haven't told me how they busted Logan."

"Some kid in the fourth grade finally spilled her guts."

"Just like that?"

"Word is her mom found some strange pills in the kid's backpack, and the little girl told her mom that Logan had given them to her."

"How would Logan ever even come in contact with a little kid like that?" November asked in disbelief.

Dana reveled in telling November the juicy gossip. She told the story with drama and flair. And she took her time. "Logan had an after-school job."

"Yeah, I know. He always had lots of spending money. He once donated a hundred dollars when we were collecting money for the hurricane victims in New Orleans. Where was he working—McDonald's?"

"Nope. He drove the ice-cream truck."

"Oh that's right, I remember. Jericho's little brothers used to break their necks when the truck came down their street."

"So did I," Dana said with a giggle. "But it turns out that Logan was selling more than popsicles and ice-cream bars. He had a huge stash of pills in the back of the truck."

"No way!"

"Yes way!" Dana's voice rose in excitement. "He told the kids that the pills came from the health food store and would give them lots of energy. He gave them the first pill, then sold them any more they wanted. And they always wanted more."

"But fourth graders are only nine!"

"No kidding. That's what made them easy prey. Little kids are gullible."

"So the cops came into school?" November asked, getting Dana back to the story.

"Yep, the principal, along with four armed police officers with their hands on their guns."

"Like somebody was gonna shoot them? Cops are so full of themselves."

"I don't know. They just looked scary serious. No smiles. No conversation."

"I bet the cafeteria got so quiet." November could only imagine what the tension must have been like.

"It was like all the air had been sucked out. Nobody breathed. Nobody said a word. Everybody watched and waited to see who the cops had come for. I got a couple of unpaid parking tickets in my car. Made my heart go flip-flop for a hot minute!"

"I don't think they come in with guns for just some unpaid tickets."

"Thank goodness! No—they stomped into the lunch-room, marched over to the table where Logan and Arielle were eating lunch, pulled Logan to his feet, and hand-cuffed him in front of two hundred gaping students."

"Busted!"

"He had only taken one bite out of his hamburger."

"Then what? Did he say anything?"

"No, he was way cool. He looked like those criminals on TV—like he was too smooth to look scared or show emotion."

"Did they read him his rights like they do on the cop shows? Girlfriend, I'm kicking myself that I missed this!"

"Yeah, they did! You could almost hear every kid there gulping. Then they walked him out. His hands were behind his back, plastic cuffs on his wrists."

"I thought handcuffs were silver."

"You're thinking cowboy shows. This is the twenty-first century. Cops nowadays use stuff that's probably impossible for anyone to get out of."

"I guess you're right. So, what was Arielle doing while all this was happening?"

"Before Logan even left the room, she picked up her books, left her lunch, and split."

"I don't blame her. Talk about embarrassing! What about Jericho? What did he say?"

"He was sitting with me and Kofi. But you know Jericho—he keeps his thoughts inside. He left shortly after Arielle did."

"You think he went to make her feel better?"

"Not likely. I think he went home. I didn't see his car in the parking lot after school."

"You know, even though Logan put up a good show, I bet he felt like he was gonna pee in his pants."

"You got that right. If I was Logan, I'd be real scared."

"I bet he gets some serious jail time," November commented.

"You know, he had a scholarship to college—basketball," Dana told November.

"And just last week Arielle was boasting that Logan had a recording contract ready to sign—big label." November shook her head.

"A girlfriend. A job. Parents with cash. Good looks. A car." Dana sounded perplexed.

"Why would he toss all that away?" asked November.

"Just stupid, I guess. Hey, I gotta go, girl. See you at school tomorrow."

NOVEMBER'S FIRST-BELL CLASS WAS
American history. The teacher, Mr. Fox,
was a retired army sergeant who seemed to
march instead of walk, and he carried himself as if he was still a soldier in dress uniform. He always smelled of cigarettes. It would
seem that a man with a military background,
someone who had been in actual battles, would
be a dynamic teacher of history. Not so.

Instead of making history come alive, as her
European history teacher had the year before—
letting them build castles and play with swords and
stage mock battles—Mr. Fox assigned a new chapter
in the textbook each Monday, passed out study questions on Tuesday, did a vocabulary review on Wednesday and a review of important people in the chapter on
Thursday, then gave a quiz on Friday. He never varied his
schedule. Talk about dull!

A lot of kids tolerated him because he didn't make them

work hard. If they turned in every single assignment and passed all the quizzes, they were guaranteed to get at least a B. Nobody ever remembered anything they learned in his class, in spite of the fact that no one ever left the classroom.

Mr. Fox never let students out of class. Ever. He had tossed his hall pass in the wastebasket the first day of school. Counselors who wanted to check a student's schedule had learned to get that person out of English or gym or band. Not Mr. Fox's class. Kids learned to use the toilet facilities before class, or hold it until after.

November wiggled in her seat uncomfortably. She really had to go to the bathroom. Her mother had insisted she drink two large glasses of orange juice before she left for school. November was sure her bladder was about to burst.

"I gotta pee!" she whispered to Olivia.

"You gotta hold it," Olivia whispered back.

"I *really* gotta go bad! Feels like a brick is sitting on my bladder. It's gonna pop like a balloon!"

Mr. Fox looked up disapprovingly.

"That's no brick. That's the baby!" Olivia hissed.

"I *really* gotta get out of here."

"He won't let you!"

"How is he gonna stop me?" November retorted. She stood up.

"May I help you, Nelson?" Mr. Fox said, looking up from the book he was reading.

"I need to be excused, sir."

"Sorry. You know my rules."

"But this is an emergency."

"Lack of planning on your part does not constitute an emergency for me."

"Nobody plans when they have to pee! When you gotta go, you gotta go! And I gotta go."

"It's almost the end of the school year, Nelson. Surely you know I don't let students out of class. I have not yet, and I do not intend to do so. Now sit down. You can wait thirty minutes."

"But I can't!" November's voice was pleading and desperate. She hopped from one foot to the other.

"Please sit down, Nelson."

"What if I walk out? What are you gonna do—shoot me in the back as I leave?" November moved closer to the door.

"No one leaves my classroom. That's my only rule. I think that's quite reasonable."

"It not like anybody would miss anything in this boring, bootleg class!" November shouted. "A trained chimp could pass this class!"

"What has gotten into you, young lady?" Mr. Fox asked, his voice bristling with anger. The class looked at her in awe.

"What's in me? You really want to know? Well, I'll tell you! Two glasses of fresh-squeezed orange juice, one large poppy-seed bagel, one bowl of blueberry yogurt, and a baby! Yes, a real, live baby, who is at this moment doing a tap dance on my bladder."

Several students gasped at this revelation. November, flushed and angry, continued, "So you're just gonna have to mark me as AWOL because I'm walking out of that door this instant, down the hall, and to the bathroom before I pee all over your floor!"

She dug her fingernails into her palms to keep from crying, then stormed out of the room. She could hear the class cheering as the door slammed. She knew Mr. Fox would silence their outburst with just a look.

Well, there goes Mom's big secret, she thought a few minutes later as she washed her hands. *It's not like it wasn't gonna creep out eventually*. She sighed. *Now it begins*. She wandered the halls until the bell rang, when she darted into the room, grabbed her books, and scooted back out. She avoided looking at Mr. Fox or anyone else.

By the end of the day, everybody at school knew that November was pregnant. Cell phones had come out like buzzards after a kill as kids sent calls and text messages to one another, passing along the news and trying to get more details. That's all anyone talked about—November, and the fact that Logan had been arrested at school. It was better than reality television.

The conversations in the hall hummed with half truths and rumors.

"I heard Logan was caught doing drugs."

"No, he wasn't doing drugs—he was dealing!"

"To little kids!"

"That's pretty low, if you ask me."

"I heard one kid almost died because of what Logan gave him."

"I think it was a cop's kid."

"Somebody said they searched Logan's house and found a garbage bag full of stuff."

"I wonder what cops do with a big stash like that."

"I bet they divide it up and take it home."

"You think?"

"You so dumb. You believe anything."

"Logan's dad hired a big-name lawyer, I heard."

"He's gonna need one!"

"What about Arielle? They find anything on her?"

"I don't think so."

"Too bad."

"You too cold."

"Yeah, tough break for November, too. She deserves better."

"Straight up."

"Naw, Miss Thing got what's comin' to her."

"How you figure?"

"She used to think she was all that, but now she ain't nothing but!"

"Girl, you just be hatin'!"

"I wonder who else she been with."

"She keepin' the baby?"

"She got a dead baby-daddy. That sucks."

"I've seen some live baby-daddies that ain't much better than a dead one!"

"Straight up."

"I wonder what Josh's parents think about the kid. They have lots of cash, somebody said."

"So?"

"Well, if you got enough money, you can do anything!"

"Would you give up your baby to its grandparents?"

"Not me. But my man's parents are whacked. I wouldn't do that to a kid."

"I might think about it—I could go out and have fun and not have to worry about some cryin' baby back home that needed changing!"

"Then you better keep your pants on, girlfriend. You ain't fit to be a mother!"

November knew what the kids around her were saying, and not only did it embarrass her, it ticked her off. It made her blush to imagine what kids were saying about what she and Josh had done, and she felt like smacking some of the self-righteous girls who tried to look down on her. Arielle was one of them.

"What's up, November?" Arielle said one day after school.

"Nothing much," November replied, trying to dig her English book out of her locker in a hurry so she could avoid talking to her.

"Word is you and Josh were a lot closer than you let on."

"Why you tryin' to be all up in my business?" November slammed her locker door.

"So you're keeping the baby?"

"It's really none of your business, Arielle," November replied tersely as she snapped the lock onto the metal hasp.

"You don't have to get all salty," Arielle replied, rolling her eyes. "I thought we were tight."

"We used to be," November said after a pause, a hint of sadness in her voice. "But lately you been acting like you all that and a bag of chips!"

Arielle leaned against the lockers. "It wasn't me who changed. When I broke up with Jericho, you and Dana acted like I'd dumped you as well. So I moved on."

"Well, keep moving. I gotta get to lunch."

"I'd wondered why you were gaining so much weight," said Arielle as she walked alongside November. "You used to have such cute clothes." Arielle brushed a speck of dirt from her Ultrasuede miniskirt.

"And you used to be likable," November retorted. She hurried away in the other direction—angry, embarrassed, and hurt.

She threw her books onto the lunch table and flopped down next to Dana and Olivia.

"So who peed in your cornflakes?" Dana asked.

"Teachers. Haters. Arielle." November blinked hard— she wasn't sure if the tears were from anger or frustration, but she was really tired of crying all the time.

"Don't let lowlifes get the best of you, November," Olivia said gently. "I face it all the time."

November sniffed. "I'm okay. At least for the moment. Can I have some of your fries?" she asked Olivia.

"You want to go to the mall with us after school?" Dana offered. "Shopping cures all problems!"

"I'm with you on that, but I've got a doctor's appointment after school," November told them.

"You going by yourself?" Dana asked. "I can drive you if you want some company."

"Thanks, but my mother's going with me. I guess she's finally quit pretending this will go away, and now she wants to get information so she can stress me out for the next five and a half months! Already she's got me drinking guava juice and eating raw carrots. And save me from Internet baby blogs!"

"Aw, quit complainin'," Olivia said, intently mixing a slab of butter into her mashed potatoes. "At least you got a mama to fret over you."

November and Dana exchanged glances. "What happened to your mom?" Dana asked gently.

"She died the day I was born. A rare childbirth complication called postpartum hemorrhage," answered Olivia. She buried the butter into the potato mound. "Basically, she bled to death."

At the words "childbirth complication" November shifted uncomfortably in her seat. Complications? She'd never given a moment's thought to complications. Man, she was totally clueless. She forced her attention back to Olivia. "That's so sad," she whispered.

"I didn't know," Dana added softly. "I'm really sorry, Olivia."

November inhaled. "My dad died when I was ten. I still miss him."

"You got memories of him?" Olivia asked.

"Yeah, lots of good ones, although it's like they fade as I get older," November mused. "I hate that."

"I don't have one single thing to remember," Olivia said, her eyes filling with tears. "It's like a clean notebook—full of pages with nothing written on them."

"My mother makes me itch," Dana told them, "but I wouldn't know how to breathe without her. It must be really hard."

"You know what it's like not having a mother?" Olivia asked.

"I can guess, but not really," November replied.

"Imagine being born without your right hand. You learn to do stuff without it. You eat with your left hand and fig-ure out how to tie your shoes. You only need one glove in the winter. But you can't clap."

November rubbed her hands together unconsciously. "Deep."

"You function, sort of, but you're missing something vital. Feel me?"

"Yeah," said Dana.

"My daddy raised me. He did a pretty good job, and he loves me something fierce. But he never much cared about what I ate, so I grew up on Froot Loops and french fries, and he never once took me shopping for anything other than groceries. I've always envied girls who go to the mall with their mothers. I bought my first bra by myself."

"I think I'd rather do that trip without my dad," Dana said with a smile.

Olivia smiled back. "Don't get me wrong. I owe a lot to my dad. He used to read to me every night, and that's how I learned to love books. He made me study so I could make good grades, and he taught me to be tough so I could face airheads like Arielle."

"Sounds like you got her on your mind," November teased.

"I could care less about that little twit. She's the one who's thinking about me. Every time I see her in the hall, I make a fist and mouth, 'I'm gonna pay you back!' She wrinkles up her face like she's about to cry or puke, then runs in the other direction." Olivia laughed. "The threat of terror is a powerful thing!"

"Are you really going to get her?" Dana asked.

"Of course not. But she doesn't know that. It's the intimidation factor that makes me powerful. As long as she's scared of me, she won't bother me."

"Arielle's been laying kinda low anyway since Logan got busted," Dana added.

"I heard she dumped him just like she dumped Jericho. The girl does not deal well with stress!" November said.

"Anybody know what's going to happen to Logan?" asked Olivia. "Not that I care."

"Lots and lots of jail time."

The bell rang and the three girls put away their lunch trays and headed for class.

AFTER DR. HOLLAND FINISHED HER EXAMI-nation, she snapped off her gloves and told November, "You seem to be doing fine, dear, but your blood pressure is a little higher than I'd like to see, and it's a little early for your feet to be swelling like they are. I want you to eliminate salt from your diet."

"No salt? I'll shrivel up and die!" November wailed.

"If we don't get that blood pressure down, that's a real possibility," the doctor warned.

"For real?"

"My job is to keep you and that baby as healthy as possible. Your job is to do your best to follow my guidelines so we don't have to worry about such serious complications, okay?"

November immediately thought of Olivia's mother and nodded. "I'm trying. I take those stupid horse vitamins every day. My mom has become a health food addict, and I even try to exercise a little."

"Good." Dr. Holland scribbled notes on November's chart. "Do you have any other questions for me?"

"Uh, I don't want to sound stupid, and I read a bunch of stuff on the Internet, but it just seems amazing that a little mini-me knows what to do in there, how to grow and stuff."

"You're right. It is incredible. I think that's why I stay in the business. The creation of life is truly awe-inspiring. Your baby has a heartbeat now, you know."

"Really?"

"Would you like to hear it?"

"Can I?"

"Sure. Would you like your mother to come in and listen with you?"

November agreed, and her mother was called into the examining room while Dr. Holland hooked up the fetal monitor, explaining that it could both detect as well as project the sound of a tiny heartbeat.

"Good afternoon, Mrs. Nelson. Are you ready?" the doctor asked.

November's mother sat down in a chair and nodded. Her face showed a mixture of excitement and resignation. "I suppose there's no turning back now. The whole idea of my daughter being pregnant is something I've had to get used to," she admitted.

"I understand completely."

As the doctor adjusted the dials on the machine, Mrs. Nelson asked, "Is November okay? Is the baby healthy?"

"Everything is fine right now, but I'm little concerned

about her blood pressure. I've advised her to stay away from salt."

"Really? Is there a problem? Should I be concerned? Should we call a specialist?" Mrs. Nelson rattled off questions like machine-gun fire. "I'm looking this up on the Internet as soon as we get home."

November put her hand on her forehead and shook her head. "Now you've done it, Dr. H. You've told the queen of healthy eating that I can't have salt. She'll be checking labels and making me eat tasteless food for the rest of my life!"

Dr. Holland laughed. "You should be thankful you have such a concerned mom, November." To Mrs. Nelson she said, "Moderation is the key right now. I'm keeping a close watch on her."

Mrs. Nelson didn't seem to be completely convinced, but she nodded in agreement.

Dr. Holland adjusted the ultrasound machine as well as the probe that was connected to November's belly. "Here we go."

The room was silent for a moment, then November could hear the softest little rhythm, *LUB*-dup, *LUB*-dup, *LUB*-dup. It sounded like the heartbeat of a mouse. Dr. Holland adjusted the volume, and the rhythmic thuds almost boomed in the small room.

"Is that my baby?" November asked, her voice full of awe.

"Yes, it is."

That's my baby! she thought. *A real baby!* Somehow the heartbeat made it all completely real.

"How big is it?" she asked.

"About five inches long now—the size of a baking potato."

"When do I find out if it's a boy or a girl?"

"We'll do a sonogram next month, and, if the baby cooperates, we'll find out then."

November glanced over at her mother. She was amazed to see tears streaming down her mom's face. "Are you okay, Mom?"

Mrs. Nelson pulled a tissue from her purse and wiped her eyes. "Of course, honey. It's just . . . it's just so overwhelming!"

"I'm glad you came with me, Mom," said November with feeling as the doctor unhooked the machine.

"Me too, sweetie."

"When will I feel it move?" November asked the doctor as she touched her belly gingerly.

"Soon. It might feel like you swallowed a small fish that's wiggling around, or like there's a butterfly fluttering around in there. Did you know that the fetus can already suck its thumb?"

"Wow."

"What can I do to help, doctor?" Mrs. Nelson asked.

"Make sure she drinks lots of water, eats several healthy meals a day, and no more fast food. We don't want this kid coming out craving burgers and fries! Also, November probably needs to take a nap after school."

"School is almost out for the summer, so she'll have lots of time to eat well and rest."

"What about my job at Stepping Stones summer camp?" said November. "I volunteer there every summer, working with the disabled kids. Can I still do that?"

"Is it safe?" Mrs. Nelson asked the doctor. "Some of the clients there are heavy to lift, and some are a little hard to control. I wouldn't want November to endanger her health or the safety of the baby."

"Oh, Mom. I always work with the three-year-olds. I'd be fine."

"I know," said her mother, glancing at the baby ducks in the picture on the wall. "But you know what the old people say. . . ." She let her voice trail off.

"Disabilities are not contagious, you know," the doctor said softly.

"Oh, I know that. In my brain I do." She turned and faced the doctor. "Did November tell you about her older brother? He has Down syndrome."

"Yes, it's in her medical history. Now that is something that *is* inherited and can be passed down genetically." Dr. Holland looked directly at November's mother. "Perhaps we should schedule an amniocentesis—to make sure the baby is developing normally."

November, who had been sitting slumped and dejected, raised her head then, silenced her mother with a glance, and told the doctor, "We'll let you know."

The doctor jotted some information onto November's chart. "I'll leave that decision to the two of you. Maybe a summer of reading, relaxing, and light exercising might be better for all concerned," she commented. "Maybe you can take a parenting class or a predelivery class instead. Here's a flyer on a program I think is pretty good. Call them. The more you know about what to expect, the less afraid you'll be."

"I think we're both pretty scared. Thank you, Doctor," Mrs. Nelson said as they got ready to leave.

"I'll see you, November, around the end of June or first week of July," the doctor said. "Call me if you have any concerns."

November answered, "Okay." She picked up her purse, then hesitated and looked back at the small machine that had detected the heartbeat. "Amazing," she whispered.

WHEN NOVEMBER AND HER MOTHER GOT
home, the telephone answering machine
was blinking. November sunk down on the
sofa, picked up the phone, and dialed the
code to check the messages.

The first was from Dana. "Hey, girl. Just
checking on you. Maybe the doctor made a mistake and you're not pregnant after all; it's just a
case of too many mashed potatoes!" November
grinned as she listened.

"Seriously, let me know if everything is okay, or if
you need any help. I sure am glad school is almost
out. When I get back from the Black College Tour—
did I tell you Kofi was going in your place? Yum. A
week on the road with my dude. Anyway, when we get
back, I'm working at the mall. You know that new bou-
tique store that sells the fly outfits? With my employee
discount, I won't save a penny, but I sure will look good in
my new rags when we bust in there as seniors!" Then there

was a silence. Dana continued, "Hey, sorry. I forgot you won't be able to wear cool clothes—at least for a while. But we'll get you hooked up after the baby is born. Don't worry. Hey, I gotta go. Kofi's on the other line. Call me when you get a chance."

November sighed. Dana was right. Senior year. Everyone had said it would be the best time of her life. Dates. Parties. Clothes. The prom. All of it screwed up because of this.

She clicked over to the next message. This one was from Olivia, sounding a little hesitant. "Hi, November. This is Olivia. I hope your doctor visit went well. Guess what? I bought a baby memory book for you from the home shopping channel. It's so you can keep a record of everything that kid does and says and how you feel about it. I hope that's okay."

November pictured Olivia's earnest face and smiled. She was definitely glad she'd gotten to know her better. Olivia continued, "You know, we talked a little today about shopping. Maybe one day during summer vacation, if you're not too busy, I mean, maybe me and you can go to the mall and look for a couple of maternity tops for you. Maybe even some baby clothes. But if you'd rather do that with Dana or your mom, I understand. I just thought it might be fun. I'm going to work this summer down at the public library. I work there every summer. It's quiet, nobody bothers me, and I get to read a million books. Besides, it's a nice break from all the noise of band practice. Call me if you feel like it."

November promised herself she'd call Olivia after dinner. She clicked over to the third message. The caller ID indicated it was from somebody named Henderson Grant, attorney-at-law. *Probably one of those annoying salesmen*, November thought. But her heart began to thud as she listened. "This message is for April and November Nelson. We would like to meet with you at your earliest convenience to discuss the future of your unborn child. Our clients, Brock and Marlene Prescott, would like to make this process painless as well as profitable for you. A meeting has been set for June twenty-eighth, at ten in the morning, in our offices downtown. We look forward to working with you."

Stunned, November held the phone in her hand until it started making that irritating beeping noise to remind her to hang it up. "What the hell . . . ?" she muttered.

Her hands trembled as she redialed for the rest of the messages. There was one left, and it was from Jericho. "Hey, November. I just want to give you a heads-up. My uncle Brock and aunt Marlene have lost their minds—both of them. I guess you know they found out about the baby. News like that travels fast. Anyway, Aunt Marlene has decided she wants custody of the baby when it's born. Their lawyer is gonna call your mother soon—offer you money to give up the baby. I just wanted to warn you. Take care, girl. This is a mess! Catch you later."

November stood up, gulping hard. *I don't get it. Why would they do this?* Her stomach churned so badly she felt like she had to go to the bathroom.

Finally she called to her mother, who was upstairs using the computer. "Mom, I think we have a problem. A big one."

In an instant her mother's feet were pounding down the stairs. "Do you feel sick?" she asked frantically.

"No, not that kind of trouble, Mom."

"Then what's up?" her mother asked, hurrying into the room.

"Josh's parents found out about the baby. They've hired a lawyer. Can you believe that? They want us to meet with them next month. I think they want to offer me money to give them the baby." November was surprised at how furious she felt. "Is that even legal?"

"What? Why would they do that?"

"I don't know . . . Yeah, I do. Because it's part of Josh. Maybe they think I don't want the baby. Maybe they think they'd be better parents." November looked at her mother in anguish.

Her mother took November's face in her hands. "Sweetheart, calm down. I'm not one hundred percent legally sure, but they can't simply walk in and claim the child," she told her. "Not unless you want to give the baby up to them voluntarily."

"What? Give it away?"

Her mother paused. "It *is* an option," she said hesitantly.

November stopped cold. What was her mother saying? "What do you mean? That the baby would be better off with *them* than *me*?"

"No, of course not. But . . . maybe it's something to consider." Mrs. Nelson sat down next to November.

November glared at her mother. She was suddenly, completely, utterly infuriated. "How can you even consider giving up your grandchild? What kind of monster are you?"

"Just listen, November. You're so young, with such a great future ahead of you," her mother said in her most soothing voice. "When all this is over, it's not impossible that you could still get accepted to Cornell, or another fine university. Maybe letting them adopt the baby might not be such a bad idea."

"How can you say that? You talk like after the baby is born, this will all go away like a bad dream! How *dare* you take their side!" November's eyes flashed.

Her mother looked at her for a moment and touched her daughter's hair. "Not at all, sweetie. This situation is just so difficult." She choked back tears.

November pushed her mother's hand away. "This is *my* gut that's stretching, and *my* nose that keeps getting stopped up. It's rough for *me*, not you!" she screamed.

"And if you had kept your pants on, none of this would have happened!" her mother yelled back. She stopped then, and they stared at each other in shock.

"Well, I'm glad you finally said it!" November shrieked, jumping up off the couch. "You think I'm a slut!"

Suddenly the room was very quiet. Neither mother nor daughter said anything. Both of them were crying.

Finally Mrs. Nelson said, her voice steady again, "We're going to get through this together, baby girl. Together, you hear?" She reached out to her daughter.

November fell into her mother's arms. "Oh, Mom. I wish Josh was alive and none of this had happened." She cried for a long time.

When November's shoulders stopped heaving, her mother said, "You don't have to decide anything right away. Let's think about this, and pray about it, okay?"

November sniffed and took a deep breath. "What about finishing high school? Going away to college? That's pretty much screwed up if I try to raise this kid myself."

"Not necessarily."

"What do *you* think I should do, Mom?" November asked glumly.

"It's your decision, not mine. Just like you made the decision to make the baby, it will be your choice to determine what happens to it."

"I didn't *decide* to make a baby!" November replied, her anger flaring up again. "I didn't plan on any of this!"

"Well, it's time for some serious planning now. I love you, November, and, yes, I love that child you're carrying. But we're talking about a life here. Sometimes doing the right thing is the most difficult decision to make."

"How can you be so cold?" November looked at her mother pleadingly.

"I'm going to try to keep *my* emotions out of this. It's up to you, November. You have to think about your life, and the life of that baby—not just the first year when it's cute and cuddly, but also through grade school and chicken pox and knee scrapes and braces and college—everything will be *forever* affected by what you decide."

"I'm so mixed up, Mom. How do I know what's the right thing to do?"

"Take your time. You'll know."

November had never felt so confused and alone. Forever was a long, long time.

CHAPTER 22
JERICHO
MONDAY, JUNE 14

JERICHO TROTTED RELUCTANTLY ONTO THE
field behind the high school. *What have I
signed myself up for?* he thought. *What was
I thinking, telling Coach Barnes I'd play football?* At least the summer practices were not
full-fledged workouts, he tried to convince
himself—more like conditioning and physical
fitness stuff. He stretched a little, took a huge
gulp from his water bottle, and nodded to the
other guys who were doing the same. Aside from
Luis, the quarterback, the only boys he knew well
were Rudy and Cleveland, who had pledged the Warriors with him. No one had much to say, which was
how Jericho liked it. He wasn't here to make friends. *I
can't believe how hot it is*, he thought, *and it's still
June. No one in his right mind should be out in this sun.
What am I doing here? Now I remember why I gave it up
in ninth grade.*
Since the Ohio High School Athletic Association's rules

about preseason play were very strict, Jericho had figured he could handle the ten days of conditioning between now and the time the season officially started, but he hadn't planned on this heat. But the days when he didn't have practice were worse—those were the days that he had nothing to do but think. Vacation was the pits.

He looked up at the blazing sun, and a thought struck him. Josh had no idea what the weather was, or whether a hurricane or tornado had messed up some city, or that November was having his baby. Josh knew nothing. It was still unimaginable.

The coaches, clipboards in hand and whistles around their necks, started barking orders. "Gimme a lap around the field!" Coach Barnes yelled. Jericho and the others fell into place and started running.

He jogged at a steady pace. Jericho couldn't help remembering all the running and exercising he and Josh and the others had done to get into the Warriors of Distinction. Josh had bounded effortlessly through the whole process—that is, until the very last night.

Get outta my head, Josh! Jericho thought, sweat starting to roll down his back. His brain felt crowded and jumbled, as if all the doors in his head were nailed shut. Then he almost panicked, fearing that his memories of Josh would fade. It was making him crazy. *Stay with me, Josh! I don't know how to do this without you, man!* Josh lived in that mess in his head now, and no matter what he did, Jericho could not escape. He ran even harder. He had no idea if he could sweat the pain away, but he was damn well going to try.

"Okay, men," the coach called, "let's break down into groups and try some reaction drills. Backs, you go with Coach Crawley. Linemen, you stay with me."

Jericho, the biggest lineman in the group, took his position in the front of the pack. Just before school had let out, the coach had taken Jericho aside.

"So you're coming out for my team—finally ready to step up and be a man," he'd said with a grin.

"I guess."

"I need commitment, Jericho. I don't want you out there if you can't give me one hundred and ten percent!"

"I'm ready, Coach. For real."

"I dug up the tapes of your games when you were in junior high. There was a lot of raw talent there. You're a natural."

"I am?"

"It's like riding a bike. You never forget the skill. You just have to get back in shape."

"If you say so." But Jericho had been doubtful. "I guess it's like playin' my horn. The music is always there—stuck in the back of my head."

"Are you sure about leaving the band?" Coach Barnes had asked. "I talked to Tambori and he's really pissed that you've given up your instrument."

"Yeah, I know. He thinks I have talent. I had a chance to try out for Juilliard, but I blew it." Jericho avoided looking at the coach. "I always figured I'd be tryin' for a music scholarship. I guess stuff just changes," he continued, thinking again of Josh.

"Well, I think you have real potential as a football player. I want you on my line—as a tackle. You do have an opportunity for a football scholarship, you know. Colleges will be looking at you seniors, and even though you haven't played recently, you've got the size and the weight to be a great tackle. But do you have the heart?"

"Yeah, Coach. I got what you need," Jericho had promised. But he still wasn't sure if he'd made the right decision.

"All right, now! Keep those feet moving! Come on—chop it up! Way to work, Jericho," yelled Coach Barnes.

Jericho didn't acknowledge the compliment, but it made him feel good that he was the only man out there who the coach had mentioned by name. *Maybe it's because he knows I'm not sure if I want to be here. Maybe he's just trying to make me feel good so I won't quit and go back to the band.*

Despite his size, Jericho's reactions were quick and deliberate. Leading the group, he sprinted out when the coach's hand was raised, then returned to the back of the line, getting ready for the next drill.

"Over and under in a figure eight!" the coach bellowed. "At the sound of the whistle, the middle man hits the dirt and rolls to the right. The man to the right goes over him and rolls to the left. Hustle, men! Don't stop until you hear the whistle. Go!"

The rhythm of the physical leaps and runs and rolls had a surprisingly calming effect on Jericho. For an hour or so, his head was free of guilt and turmoil. Jericho began to hope that Coach Barnes, who had been drafted by the Cincinnati Bengals back in the day, might be the one to help him work out the kinks he felt inside.

"When you hear the whistle," the coach said next, "spring up into a ready position and keep those feet choppin'! When I raise my hand, sprint, and I mean *sprint* to the side and get back to the rear of the line!" The whistle shrieked.

Jericho was already dripping with perspiration, and now, because the tackles and guards did their drills on the section of the practice field that overlapped the baseball infield, he felt like one big dirt demon.

Mr. Barnes cried out, "Let those pretty boy backs have the grass. The real men, those of you on the line, don't care about a little dirt! Do it again—this time with power! Sometimes winning is a dirty job. Let me hear you say Po-wer!"

"Po-wer!" the boys on the line shouted back enthusiastically.

After a couple of hours of drills and sprints, Jericho was relieved to hear the coach blow his whistle. "Bring it up and take a knee, fellas."

Gathering in a circle around him, the players crouched, one knee on the ground, guzzling from their water bottles. "Okay, men, I want to talk about the upcoming season. The Douglass High Panthers have not had a winning season in five years. As a matter of fact, the last time this school was in the state play-offs was twenty years ago, when *I* was the quarterback of the team—and that's back when dinosaurs ruled the earth!"

The players chuckled.

"But this year we are going to turn it around. We are a small team, but we have good hustle and speed. You looked good out there today. We've got our strengths, and

I've spotted a few weaknesses, but that's what conditioning and practice are for. We've got time to get ready for a great season. The Panthers will prowl this year!"

"Panthers!" the players yelled together. "Panthers prowl! Panthers win!"

Jericho found himself caught up in the sweaty excitement of the boys and the coaches as he shouted with them. *Sorta like the chants we recited as we pledged for the Warriors of Distinction*, he thought, vaguely uneasy, but he brushed the thought away. *This is football. The real deal. Pathway to big-time college football and the NFL.*

Coach Barnes continued, "I believe we'll take a lot of people by surprise. This season we're playing our usual opponents—Hazelwood and Fairfield and Lakota. We've got a bye for the first week, which is good because that gives us another week of practice." He paused.

"Who's our first game with, Coach?" asked Luis.

"It's a team we've never played before," the coach replied with a grin. "You're gonna need all your quarterbacking skills, Luis, as well as the rest of you."

"So who do we play—the Bengals?"

"The Bengals might be easier to beat!" the coach joked. "Our very first game, September fourth, is against the Excelsior Academy from Cleveland." He let that sink in.

"Excelsior the Excellent," one of the seniors said, elbowing the guy next to him.

"Damn. Richest school in the state," said the other boy, elbowing back.

"They've got ninety kids just in their *band*!" Jericho told them, remembering. "Every year they get brand-new gold and blue uniforms that light up in the dark. They use lasers and smoke and electronic instruments, and their half-time show was on HBO *and* CNN last year."

"Forget the band—what about the team?" Luis asked.

"More than fifty of the best-trained athletes in the state," Coach Barnes told them honestly. "Parents move into that area just so their boys can go to that school. Boosters and alumni pay for everything. They have a stadium that's almost as elaborate as the one the Bengals use."

"What's their record, Coach?" asked Jericho.

"They have gone to state finals eight of the last ten years, and for the past three years they have been undefeated. It's some kind of national record."

"Nobody's beat them?" a freshman asked in disbelief.

"Nobody. And they don't just win, they defeat their opponents by several touchdowns."

"Oh, man!" Cleveland groaned. He was playing halfback this year.

The coach continued, "And every time they score, they celebrate by shooting off fireworks and a cannon. It's quite intimidating," he told the boys, a small smile on his face.

"They're gonna kill us!" said Cleveland.

"What kind of attitude is that?" the coach asked. "I thought we were grooming winners out here today!"

"Groomin' us to get stomped on," Cleveland muttered.

"I don't want to hear talk like that, men. That team uses intimidation to terrorize their opponents. The lights, their new uniforms, their band—it's all designed to make you feel like a loser when you run onto that field. But we're not going to let that change our fighting attitude!"

"I still don't understand why we gotta play them," Luis said, scowling. "Especially on *their* field. We've never played them before."

"We're playing them for several reasons. One, since it's a nonconference away game for us, we get a nice little check from their gate receipts. They're likely to have twenty thousand people in the stands."

"This is gonna be humiliating!" a player named Roscoe said with a frown. "Why do we wanna sell our souls for some cash?"

"I would have scheduled you for this game even if they paid us nothing. I want you to see the professionalism and polish of a first-rate team. I want you guys to see what it's like to stay in a luxury hotel where you have to use table manners to eat!" He laughed. "I want you to experience the roar of a large crowd."

"Laughing at us?" Roscoe asked, his voice full of doubt.

"No, cheering for us," replied the coach with assurance. He continued to wear that strange, confident smile.

"How you figure they be cheering for us?" Jericho asked. "Face it. We're from a nobody school in the inner city."

Ignoring him, the coach demanded, "Stand up, men. Stand up tall!" The boys got out of their crouches and looked at the coach closely. He seemed to be glowing with enthusiasm.

"They are going to cheer for us because"—the coach took a moment to look at each of the players—"because we're . . . going to beat them!"

"Beat them?"

"Starting today, starting this very moment," Coach

Barnes said clearly, "we become winners! Champions! Believers in our skills and abilities!"

"Defeat the Mighty Excelsior Wildcats?" The guys on the field looked at the coach in disbelief.

"You trippin', man!" Roscoe grumbled.

"Take a lap, my young friend. As a matter of fact, take two! In order to succeed with us, you must believe with us." The coach pointed to Roscoe and jabbed his thumb toward the fence. Roscoe started to protest, but then he got up and began to jog slowly.

Another guy complained, "We're gonna look like animals going to slaughter when we walk out on that field." Jericho, who had no intention of running another step, couldn't believe the kid was stupid enough to complain, especially after he'd seen what Roscoe was doing.

"Join Roscoe," the coach commanded. "Anybody else want to say we can't win? I've got all day to sit here and watch you run."

No one else said a word.

The coach then burst out with, "A-gile! Mo-bile! Hos-tile! Say it with me, Panthers. Feel it!"

"A-gile! Mo-bile! Hos-tile!" the team chanted, but the enthusiasm wasn't there.

"Maybe we need to run a little more to find our passion," the coach threatened. "I said, 'Panther Pride! A-gile! Mo-bile! Hos-tile!' Say it like you mean it!"

"A-gile! Mo-bile! Hos-tile!" the boys repeated, louder this time.

"Good. Now we can start the process of learning how to be winners. You ever hear the story of David and Goliath?

The tortoise and the hare? These are tales where the underdog, the one that everyone expected to lose, and lose big, turns the tables, defeats the odds, and wins! Do you hear me? They won!"

"How?" shouted Cleveland, a hint of defiance in his voice.

"Through courage and cunning. Through skill and agility. And that's what we are going to learn to do this summer. We are going to learn to be champions! Are you with me, men? WE WILL WIN!"

Hesitantly at first, then more and more confidently, all the boys on the team joined the wave of the coach's enthusiasm. "WE WILL WIN!" they chanted. "WE WILL WIN!" Jericho joined the rest of them, yelling and screaming and hooting the name of the school and their team, but he doubted it could really be done.

AFTER PRACTICE, JERICHO DECIDED TO WALK
home rather than wait for his dad to pick
him up. He realized with dismay that he'd
left his water bottle on the field, but he didn't
go back. In the distance he heard music—the
familiar thumping of the drums, the bronzed
tones of the saxophones, and the crisp metallic
echoes of the trumpets. Band practice.

He couldn't help it—he headed straight for the
field where the band learned their steps, and stood
by the fence, watching. Mr. Tambori stood on a plat-
form, shouting instructions from a megaphone. "Backs
straight! Knees up! Keep those lines straight now!"

Jericho thought the band sounded pretty good. They
were practicing today without marching in the intricate
patterns that looked like squares or circles or other
designs. The clarinets sounded a little off-key, he thought,
but the brass instruments shone in the sunshine and
sounded like it as well, as far as he was concerned. The

sound washed over Jericho. It was the first time all day he'd relaxed.

"Hold your horns up," Mr. Tambori was calling. "Don't play to the ground—let the audience hear you! Swing those horns in rhythm! Move, trombones, move!"

Jericho spied Olivia Thigpen blowing her sousaphone with everything she had. It was clear she loved what she was doing, her cheeks puffing in and out and her feet marking the beat as she stood in place.

Jericho knew a lot of kids didn't get marching band. They thought the football players and cheerleaders were the ones who really worked. But he knew that marching band members were the tough ones. It was so much more than simply playing an instrument—it was about being a team player, memorizing every piece of music, holding the instrument correctly, learning new ways of moving and breathing. It was a lot of work. Some of those tenor drum sets could weigh up to fifty pounds. Tambori bellowed out, "Let's try that cadence again!"

Jericho laughed out loud as he looked across the field to Crazy Jack in the percussion section. Jack Krazinski loved to play the cymbals. He'd crash them on beat and off beat whenever he felt like it—before, during, and after practice. It wasn't uncommon to hear Crazy Jack smashing his cymbals together in school as he walked down the hall. Teachers would frown and write him disciplinary reprimands, but the next week he'd be at it again, making as much noise as he possibly could, grinning the whole time.

Jericho noticed that Olivia had put down her instrument as the woodwinds took up the song. The trilling of the flutes and piccolos, weaving in and out of the wailing of the clarinets, sounded like birds in the hot summer air. Olivia glanced over to where Jericho stood. She waved when she noticed him, then pointed to the area where the trumpet players stood, where Jericho would have been standing. He waved back but shook his head.

He looked at the kid who had taken his place as first trumpet and sighed. A sophomore! And a girl? He couldn't believe Tambori gave such an important position to somebody who'd only been playing for a couple of years! But then he realized he had no right to complain. He was the one who had quit the band. He watched quietly for a few more minutes, then picked up his bag to head home as band practice was dismissed.

He heard Mr. Tambori called out, "How was football practice?" He was walking toward Jericho.

"It was aight," Jericho answered, saying the word carelessly. But every muscle in his body seemed to be aching.

"There's still room for you here, you know." Mr. Tambori dangled the words like temptation. "Carole is an adequate player, but she's not you. She just reads the notes off the page of music. You feel them."

"So why did you make her first chair trumpet?"

"Because she was the best I had left."

"Hey, I appreciate what you're tryin' to do, Mr. T, but I gotta go. I hope the band has a good season."

"Take care, Jericho. Remember I'm here if you need me."

"Thanks, man." Jericho headed away from the fence and trudged down the street. *This must be what hell feels like*, he thought. *I need me some air-conditioning!*

"Hey, Jericho!"

Now what? He turned and saw Olivia Thigpen waving and hurrying in his direction. "What's up, Olivia?" Jericho really didn't feel like being bothered with her or anyone else today.

Her bright red, long-sleeved sweatshirt, tight over her arms and belly, was damp with sweat. She carried her sousaphone case, bulky and black, in front of her. "This is the kind of day I wish I played the flute," she said with a laugh.

"Hey, let me carry that thing for you," Jericho offered. "You look like one of those soldier ants carrying a big piece of food from the picnic table!"

"More like a beached whale carrying an elephant!" she joked, but she gave him the instrument.

"I told you about blasting on yourself," he chided.

"Forget about me—what did you think of football?"

"I like it."

"For real?"

"I think I'm gonna be pretty good at it. Coach Barnes says I'm really fast for a big dude."

Olivia made a face. "Gee, you smell like you want to be by yourself!" she teased.

"Maybe I do," he told her. "But you ain't no peaches-and-cream cologne either!"

Olivia grinned broadly and nodded in agreement. "You got that right! So, did football give you that man-savage feeling that dudes act like they need?"

"I guess so. We had chocolate-covered rocks as a snack when we finished."

She laughed again and wiped beads of sweat from her forehead. She had a natural, comfortable laugh and was the easiest girl to talk to that Jericho knew.

"Mr. T was telling us about the first game," she said. "I can't believe they scheduled us to play Excelsior! Their band is, like, the best in the nation!"

"So is their football team."

"We're gonna get destroyed! Our band uniforms, the same ones they used back in the eighties, are just plain embarrassing. We're gonna look like refugees from the thrift store."

"I hear at least we're supposed to be getting new football uniforms—white with red numbers, I think. Coach said the athletic director knows somebody who owns a warehouse and he's getting them for us real cheap."

"It sure would be nice to show up at Excelsior with some band threads we could be proud of," she said as she fell into step with Jericho.

"Yeah, but it's not likely," he told her. "You know the school board doesn't have the money for stuff like that."

"But our band sounds good, even if we do show up lookin' like leftover soup," Olivia asserted. "Mr. T is the best band teacher around." She paused and glanced at Jericho. "I saw him talkin' to you."

"He's a good man, but he just doesn't understand."

"Maybe not. But maybe you're tossing away the wrong thing. Hey, here's my bus stop. I'll see you around, Jericho."

"You're taking the bus with this big old instrument?" Jericho asked as he handed it back to her.

"Hey, at least I got some kinda wheels. You seem to

be doing the two-foot shuffle home. What happened to your car?"

"My stepmother's car is in the shop, so she's driving mine today. I can't complain—she and my dad make the payments on it. And I really don't mind the walk. It feels good sometimes."

"I feel ya. Here's my bus. Catch you later." The bus swallowed Olivia and her sousaphone, and Jericho was left alone in the heat of the summer afternoon.

NOVEMBER USUALLY LIKED BEING DOWN-town. The tall buildings, the moist breezes from Fountain Square, the thick, rich smells from the German and Chinese and Italian restaurants, all seemed to add a heightened sense of excitement to every trip. Sometimes she'd spend a whole day at the main public library, browsing for books, doing research for some school report, stopping at lunch to get a bagel sandwich from Busken Bakery. But today she was filled only with dread.

She and her mother walked up the stone steps to the wide glass entrance doors of the building. Their meeting was on the seventieth floor. November glanced up at the structure, tiny windows going up one side of it like eyes with no face.

"Who do you think works in all those offices, Mom?" she asked.

"People who make the business world function, I

imagine," her mother replied. "Auditors and account-
ants and advertisers . . ."

"And that's just the ones that start with the letter *A*,"
November said, shaking her head. She was much too nervous to laugh.

"Most of these office folks just try to do their job well
and go home to their families in the evening, I guess. Lots
of them work in tiny little cubicles without even a window
to see the sunshine."

"I'd hate to have a job like that. How depressing!" said
November.

"Thoreau said, 'The mass of men lead lives of quiet desperation,'" Mrs. Nelson commented as they entered the
granite-tiled lobby and searched for the name of the law
firm on the directory in front of them.

"Hey, I recognize that quote!" November said, pleased
with herself. "It was on the American Lit final that Mrs.
Brisby gave us. We read *Walden* last year."

"Did you get the question right?" her mother asked.

"I must have," November told her. "It's rare when
school stuff actually shows up in real life—except maybe
like on *Jeopardy!*"

Her mother smiled. "It happens every day, baby girl.
You're just too young to notice. How do you think I do my
taxes or measure for wallpaper or figure out how much to
tip the waitress?"

"Math, I guess." November wished the elevator would
hurry up. She hated it when her mother went into "teacher
mode." "I hate math, though. I want to work with people—
like maybe be like one of those social workers who helped

the people after the hurricane in New Orleans."

"That's a great career goal, November. But it requires a college education, you know. Probably some math as well," she added.

November's shoulders slumped as the elevator doors finally separated. She knew where her mother was heading. Neither of them said anything as they rode up to the seventieth floor. Not that this surprised November— she and her mom had been avoiding talking about this meeting—something *so* important—for a week! It was weird, she thought. Before she got pregnant, she and her mom could talk about *anything*—even sex. But now they were on pins and needles around each other. The elevator deposited them into a tastefully decorated lobby, done in tones of beige and pink.

"I can venture a guess at how much this lawyer's fees are," Mrs. Nelson commented.

As they walked down the hall toward where the lawyer's offices were located, November couldn't stop herself from grabbing her mother's arm. "What should I tell them, Mom? What's the right thing to do?"

Mrs. Nelson dropped her purse and pulled her daughter into a hug. "Do what's right for that child, November. That's all I can tell you," she whispered in her ear.

November drew away, disappointed. Although she knew better, she still wished her mother could wave a magic wand and make everything all better. She wondered if she'd ever have the power or the knowledge needed to wave a wand for a little kid in trouble. *Probably not*, she thought glumly.

They were greeted at the door by a secretary dressed in the same tones of tan as the wall and the carpet of the offices. It was as if she dressed specifically to be color-coordinated with the place, November thought. "Please come in," the woman said with a smile. "They're waiting for you in the first conference room on the left."

November hesitated. "Where is your restroom?" she asked quickly, looking around with an anxious face.

"It's the first door on your right," the secretary said in a voice that was modulated so pleasantly that it sounded artificial.

November took as long as she could in the bathroom. She looked at herself in the mirror. Her jeans had given up trying to find a waistline and had settled in that space just below her ever-expanding belly. She didn't like the tight T-shirts mothers-to-be seemed to be sporting these days, so she wore a short-sleeved white blouse that fit loosely and comfortably.

Still, she thought she looked like one of those mirror images from the fun house at the amusement park. She put on a little lipstick. *I'm bloated, my face has grown a whole village full of pimples, and my arms look like sausages. Plus, my back is killing me!*

Unable to stall any longer, she washed her hands and emerged from the bathroom. The perfect secretary escorted her to the conference room. Sitting around a highly buffed mahogany table were Josh's parents, her mother, and a man she figured had to be the lawyer.

"Hi, November," Mrs. Prescott said softly. November was startled at how much better Josh's mom looked than

144

she had that night at the store. Her hair was freshly curled and shining, and her face looked somehow fuller. She smiled, but November didn't return the gesture. She glanced at Mr. Prescott, who was clasping his wife's hand. He too looked different, yet still intense. He offered November his other hand, but she pretended not to notice and took a seat at the other end of the table.

The lawyer, who was grinning at her like a hunter sizing up his prey, had blond hair—actually, it was an unusual shade of beige—and he wore tan slacks with an off-white, thick-cabled sweater tied around his shoulders over a softly tailored pale yellow shirt. Not only did he match his office, November thought, he looked like something out of one of those slick fashion magazines that advertise to men who had lots of money. The man's teeth were perfect, his eyes were deep blue, and as he shook her hand with a powerful handshake, November knew without looking that his fingernails were covered with clear polish. She hated him immediately.

"Welcome, November!" the lawyer said a little too loudly. "I'm Henderson Grant. I think you know everyone else. I've just been chatting with your mom here, getting to know her a little. You know she's your biggest fan!"

November looked at her mother as if she had joined the Confederate army. Mrs. Nelson gave her daughter a big smile of encouragement, but November narrowed her eyes. *I know you want me to make this decision by myself, Mom, but it's kinda cold of you to be grinnin' in the face of the enemy. Whose side are you on, anyway?*

"Would you like something to drink? A cola? Perhaps

some fresh fruit juice? We'd better eat healthy for that little one!" Mr. Grant said in a booming voice.

This perfect-faced, perfume-smellin' phony is gonna make me gag. He sounds like all the announcers I've ever heard on the home shopping channel, rolled into one greasy salesman.

"Who is *we*?" November finally asked, her voice a croak in the silence. "Who else has to eat healthy for that 'little one,' as you call it?"

The lawyer, not really answering her and using what November knew had to be his most soothing voice, responded, "I suppose you've brought us to the reason why we're here today—the health and future happiness of Joshua Prescott's child."

Oh no he didn't! she thought, anger coursing through her. "Excuse me? This baby is my child as well." November glanced at her mother and was glad to see that she was suddenly sitting at attention too.

"Of course, dear," Mr. Grant said. "But I represent the Prescott family, and our purpose here today is to see if we can come to a determination that will please everyone. Did you bring a legal representative to advise you?"

November looked again at her mother, this time with alarm. *Maybe we didn't treat this mess as seriously as we should've. Say something, Mom!* she thought desperately.

"No, we didn't," Mrs. Nelson replied. "Not at this time. We have come today simply to listen to your proposals. If we find we need formal representation, we will pursue it at a later date."

"I see. Thank you. That will be fine." The lawyer

scribbled something on a legal pad. He seemed to be pleased.

November looked over at Josh's parents. *His mom's gained a little weight—she needed that*, November thought. *And she's got her hair and nails done too. New hookup as well—DKNY—nice stuff. Dag! She's almost glowing!* Josh's father, looking fit and trim, smiled warmly at her, but November still couldn't quite smile back. *With that gray at his temples and that leather jacket, he looks dignified, and I gotta admit, downright responsible. Looks like they've been to that* Extreme Makeover *TV show.*

And me? I look like . . . like a scared sixteen-year-old pregnant girl. But that doesn't mean I don't have rights! Where do they come off with this stuff?

So she asked outright, "Do you plan to try to take my baby?" She stared directly at Mr. and Mrs. Prescott but found she was trembling.

"Of course not, but we would like to make you an offer, November," Mrs. Prescott said gently. "We'd like to adopt the baby and raise it as our own."

November's thoughts churned. Her first reaction was to scream, "No way!" Then she immediately wondered what would happen if she agreed to this ridiculous proposal. *Would I get to see it? Would they let me?* And, a moment later, *Would I want to?*

"You wouldn't have to be burdened with this unplanned responsibility for the rest of your life," Josh's father added.

He's right! I'd be free! Her heartbeat quickened. But then she immediately felt overwhelmed by guilt. She gulped. *How can I turn against the baby like this? What kind of mother even thinks about giving her baby away?*

"We'd make it worth your while." The lawyer inserted himself into the conversation. "You'd be financially set for years to come."

November knew they had recently come into a lot of cash—Josh had told her how his mom had inherited it from her grandfather. How was she supposed to fight all this?

Henderson Grant cleared his throat. "Your mother tells us you've been accepted to the Cornell Summer Academic Program. What a stunning achievement! Please allow me to offer my congratulations."

November, furious at her mother, shot her a look of pure hatred. *How* dare *she tell these people my business!* Mrs. Nelson looked away.

The lawyer, his voice smooth and convincing, continued, "Not only would you receive a generous settlement check when the baby is born, but all your college expenses would be paid as well—tuition, books, dorm, everything—for the full four years."

These folks are off the hook! I can't believe what they're doing! They're practically offering to buy my baby! November didn't know if she felt insulted or excited about all the possibilities they were dumping in her lap. Her thoughts swirled at a dizzying speed. *I could go to Cornell for the summer after all!* she thought guiltily. *Mom wouldn't have to get a second job. I could concentrate on books instead of bills.* Then she realized what she was considering, and she slumped once more in despair.

Mrs. Nelson gasped and looked at her daughter but gave no indication of what she was thinking. November felt like one of those unfortunate animals on the nature channel who sits and waits for the stronger, fiercer animals to come and devour it.

I'm way out of my league here. And I think they know that.

"Of course we'll do a DNA test to establish paternity— just a formality, I assure you—then the formal adoption papers will be filed." The lawyer gave November another of those magazine-model paper smiles.

November jumped up. *Now wait just a minute! They can't just dis me like that!* "You think this is somebody else's baby?" she asked angrily. "You think I slept around with every boy in Douglass High School?" She headed for the door.

"Don't be upset, dear," the lawyer said, comforting her and directing her back to her chair. She jerked her arm away. "These things are simply legal formalities. Of course we know the baby belongs to Josh. That's why we're here."

November sat down warily. "What if I turn down your offer?" she asked harshly.

"That doesn't make a whole lot of sense, now, does it?" Mr. Grant said soothingly. "You have limited financial resources, you're only sixteen, and you have nothing to offer this child. The Prescotts already know how to bring up a baby. They have a comfortable home and can give the child everything it deserves or desires."

November grew increasingly dismayed. *Everything he says is true*, she thought.

"He'd have his own room," Mrs. Prescott added, her voice pleading. "A puppy. A bicycle. A backyard swimming pool."

Josh never had a puppy or a pool, November recalled.

"If it's a girl, she could take piano lessons and ballet lessons and go to Paris to study if she wants," Mr. Prescott added.

Give me a break! Paris?

November glared at her mother, who, although looking drained, said nothing. *You're not helping here, Mom. I feel like I'm drowning!*

Her mother remained silent, so November finally stated the obvious. "You didn't tell me what would happen if I turned down your offer."

The lawyer sat down on the edge of the gleaming table, close to November. He dropped the fake smile and the soothing voice. He looked directly at her and said pointedly, "Well, there are all sorts of legal parameters we could use—unfit mother, perhaps—and we'd hate to have to sue for custody, but we would." He paused. "And we would win."

He is straight-up serious, November realized. She twisted around to her mother, who clearly had finally had it. Mrs. Nelson stood up, lifted her chin, and said with a quiet fury, "How dare you speak to my daughter like that? She is no more unfit than you are! Don't you dare threaten her!"

Way to go, Mom! 'Bout time! November gave her mother a small smile of thanks. *But this slimy dude doesn't seem to be fazed. He's looking at Mom like she was a fingernail clipping.*

"I don't threaten, ma'am. I succeed." The lawyer got up, flicked a speck off his slacks, and went back to his seat.

Mrs. Nelson looked as if she were going to protest more, then she pressed her lips closed. The room was silent except for the piped-in classical music that November had not noticed before. Everyone's eyes were on her.

November refused to look at any of them. She leaned back in the cushioned chair and placed her hands over her belly. She looked down past her scuffed shoes to the thick, off-white carpet on the floor.

Oh, Lord, what shall I do? she prayed. *It seems like they're asking me to sell my baby! Can that be right? Maybe the right thing to do is what's best for the child, like Mom says. I didn't really love Josh. I don't really want a baby. I could go away to college after graduation*, she thought wistfully. *Maybe this is my chance to make everything right. The Prescotts sure do need something to make them happy again.* She felt like she was on one of those amusement park rides that turn you upside down and sideways.

November raised her head and looked at the people around that table. The room was ripe with expectation. She opened her mouth to speak, then closed it. She gulped. "There's no need to drag this out all summer. I've made my decision," she began. "I have chosen to—" Then she suddenly stopped. She lifted her hands off her lap as if they'd been stung, and looked down at her belly with wonder. "Oh my God! The baby kicked me. That's the first time I felt it move!"

MRS. NELSON RAN TO HER DAUGHTER'S side, knelt down beside her, and placed her hand on November's tummy. "I think I feel it too!" she said hesitantly, her voice full of joy. November smiled, relief spreading through her. Her mom had been trying so hard to stay neutral in this mess and pretend that she didn't care what November decided. But it sure felt good to see her acting all stupid and excited, and in November's corner again.

The lawyer seemed uneasy with the unexpected commotion. He removed his sweater and paced the length of the room.

Josh's parents also got out of their seats but seemed hesitant to come any closer to November.

"I've felt little twinges before, but I wasn't sure what they were," November murmured to her mother. "But nothing like this. It feels like a whole football team is in there!"

"Would you like a glass of juice?" the lawyer finally said, trying to reestablish control of the situation.

"No, thank you, I'm fine," November answered.

"Well, let's get back to business then," Mr. Grant said, looking a little more self-assured. "You were about to tell us your decision about our proposal."

The Prescotts sat back down and looked hopeful and expectant. "Please, November," Josh's mother whispered from across the table. *She looks just like Josh did when he was trying to get me to skip school to go take that ballroom dancing class*, November thought with a pang.

She stood up. "Give me all the paperwork," she said decisively. "And your stupid DNA test as well," she added. "I'm not going to sign anything today, or tomorrow, either, for that matter. I intend to take all of it home and read every single line. Then my mom and I will get a lawyer to read it all again."

Mr. Grant handed her a folder thick with papers and said (trying to sound officious, November thought), "I'll need these back within thirty days."

"You'll get them back when I'm finished with them," November said firmly. She felt like she was back in control again, and it felt good.

"And then you'll sign?" asked Mrs. Prescott hopefully.

"No, then I'll go get ice cream!" November said with a smile. "I can't make a decision like this in a minute, or an hour, or a day. I need time to think, to pray, and to know what I should do. The baby isn't due until the first week of November. We have plenty of time."

"But if you just—," the lawyer began.

November pulled the papers out of the folder. "Give me some space, mister, or I'll rip these papers into shreds and never come back." Mr. Grant backed off, hands in front of him to show he had given in.

"If there's anything we can do for you while you're thinking about all this," Mr. Prescott said to November, "please don't hesitate to ask."

"Thanks," said November, "but I think me and my mom got it covered right now. You ready to go, Mom?"

"Yes, let's go, baby girl," Mrs. Nelson said triumphantly. "I knew I could trust you to know what to do," she told November as they left the lawyer's offices.

"But I didn't, Mom. I still don't," November protested.

"You did exactly what you should have. Let's go home."

As the two of them walked out, November asked hesitantly, "You want to get lunch?" It felt good to have her mother on her side once more.

"Sure, why not?"

Feeling as if a weight had been lifted, November wanted to jump off the stone steps like she had when she was four or five. Remembering her condition, however, she walked down the steps carefully and followed her mother into the diner across the street. They found a seat by the window, where all those people with "lives of desperation" hurried past them, awash in their own problems.

"I'm starving!" November said as she scanned the menu.

"Me too. I think I'll even let myself have dessert today."

"Are we celebrating, Mom? And if so, what?"

"I think we won a moral victory today," Mrs. Nelson

answered as she ordered vegetable soup and a Caesar salad from the waitress. "I didn't like that lawyer very much."

November ordered a pasta casserole and a glass of orange juice. "I still haven't made a decision about what they offered," she said, crunching a package of saltines in her hands.

"I know. But they were pressuring you to sign right away. You need time. I feel like we can breathe a little."

"Yeah, at least for a little while. It really is amazing what they're willing to do, Mom, but somehow it makes me feel dirty inside—like I'm washing my hands in muddy water."

"I understand completely. How could an office that looked so clean make you feel so unclean?"

"Too much beige," November said with a grin. "Covered up the dirt under his rug."

The food arrived quickly and they ate in silence, November brooding and her mother nervously sipping two servings of Diet Coke.

Finally Mrs. Nelson suggested, "Let's see what's in the folder."

November pulled out the first sheet of paper and read it, then handed it to her mother. She felt suddenly cold. "They make it seem so simple," she said, as she burped from the heavy, garlic-seasoned casserole. "It's just a few lines. But they can change the world of everyone involved."

CONSENT TO ADOPTION
In the Matter of the Adoption of _____
by Brock and Marlene Prescott:

I, November Rochelle Nelson, mother of
_____, a minor child, as yet
unborn, hereby consent to the legal adoption of this
child by Brock and Marlene Prescott, paternal
grandparents, as sought in the attached petition. I
hereby forever waive all my rights to the custody and
control of the child.

Dated this _____ day of _____, _____.

"ARE YOU SURE YOU'LL BE OKAY GOING TO the doctor by yourself?" Mrs. Nelson asked November for what seemed to be the millionth time. "I really can't change this meeting I have at the YWCA."

"I'll be fine, Mom," November called from the kitchen. "And I won't be alone. I talked to Dana yesterday and she said she'd go with me. Jericho might show up as well."

"Jericho?"

"Yeah. He's been acting all fatherly and stuff. Like he's responsible somehow."

"Does it bother you that he's so interested in the baby?"

"No, actually, it's kinda refreshing. Boys are usually so clueless!"

"You kids be careful, you hear? I'll be back late this afternoon. And you let me know everything that Dr. Holland tells you, okay?"

"I will, Mom. Now get out of here. You're gonna be late."

November was relieved to hear the door shut and her mother's car start up in the driveway. She fixed herself a peanut butter and jelly sandwich, then sat down on the softest chair in the living room because her back, once again, was aching. She looked down at her feet, which were swollen, and her belly, which no longer seemed to belong to her. *And it's just July*, she moaned to herself.

The phone rang. She looked at the caller ID, saw it was Dana, and said casually, "What's up, girl?"

"Nothin'. Just chillin'. Or tryin' to in all this heat. Getting ready for my date tonight with Kofi. How are you dealin' with it, little mama?"

"I'm sitting here looking at my feet and they look like two tree trunks. I don't think I'll ever be normal again," November complained.

"I'll be by there in a few minutes. Anything you want me to bring you?"

"Yeah, my life back."

"Okay, one normal life on a platter—coming right up!" Dana laughed and hung up.

Before she could put the phone down, it rang again. This time the digital screen listed Jericho's number.

"Hey, November. How's it goin'?" he asked.

"You don't want to know."

"You're probably right. I just wanted to know if you're still speaking to me."

"Why shouldn't I?"

"Because of what my aunt and uncle are trying to do to you—you know, about adopting the baby."

"You're not responsible for what they're doing, Jericho."

"Yeah, in a sense, I think I am."

"How you figure?"

"If Josh hadn't died, none of this would be happening. It's my fault he's dead."

"Jericho, you have to quit talking like that! What happened to Josh was an accident. Loosen up, man." Deliberately changing the subject, she asked, "Hey, how's football?"

"Maybe because I'm so big, or maybe it's all comin' back like Coach said it would, but it's easy for me—and fun. I'm pretty good at it. Coach has me playing both offensive and defensive tackle."

"Whatever that means. I tell you what. I'll spare you the details of childbirth, and you don't try to teach me the rules of football—bet?"

"Bet." He laughed, then his voice turned serious. "So did you decide what to do about Brock and Marlene?"

November could see Dana's car pulling into the driveway. "I decided not to make a decision yet. I know it's stalling, but I have to be sure."

"Is it still okay if I drop by the doctor's office with you and Dana? You sure I won't be in the way?"

"As tiny as you are—who's gonna notice?" November replied. "Hey, Dana is here. She's driving me there. I gotta go. See you there, maybe."

"Let me know if you need anything, November."

"You willing to babysit for the next fifteen years or so?"

"I don't know about all that! Talk to you later."

"Peace out."

"CAN MY FRIENDS COME WITH ME INTO the examining room?" November asked the nurse. Jericho had shown up, freshly showered and nervous, just before November's name was called.

"They can come in after the doctor has finished her initial examination. You're scheduled for an ultrasound today, right?" the nurse said with a bright smile.

"That's what Dr. Holland told me last time," said November.

"Good. Your friends can be with you for that. You might even get to see the sex of the baby today. Won't that be fun?"

Part of the woman's job description must be to be cheerful all the time, November thought as she made a face behind the nurse's back. She let the woman lead her back to the same overly chilly room with the ducks. She undressed, put on the paper gown, and climbed up on the paper-covered table.

I wonder how many women have sat on this table in this cold room. I guess the ones with husbands out in the waiting room are happy and excited, 'cause that's the way stuff is supposed to happen. What about girls like me? Her thoughts were interrupted by Dr. Holland, who greeted her warmly, snapped on a pair of latex gloves, and began the probing and palpating that November hated.

"Are you having any problems?" the doctor asked after her examination.

"I feel swollen. My back hurts. I'm constipated. I burp all the time. I'm always sleepy. Other than that, I'm just peachy!" November replied sarcastically. "How am I going to make it until fall? Last week I had some garlic pasta and I think I burped and farted that stuff for three days!"

The doctor laughed. "You'll survive. Somehow we all manage to make it through this ordeal. I'm a little concerned about the swelling, however, and your blood pressure is still a little high. Did you lay off french fries like I told you?"

"For real, I did," November told her. "I've had no salt at all since I was here last. My mom even checked the salt content on the toothpaste!"

The doctor frowned slightly. "Good. But I want you to drink even more fluids, increase your intake of fresh fruit and fish, and take a walk once a day. Can you do that for me?"

"Yes, ma'am. I have nothing else to do all summer. I withdrew from the summer college program I had planned to attend, and I decided . . . I decided not to work or volunteer. So I'm just home feeling sorry for myself and watching myself swell up into a balloon."

"Well, there's a reason for that," the doctor explained. "Your baby weighs about a pound, and he's more than a foot long."

"Footlong. That's funny," November mumbled, almost to herself. Then she looked up at Dr. Holland. "You said he? Are you sure it's a boy?"

"I certainly can't tell by examining your belly. I'm good, but I don't have X-ray vision," she replied with a laugh. "We'll find out the sex of the baby in a few minutes when we do the ultrasound. Have you felt movement yet?"

"Yeah, I did—just last week," November reported, her voice full of amazement. "Now almost every day I get a little kick or wiggle." Unconsciously she rubbed her belly.

"You'll feel that all the time now. You'll find the baby has a rhythm—it will have active periods and rest periods—just like it will after it is born."

"Really?"

"Yep. It can even get the hiccups."

"That's funny."

"How's your mom adjusting?" the doctor asked as she made notes on the chart.

"She goes back and forth between being excited and supportive, to trying to use that tough-love stuff and make me realize how hard this is going to be. She's got more mood swings than I do!"

"So you'll be keeping the baby?"

November looked up in surprise. "How did you find out about the Prescotts?"

Dr. Holland looked confused. "I don't know what you're

talking about. I'm not trying to pry—I just need the information for our records."

"So you didn't get a call from a slimy lawyer guy named Grant who wanted information about my baby?"

"If I did get such a call, he would get absolutely no information from me or anyone on my staff. That is privileged and, trust me, very safe." Dr. Holland put a hand on November's shoulder. "What's going on?"

November relaxed a bit as she tried to explain. "The parents of my baby's father want to adopt the child when it's born. They've got a lawyer, and they're not playing."

"Why would they want your baby?"

"I guess the baby would replace their son." November shrugged.

"And you're considering this?"

"I guess." November looked down at the floor and wished the doctor would leave the room so she could get dressed.

"Let me offer you some advice. Don't sign anything until you're sure. It's your baby and no judge will take that child from you unless you spend every weekend doing the hoochie-coochie dance down on Vine Street!"

"Not likely," November replied with a small smile.

The doctor chuckled. "I've seen cases worse than that where the judge decided in the mother's favor. So relax."

"But what if the baby really would be better off with Josh's parents?" November continued.

Dr. Holland seemed to be uncomfortable with the direction the discussion was taking. "Can't help you there, my dear. I'm the doctor, not your moral counselor. You have a lot to consider. But, for the moment, there's something else to think about. Are you ready for this ultrasound? Get dressed and meet me in the room next door."

"Is it okay for a boy to be in the room?" November asked.

"Sure. If he can handle it, I have no problem with him being there with you. You need all the friends and support you can gather. And this part is fun!" Dr. Holland breezed out of the room.

Dana and Jericho were called in to the ultrasound room. Jericho seemed to fill the room, and his pine-scented aftershave made November feel slightly ill. But she said nothing.

He looked excited, but really out of place. When the doctor lifted November's T-shirt to reveal her tummy, Jericho backed toward the door.

"Get it together, son," Dr. Holland said, glancing at him. "You've seen more stomach in a Victoria's Secret commercial."

"Yeah, but not on November," he said nervously. But he stayed.

The doctor adjusted dials as she slowly slid a monitor back and forth over November's abdomen. The room was silent except for the beeping of the machine and Jericho's anxious breathing. Gradually a vague figure emerged on the screen. November could see an incredibly small shadow of a person. Jericho and Dana leaned in closer to get a better view.

"Oh my God," November whispered. "It's got a tiny little head, and ears and legs. And are those eyebrows? Wow."

"She looks like she's sleeping," said Dana. Both girls

spoke softly, as if anything louder would disturb the child. Jericho's eyes were wide.

"Did you know the baby can recognize your voice, November?" Doctor Holland said.

"For real? I better be careful what I say!"

"He's got a big nose," Jericho said softly. "At least I think that's what I'm looking at."

"Yes, that's a nose, and those are arms," the doctor said, pointing at the monitor.

"Josh had a big nose," Jericho commented to no one in particular.

November had forgotten all her pains and discomforts. "Can you tell if it's a boy or a girl, Dr. Holland?"

"Let me see," the doctor replied as she moved the monitoring device, trying to get a clearer picture. "Hmm, I see one leg. Two legs. Aha!"

"What? I can't tell from the picture," November said, trying to turn her body so she could see the screen better. "Is something wrong?"

"I didn't mean to alarm you. Nothing's wrong. I just got a clear picture. Here—take a look."

November stared at the grainy image on the screen. "It's a girl, Dana," she said with wonder. "Look at that— it's a little girl."

"Josh woulda been freaking out right about now, man," Jericho said, shaking his head. "He'd be jumpin' around like a little boy, boastin' about what a man he is. Jeez, I wish he could see this." His voice broke. "November, I gotta go!" November and Dana looked at each other in alarm as Jericho fled the room.

WHEN NOVEMBER GOT HOME, SHE SAT down and forced herself to eat a tuna salad sandwich, even though she usually avoided fish, and she drank two bottles of water. As she chewed, she thought about all the good stuff her baby was getting. But who was getting her baby? Was she eating well so the Prescotts could buy a healthy kid?

Feeling restless, she flipped through the television channels, stopping at something on the Discovery Network called *Critical Delivery*. It was all about mothers who had had complications having their babies. *I don't need to be watching this*, she thought. *Especially today.* But once it was on she couldn't turn it off—it was horrifying and mesmerizing. One mother's baby died. Another mother was trying, painfully, to deliver two breech babies. She ended up having surgery, but her twins were beautiful when they were shown close-up at the end of the show.

I wonder what this baby will look like, November wondered as the show paused for commercials. *Sandy hair and freckles? Skinny legs? Curly dark hair like mine?* Strangely, she always visualized Josh rather than herself when she thought about the baby's looks. Somehow she never pictured a tiny little November in her arms. Only a small Josh.

Finally she forced herself to switch the television off. "I've got to get out of here," she said out loud. She dug in her purse, checked her wallet to make sure she had bus fare and enough to buy a magazine or two, and headed down the street to the bus stop. She figured a trip to the library might help clear her head. She couldn't remember if Olivia was working today, but she hoped she could hook up with her for a few minutes.

November breathed deeply in the warm summer air—Mrs. Miller's roses were in full bloom, and the smell was finer than any perfume. The sun on her skin was just warm enough. She almost felt as though she were being bathed in gold. It made her think about one of the best vacations she'd ever had, when her mom had taken her to Myrtle Beach a couple of years ago. She had spent hours lolling on the sand, listening to the rhythm of the surf, and basking in the sun. *I love sunshine*, November thought happily.

The bus rumbled to her stop and November sat down in the first empty seat. She closed her eyes and thought back to that grainy image on the sonogram. *A girl! A baby girl! I wonder how Mom felt when she found out she was pregnant? Did she love me right away? Would she have given me away?*

"When are you due?" a young-sounding voice said, interrupting November's thoughts.

Startled, November looked over. A very pregnant girl was sitting next to her. "Uh, I've got about four more months. How about you?"

"The doctor at the clinic says any day now." The girl wore a very tight hot pink T-shirt stretched over her huge belly and matching pink flip-flops covered with tiny pink daisies. Shiny silver-sparkled eye shadow decorated her eyelids, and she wore her blond hair brushed back into two long braids. *This kid looks like a baby herself!*

"How old are you?" November asked.

"I'm twelve."

"Twelve? You're in middle school?" November's jaw dropped. She was the same age as Jericho's brother Todd. "What school do you go to?"

"Hazelwood Middle School. I'll be in seventh grade next year."

"Do you know a kid named Todd—cute, curly black hair, runs track?"

The girl grinned, showing off a mouth full of braces. "Yeah, I know Todd. He sat next to me in math last year."

November gulped. "How did you, you know . . ." November pointed at the girl's bulging tummy. "How did you . . . I mean, uh, you're twelve."

"How did I get pregnant? Same way you did," the girl said casually.

"But you're just a kid—shouldn't you be playing with Barbies or something?"

"I know I'm young, but I'm very mature for my age,"

the girl replied. Her fingernails were painted bright green. She dug in her purse, which was decorated with Disney princesses, pulled out a pack of Jolly Rancher candy, and popped two in her mouth. "Want one?" she asked November.

"No, thanks. My doctor doesn't want me eating a lot of sugar. Didn't your doctor say anything about that?" November suddenly felt like an adult, which made her feel really uncomfortable. She shifted in her seat.

The girl rolled her eyes, the same eye roll November had used on her own mother for years. "Give me a break. You sound like my mother."

"I guess," November replied. They rode in silence for a few minutes, then November asked, "Do you know if you're having a boy or a girl?"

"It's a boy. I'm going to name him Hector, after his daddy. What about you?"

"I just found out today," November said, wonder still in her voice. "It's a girl."

"You got a name picked out yet?"

"Yeah," November said, "I do. Her name is Sunshine." The name just appeared on her lips, like a lovely song. But when she said it, she knew it was the only name that would work.

"That's a really pretty name. I wish I was having a girl. You get to buy all that cute pink stuff. Girls' clothes are way cuter than boys'! Pink is my favorite color," the girl added wistfully.

November wondered how this kid was going to take care of a baby, and she tried to figure out a way of asking that wouldn't offend the girl. "So, are you going back to school in September?"

"Yeah, my mom says I have to."

"So who'll watch the baby?"

"My mom will. She's already watching my older sister's kids, so she won't mind."

"How old's your sister?"

"Sixteen. She's got two kids—Lacey is three and Mickey is almost two."

"So, you have a boyfriend?" asked November, feeling slightly incredulous.

"Sure! Don't you?"

"Not really," November replied as she shifted her gaze past the girl and out the window.

"Did he dump you when he found out about the kid? That happened to my sister the first time."

"No, he died."

"Ooh, bummer. Well, here's my stop. It was nice talking to you."

"Good luck," November told her.

The girl waved a brief thanks, then waddled off the bus and disappeared into the crowd.

When people look at me, do they think I look as foolish and pitiful as that kid? November wondered. *Probably so.* She'd always imagined that when she got married and had kids she'd have it all together with a fine husband, a great career, and a nice house in the burbs—the storybook stuff. By then she'd be able to welcome a new baby with the best of everything—designer blankets and sophisticated educational toys. She'd even pictured the expensive stroller she'd push through the mall. But here she sat, with barely enough money to ride the bus and the very real possibility of having to apply for welfare so she could feed and care for her child. Unless, of course, she gave in to the Prescotts' demands. *Not fair!* she thought sullenly. *This is so not fair.*

WHEN THE DOORBELL RANG AT ELEVEN in the morning, November, still in her pajamas, peered out to see Dana and Olivia on her doorstep. Olivia held a box of Krispy Kreme doughnuts.

"You gonna open the door, or do we have to stand out here all day?" Dana called out when she saw November peeking through the curtains.

November swung open the door and the two girls marched in as if they were on a mission. "Mmm, those doughnuts smell yummy," November murmured.

"They're still warm," said Olivia enticingly, as she set them down on the kitchen table and opened the box. The sweet smell of sugar glaze and soft dough filled the room. "We got your favorite—chocolate cream."

November took one and bit into it with a deep sigh of satisfaction. "Wow. There's nothing better on a Saturday morning."

"My favorite fruit," Olivia said jokingly, her mouth full. She wore yellow cutoffs and a matching top.

"That's a cute outfit, Olivia," Dana told her.

Olivia blushed. "Thanks," she said. "I feel like a big banana."

Dana went over to the refrigerator and poured them each a glass of milk. "Drink up, little mama," she told November. "You need the calcium."

"I probably don't need these calories, and I definitely don't need this sugar," November said as she grabbed a second doughnut. "Look how big I'm getting. Doctor said the swelling is not good."

"You'll be fine," Dana said dismissively. "You just need some exercise. We came to take you to the mall."

"I don't feel like it," said November, rubbing her hands over her belly. "You two go on without me."

"We are *not* going without you. You been in this house all summer, cooped up like some old lady!" Dana told her. "Get some clothes on and let's go shopping."

"It's too much trouble, and walking makes me tired," November whined.

Olivia stood up and took over the situation like a charging elephant. "I'm not hearing it. First, go take a shower. You're pretty ripe, girlfriend. Then put on a T-shirt and let's get some fresh air." Dana giggled and nodded in agreement.

November rolled her eyes, but she got up and headed for the bathroom. When she came back down, freshly showered, she felt more cheerful. Dana and Olivia clapped, and the three girls headed for the door.

"You're wearing flip-flops?" asked Dana as they headed to her car. She wore neat white K-Swiss tennis shoes, white shorts, and a white tank top.

"They're all I got that still fits. Besides, it's hot. I don't want to be foolin' with shoes today."

"Your feet are kinda swollen, November," Olivia observed. "Shouldn't you wear something with a little more support?"

"Quit actin' like my mother," November pleaded. "Or let me stay home in my flip-flops and watch TV. I've gotten hooked on a couple of bowling shows that come on every Saturday."

"This is more than a rescue mission," Dana said to Olivia in mock seriousness as she started the car. "We've got to get this girl a mind makeover. Bowling for dollars? Give me a break!"

"You're right. Let's get out of here," November agreed with an embarrassed grin.

They pulled into a mall parking space a few minutes later—one reserved for "Ladies in Waiting."

"What's that supposed to be—a cute term for pregnant women?" November asked with a frown as they got out of the car.

"I don't know, but it works for me," Dana said. "Easy parking."

"Where do we start?" asked Olivia as they reached the large front doors of the mall.

"The bathroom," November replied. "I gotta pee."

"You just went before we left," Dana said.

"Can't help it. The kid is sitting on my bladder."

"Yuck. We'll wait for you here," Olivia declared as

November made her way to the ladies' room.

When November returned, Dana said, "Let's try Shoe Carnival first. They've got a 'buy one, get one free' sale." They headed to the left and passed a candle shop.

"Ooh, let's go in," suggested Olivia. "I want a new candle for my room."

"Something smells just like apple pie," Dana remarked as they walked in.

"And peppermint!" Olivia said, sniffing the air. "It's amazing how they get these realistic flavors into candle wax. Which one do you like, November?"

But November had hurried out of the store. She stood in the hall, breathing heavily and trying not to gag. "I'm sorry," she said as they followed her, concern on their faces. "All those smells just got to me. I felt like I was gonna lose my breakfast!"

"Well, that wouldn't have been pretty," Olivia said. "Let's just go to the shoe store."

They passed by a men's shirt shop and a card shop, then came to the shoe store. "This store smells like leather," said Dana. "Can you handle it?" she asked November, teasing.

"I'm cool."

Dana tried on a pair of red Nikes. Olivia tried on a cool-looking pair of navy blue New Balance shoes. "Nice," Olivia said as she walked on the carpet with one shoe on and one shoe off. "But a little expensive."

"Try on a pair, November," Dana pleaded. "Your feet are begging for new shoes!"

November plopped down on the wooden bench, kicked

off her flip-flops, and pulled on a pair of the fake stockings provided by shoe stores. "What are these supposed to do?" she asked, grunting as she labored to reach her feet.

"Protect your feet from shoe germs, I guess," Olivia said.

"More likely protecting your feet from other people's stinky feet!" Dana said. "People like November who go all summer without taking showers!" she teased.

November reached over and punched Dana on the arm, almost losing her balance on the small bench. "I'd like to see these in a size seven," she told the sales clerk, a skinny boy who smacked his chewing gum loudly as he waited on them.

When the gum-chomping salesman returned with the red Nikes, November reached down to put them on. "There must be something wrong with these," she told the salesman. "Are you sure you brought me a size seven?"

"Yup." *Smack. Smack.* "Your feet look bigger than a seven to me, but what do I know?" he said. "I only been working here a couple of weeks."

"Well, bring me an eight. But I know they'll be too big," November said, handing him back the shoes.

"Can I see these same Nikes in a nine?" asked Olivia. "And bring them in blue, if you have them." The boy nodded and disappeared.

When he returned with the new boxes, November pulled out the size eight shoes but still couldn't get her feet in all the way. "What's up with this? Do these shoes run narrow?" she asked the sales clerk.

"Mine fit fine," Olivia said as she slid on the size nine shoes.

November frowned, reached over, and tried on one of the shoes in Olivia's box. Her foot fit into the size nine, but just barely.

"Looks to me like you need a nine and a half or a ten, ma'am," the clerk said. "Do you want me to find those for you?"

"Did he just call me *ma'am*?" November asked. "Do I look that old?"

"He's just being polite," whispered Dana. "Ignore him."

November looked up at the boy. "No, I'm fine. I think I'll wait on the shoes today. Thanks for bringing so many out for me to try."

"No problem, ma'am," the boy replied with a grin. He looked as if he knew he was annoying her.

Olivia bought the blue Nikes and also got a pair of red sandals, since one pair was free. Dana ended up with two pairs of shoes. November bought nothing and sat glumly looking at her flip-flops while they paid for their purchases.

"What's that smell?" asked Olivia as they walked back into the mall.

"Ooh, gross!" Dana said, covering her nose. "Somebody farted!"

November looked embarrassed. "I'm sorry. Seems like I get the funky farts every day now. I can't even tell when one is about to let loose, and I have no control of it when it does. It's awful."

"Well, put up a flag to warn somebody," Olivia said with a laugh. "That sucker reeked!"

"I'll try," November said, "but it's like my body belongs to some lady from another planet now. It's not me anymore— just a big globule of indigestion."

"They should mention *that* in the sex-ed class," Dana asserted. "Hey, you want to stop in this baby store? Let's pick out cool baby stuff."

The three girls walked into the store, which smelled of lavender and baby powder. Soft music played in the background. "May I help you?" the pleasant-looking older saleswoman asked.

"Uh, yeah. My friend wants to look at baby clothes and toys."

The woman looked from November's face to her belly, obvious disapproval on her face. "Right this way, please," she said primly. "Here we have layettes and all you need to prepare the little one for his or her arrival into the world."

"It's a her," November said. "A girl."

"How nice," replied the woman. "If you want pink, those outfits are on this rack," she said, pointing.

"This is so cute!" Dana exclaimed as she held up a tiny pink dress with satin bows and lace ribbons.

November looked at the tag. "It's sixty-five dollars! You gotta be kidding!"

"That's the starting price for most of the outfits in this store," the saleswoman said smugly.

November touched the incredibly soft fabric to her cheek and sighed. *I should be able to afford everything in here—this is the store I dreamed of, the store my baby deserves.*

"What's the name of this place—the Highway Robbery

Baby Store?" Olivia asked, glancing at other overpriced items on the shelves.

The saleswoman did not reply, but turned her back and went to wait on another customer.

"Let's raise up out of here," Dana said. "We don't want the baby growing up to be a snob."

"I gotta pee," November told her friends as they headed out of the store. Her back was killing her as well.

"Again?" Dana said.

"Sorry."

As she headed to the bathroom, she could hear Dana say to Olivia, "She walks like an old lady."

Well, why don't you *try carrying an extra twenty-five pounds around your waist?* she thought wearily as she got to the ladies' room.

In the bathroom, November leaned heavily against the cool marble wall of the toilet stall. Her feet were throbbing, her back ached, and her stomach kept gurgling. She hoped she could control the gas that was trying to escape from her irritated digestive system.

"You about ready to go?" asked Dana, when November joined them in front of the food court.

"No, I'm good," November lied. "Let's go look at some clothes."

"Are you hungry?" Olivia asked.

"No, not really," November replied. "Besides, the smell of pizza, my favorite food in the whole world, makes me nauseous. And if I eat it, I get the farts again!"

"Then we are heading in the *opposite* direction, girl-friend!" Olivia said.

"Girl, you're just plain messed up," Dana told her, but she put her arm around November's shoulder and gave her a hug.

"Tell me about it," said November, sighing.

November watched and pretended to enjoy herself while Dana and Olivia tried on a few outfits. "That's sharp, girl," she told Dana, who showed off in the mirror.

"This one will make Kofi melt," Dana said with a sly grin.

"Kofi turns to jelly every time you blink," November said, almost enviously. "You don't need tight leather pants."

"Just workin' on my ammunition," Dana replied as she put her hands on her hips. "Never know when I might need to protect my territory!"

Olivia shyly tried on a pair of blue jeans. She was obviously a little uncomfortable.

"Those make your butt look smaller," November told her.

"Well, then I'm buying six pairs!" said Olivia with a laugh. "Now if we can find some pants that eliminate thunder thighs, they can have my life savings!" She paused. "This is so much fun. I don't usually get to shop with friends."

Dana's cell phone rang then, interrupting the awkward moment in which no one knew quite what to say. "Hey, Kofi Cutie. Yeah, we're still shopping—we might be here for another hour or two," she told him. "Wait till you see what I bought!" She giggled at whatever he said on the other end. "Gotta go. Love you! Bye." She snapped the phone shut.

"I'm getting those leather pants!" she said. "Umph! That boy turns me on!" Then she turned to glance at

November, who perched uncomfortably on the bench in the dressing room, belly hanging out of her too-small jeans.

"Oh no, not again!" cried Olivia as the small room was filled with the distinct odor of putrefied fruit. "The fart monster strikes again! It's time to go home."

Even November, who was used to the gaseous emissions that plagued her, was horrified. "Good Lord, that stinks!" she said. "I'm so sorry. Let's get out of here."

The girls hurried out of the small room, carrying their packages and the clothes, Dana and Olivia laughing and gasping for breath. "I feel sorry for the next person who uses that room!" Olivia joked.

But November was embarrassed and tired and uncomfortable. What used to be so much fun on a Saturday afternoon was now a chore. And she didn't want to tell them that she had to go to the bathroom again. "Can we go home now?" she asked quietly. "I don't feel so good."

"But you didn't get anything!" Dana protested. Then she looked at November's wan face. "Oh. You're probably tired. But this was fun. Want to go shopping again next week?"

"Yeah, sure," November replied as Dana and Olivia paid for their clothes. But she knew she wouldn't be doing this again any time soon.

WHATEVER POSSESSED ME TO PLAN THIS *cookout?* November thought as sweat rolled off her forehead. The underarms of her extra-large T-shirt were stained and dark, and she could feel sweat trickle down her back. The temperature was supposed to hit ninety degrees this afternoon, and the sun beat down with no mercy on the patio in November's backyard.

The coals in the grill shimmered, adding to the heat as they waited for the burgers and hot dogs she had prepared earlier.

She carried a plastic card table out from the kitchen and set it up, satisfied that it was only a little wobbly. Then she went back and forth four times, bringing out a folding chair on each trip. She sat down after the last chair, breathing heavily.

"You know I woulda brought those out for you, November," Jericho called, startling her. "You're always so independent!"

"I didn't hear you come in," she said, fatigue in her voice.

"You left the front door wide open," he told her. "Here, I brought you some lemonade. Actually, Geneva made it for all of us. It's good, and it's cold. You look like you could use something to drink."

She nodded gratefully and let him pour her a glass. It tasted like cool gold. "Thanks."

"How are you feeling?" he asked.

"Hot. Sweaty. Huge. Bloated. Heavy. Tired. Take your pick." She glared at him.

"And cheerful, too!" he added, grinning. "I think it's a good idea you invited a few friends over, November. This should be fun tonight."

"It sounded like a good idea at the time, but it's just so hot today," November complained, brushing her damp hair off her face. She got up slowly and walked with Jericho back into the house.

"Why don't we cook the burgers on the grill outside, but eat inside in the air-conditioning?" he suggested.

"Good idea. I'm going to run upstairs and put on a shirt that's a little less funky," she said. "Well, actually, run is not the right word. I'm gonna wobble up the steps and get changed." She headed toward the stairs. "You want to start the burgers?"

"Sure thing," he said. "Take your time."

When November came back down, she'd changed into a pink top with a shiny silver arrow pointing south. It had the word BABY and a happy face printed on it, also in silver. "I hate this shirt," she said, "but it's all I've got that's clean." She flopped into the big chair in the living room, unable to fight the fatigue that seemed to envelop her.

"I'm cookin'. You're sittin'," Jericho ordered, pouring her another glass of lemonade. "Burgers are sizzlin'."

"I was hoping you'd say that. Hot dogs are on the counter."

"Gotcha." He disappeared into the backyard with a pile of food to be cooked.

The doorbell rang and November got up to answer it. *He shoulda left it unlocked*, she grumbled to herself.

Olivia stood there, holding a large bag of chips in one hand and a jar of dip in the other. She wore khaki cutoffs, an embroidered T-shirt, and a Cincinnati Reds hat. "Hey, November. What's up? You know, you look great."

"You need glasses or something?" November rolled her eyes.

"No. You know how the old people say pregnant women look like they're glowing? That's you."

"Ha! That's not glow. That's plain old sweat. But thanks for the boost. I needed that. And I love your outfit."

Olivia beamed. "T.J. Maxx," she said proudly. "How've you been feeling?" she asked.

"Everybody keeps asking me that," November replied irritably. "I feel like one of those blown-up elephants in the Macy's parade." Then she saw the hurt look on Olivia's face and she said quickly, "I'm sorry, Olivia. I shouldn't take this out on my friends. I'm just feeling sorry for myself today."

"Don't worry about it," Olivia told her as they headed for the kitchen. "Where do you keep your bowls?"

"In that cupboard on the left," November said, pointing. Then she made another face as she walked over to the sink to get some clean drinking glasses.

"You in pain or something?" Olivia asked. "You're walkin' funny."

November sighed deeply. "You don't want to know. Really you don't." She winced as she walked to the refrigerator for ice.

"Tell me, November. What's wrong? You walk like you got bullets up your butt."

November chuckled. "Pretty good description, actually."

"Of what?" Olivia looked perplexed.

"Girl, I got hemorrhoids. Big, fat, juicy ones. I didn't even know what hemorrhoids were a couple of weeks ago. Now I can describe them up close and personal."

"Oh, yuck. Poor baby," said Olivia sympathetically.

Just then Jericho walked into the kitchen with a plate of grilled hot dogs. "Hey, Olivia, good to see you," he said. "What are you two whispering about?"

Both girls doubled over with laughter. "Trust me, you don't want to know!" Olivia told him.

"I never will figure out women," Jericho said good-naturedly as he took another plate out to the grill.

The doorbell ran once more. "Can you get that, Olivia?" November said, still laughing. "Thanks."

When Olivia opened the door, Kofi and Dana greeted her with hugs.

"Where's everybody?" asked Dana. She wore a sleek, pale blue sundress that draped her figure like icing on a cake.

"November is in the kitchen complaining, Jericho is out back grilling, and I'm doing the door thing, just glad to be here."

Kofi, carrying a bag of cookies, a carton of ice cream,

and an iPod boom box, nodded at Olivia, but his eyes were on Dana. "Let's get this party started!" he shouted. "I have three thousand songs loaded on this bad boy."

"Have you listened to all of them?" asked Olivia.

"Yeah, most of them more than once. My iPod is my second brain," he replied.

"Hate to see your first brain," Olivia teased.

All of them gravitated to the kitchen, where Jericho was just bringing in a plate of grilled burgers. "What's up, Jericho?" Dana greeted them.

"Hey, Dana. What's goin' on, Kofi?" Jericho said as he put the plate down.

"And how's little mama today?" asked Dana.

"Better now that you guys are here," November told them. "Turn the music up loud, Kofi. My mother won't be home until late."

"What's with all the cooked cow?" Dana asked as she nibbled on a chip.

"Don't worry, girl," November said as she opened the refrigerator. "I got your skinny little veggie back." She pulled out a deli tray filled with sliced fresh vegetables and fruits, surrounded by roasted cashews and almonds. "Besides, that's mostly what I eat now as well."

"Thanks, girlfriend. I knew you'd be lookin' out for me."

Everybody began to load their plates with burgers and chips and dip, chattering about food and friends.

"Did you hear Cleveland went up to Ohio State to talk to the football coaches?" Jericho asked them. He squirted ketchup on his burger.

"If they take Cleveland, they got a Mack truck on the line," said Kofi, grunting with approval.

"They have a *dynamite* band up there, with great scholarships," Olivia said, admiration in her voice. "That's one of the places I'm going to apply to."

"You can get college scholarships for band?" November asked.

"Sure! Also for dance or singing or trumpet or whatever artistic talent you have. My dad calls them the 'artsy-fartsy' scholarships, but they pay the tuition, so what the hey! Yum, great hot dogs," Olivia said, licking her fingers. "Pass the mustard, please."

Kofi pulled up a chair, turned it around backward, and began to assemble his burger. "What you are about to witness, ladies and gentlemen, is the biggest hamburger ever to be made this side of the Rocky Mountains!" While the rest of them watched, he placed two burgers, four slices of cheese, three tomato slices, two dill pickles, a layer of chopped onions, and a handful of potato chips on top of one bun. All this he slathered with ketchup, mustard, and mayonnaise. Finally he placed the second bun carefully over that. "And there you have it!" he said triumphantly.

"Are you really gonna eat all that?" Olivia asked.

"Not only am I going to finish this one, baby cake—I might eat two more. Keep that grill going, Jericho. A hungry man is a dangerous man." Kofi made a silly face.

"You're nuts!" said Jericho with a laugh.

"You're gonna be sick," November warned.

"You're disgusting," Dana added. "Eating all that meat!"

"Man eat red meat!" said Kofi, grunting like a caveman

187

and stuffing the first bite of the huge sandwich into his mouth.

They all laughed. "Reminds me of something Josh might do," Jericho mused.

The room got quiet then, the only sound coming from Kofi's music player. "I miss him, man," Kofi finally said.

They all looked at November, who could not face their gazes. "I gotta make a quick run to the bathroom. I'll be right back." She disappeared around the corner.

"It's gonna be rough when school starts," Jericho said to the others.

"For all of us, but especially November," said Kofi.

"It's senior year," Olivia offered softly.

"Senior year won't be any fun with a kid," Dana stated.

Then Kofi whispered, "Is November having twins or something? I don't know much about this stuff, but isn't she pretty big?"

"Yep. I'm big as a whale, but it's just one kid in here," November said as she came back into the kitchen. "The doctor said I'm retaining water, which doesn't seem possible seeing how I go to the bathroom every eleven seconds!"

"Hey, I'm sorry," said Kofi. "I didn't mean to hurt your feelings or anything."

"You didn't. Really," she told him. She rubbed her bulging belly. "My mom took me out to dinner last week, and I couldn't fit into the booth. We had to switch to a table with chairs instead. It was sorta embarrassing," she admitted.

Everybody seemed to concentrate on what they were eating, not sure of what to say. "Great burgers, Jericho," Olivia mumbled, her mouth full.

November went over to the refrigerator. "I'm having strawberry ice cream. Anybody want to join me?"

"Sounds good to me," said Dana, moving quickly to fill any gaps in the awkward situation. She helped November get out bowls and spoons.

"So, how was Kings Island yesterday?" November asked with forced cheer as she licked her spoon. "Wasn't that the annual trip where Jericho's dad gets free tickets because it's Policeman's Day?"

"Awesome, man!" said Jericho just a little too excitedly. "I rode the Beast six times!"

"And me and Kofi went on that ride where you have to sit *real* close together and then you go down the hill and splash into that fake lake. I forget what it's called, but that's all we rode all day."

"*Real* close," Kofi echoed as he pulled Dana close to him and nuzzled her neck. She giggled.

November smiled. "Did you keep riding it because it got you all wet, or because you had to sit almost on Kofi's lap?"

"He's got a real nice lap," Dana said with a mischievous grin. She kissed Kofi on the cheek. He was loving it.

"Did you go, Olivia?" asked November.

Olivia added strawberry sauce to her ice cream. "Yeah, I went. Thanks for getting me the tickets, Jericho."

"Gotta look out for my band buddies," he said with a nod.

"I took my little cousin," Olivia explained to November, "so I spent most of the time in Kiddie Land, but it was fun."

"You should have gone with us too, November," Kofi said. "It wasn't the same without you."

"I wouldn't have been much fun," she admitted sadly.

"I move too slow to keep up with the rest of you, and most of that stuff probably wouldn't have been safe for the baby."

She didn't tell them that she'd cried most of the day while they were gone, missing the zooms and screeches of the roller coasters, the spins and drops of the other rides that she loved.

Last year she'd gone with Josh, and the two of them had stayed from the time it opened at ten until the gates closed at midnight. They'd gone on every single ride, even the merry-go-round. They'd eaten pizza and funnel cakes and cotton candy, then kissed under the moonlight as the fireworks exploded when the park closed.

Olivia once again brought the conversation back to what seemed to be a safe zone. "I got my schedule in the mail today. Did you guys?" She gave everyone another scoop of ice cream and a couple of cookies.

"Yeah, seems like they do that earlier and earlier every year," Jericho said. "But for once, I don't care—it's our senior year and we are getting ready to blow out of there!" He took four chocolate chip cookies.

"Dominate!" Kofi said.

"Dictate!" added Jericho, squaring off his shoulders.

"Decorate!" Dana interjected with a laugh. "Shows how silly you two sound."

"Girl, don't you know nothin' about male bonding?" Jericho teased her.

"I think it involves armpits and bad breath," Olivia joked, grinning.

"The girls outnumber you here," November told Jericho

and Kofi. "You two better be careful. We've got enough female hormones in this room to choke a horse!"

"I hear you," Jericho said. "We're just psyched about senior year."

"I'm thinking of going out for the swim team this fall," said Dana, "although if it messes with my hair, I'll quit. Hairstyles are more important than activities on a college transcript," she added in mock seriousness.

"I live and die for Friday nights," Olivia revealed. "I love the feel of the grass when we march, the chill in the air, the smell of fresh popcorn from the concession area. I love the power my horn gives me." She stopped suddenly.

"I miss the band," admitted Jericho, "a little. But the feel of a good tackle or hit on the line as the crowd cheers in the background—now that's power!"

"I'm thinkin' about trying out for the mascot this year," Kofi said. "You know—that guy who dresses up like a panther at the football games. Girls go for that thing, I've noticed. Turns them on!" He rolled his eyes at Dana and waited for her response.

Dana smacked him on the back of the head. "If you find something better than me, brother, go for it. Tell those girls this panther is taken!" They grabbed each other and giggled.

November felt an odd mix of emotions. She was relieved that the cookout had been a success, but as she listened to her friends chatter about the beginning of school, she envied them, sadly aware that she would be able to participate in none of the very ordinary school activities they mentioned. None.

CHAPTER 31
JERICHO
FRIDAY, AUGUST 27

JERICHO TRUDGED OVER TO THE PARKING lot and chugged a whole bottle of blue-colored, raspberry-flavored sports drink. Coach said it was good for them, but Jericho still preferred plain old cold bottled water. He wiped his lips, tossed his gear in the trunk of his car, and turned on the motor, but he didn't get in. He hoped the air-conditioning system was working today—it could be temperamental—so the car would be cool when Olivia got there.

Summer band and football practices were dismissed at the same time. A couple of weeks ago, when a rainstorm had exploded right after practice, he'd offered her a ride home. They'd sat in his slightly leaky, definitely ancient, red Grand Am and talked for two hours while the rain swirled around them. Since then, he had been giving her a ride home every day after practice.

"Waitin' for your girl, man?" Roscoe yelled from the other side of the parking lot.

"She's just a friend," Jericho yelled back, trying to explain.

"Pretty big friend!" Roscoe laughed and drove away.

Jericho wasn't sure how he felt about Olivia. She certainly was no Arielle—pale and dainty and desirable. Olivia was just a girl—a really nice girl, fun to talk to, but nothing more than that.

She turned the corner, lugging her instrument, and waved. She wore a navy blue T-shirt and red sweatpants. Her whole face became a smile. He waved back, genuinely glad to see her.

"Last band practice of the summer—over and done with, Captain!" she said, saluting. She shoved the sousaphone into the backseat.

"And last football practice, too! Whew! I thought Coach Barnes would never let us out of there."

"You know, it's not like it's over. We'll still have practice every night after school," she reminded him.

"Yeah, I know. But somehow this puts the cap on all we've done. The rest is just practicing the details and polishing the production."

She scowled and looked at him. "You sound like a coach."

"Coach Barnes has that effect on me. He's always talking about reaching for the stars and dreaming of unbelievable possibilities. I'm starting to believe him," Jericho admitted. He opened the door on his side.

"Is the team ready for Excelsior next week?" she asked. "This is gonna be like a Tonka truck going against a Hummer!"

"Some of those kids' toys are pretty tough," said Jericho, teasing.

"Not when they're under the wheels of the biggest SUV in the world! They'd get squashed."

Jericho laughed. "We're as ready as we'll ever be. Coach won't let us say anything negative—he's making us focus on a win."

"A win against Excelsior? Impossible. You just have to hope you don't get skunked too bad."

They climbed into Jericho's car, which had cooled enough so the seats weren't hot to the touch. "At least we got new uniforms. We'll wear them for the first time for the Excelsior game," he said as he tried to make the air blow cooler.

"Sweet. So you'll look good while you get stomped into the mud."

"Girl, don't let Coach hear you talking like that. I think he really believes we can beat them."

"He's a dreamer. What do the uniforms look like?"

"Really nice—expensive looking. They've got our names in big red letters on the back. Red stripes down the sides of the pants—really first-class."

"And the band has to show up in those same ratty-looking uniforms we've been wearing for the past ten years. Oh well, at least we get a road trip to Cleveland. That ought to be fun."

"Is the band ready for the half-time showdown?"

"Hey, our music is the bomb! If that's the only thing we had to worry about, we'd blow them out of the water. We're small, but mighty. Me, I'm just mighty!" She laughed, then added, "The trumpet section sure could use you."

"Yeah, I know." He clicked on the radio, but it just buzzed. "You get music or air in my car. Which one do you want?"

"My head is full of music, and the air feels good," she answered contentedly.

"You ready for school to start on Monday?" he asked her after a few minutes.

Olivia exhaled loudly. "I'm glad it's my senior year. I'm looking forward to my classes. But that's all. School isn't fun for me." She fiddled with the zipper on her purse.

"I feel you. Me and Josh had all these crazy plans for our senior year—like climbing to the roof of the school and putting up a flag, or letting a cow loose in the main hall. . . ."

"A cow?"

"His uncle owns a farm. It's not important—just stupid kid stuff that will never happen."

"I know how much you miss him," she said gently. They stopped at a red light. He noticed she reached over to touch his shoulder, but she quickly jerked her hand back and folded her arms across her chest. He gave her no indication he had noticed and drove on when the light changed.

He pulled up in front of her house but kept the motor running. "Hey, maybe we'll have a couple of classes together."

"Who knows? When they do class schedules by computer, anything can happen. Last year some girl had been scheduled for seven periods of gym! She was in the office having a purple fit!"

"Sounds like a perfect day to me."

"Ugh. A funky armpit day."

"Well, speaking of armpits, I better get home and get showered. I'll see you at school on Monday."

She climbed out of the car and retrieved her instrument. "Uh, Jericho?"

"Yeah."

"I really appreciate the rides home. You didn't have to do that."

"No sweat. You're pretty cool to talk to—just like one of the guys."

She gave him a funny look, then closed the car door. "See you around, Jericho."

AFTER A LONG SHOWER AND A BIG BOWL of Geneva's chili, Jericho sat in his room organizing his new book bag for Monday. Binders in red and green, fresh notebook paper, and dark blue gel pens. As a junior, he'd learned to do with the very minimum— just enough to get through the day.

Todd poked his head in the door. He wore his favorite pair of Batman pajamas, the blue logo faded and almost gray. The pj's were way too small for him, but he refused to give them up, and would not pass them down to Rory. "You excited about the first day of school, Jericho?"

"Only because it's my last first day. Everything after this is countdown to graduation!"

"You'll have a first day of college," Todd said, "won't you?"

"Yeah, I suppose. But that will be different. What about you, kid? Ready for the first day of seventh grade?"

"I'm a little scared," his stepbrother admitted.

"How come? You're at the same school as last year, aren't you?"

"Yeah, but every year in June the seventh graders have a dance that they have to invite a girl to, and I'm afraid nobody will want to go with me."

"You're worried about a party that's almost a year away?"

"I'm not cool and popular like you, Jericho. You're a big football star, and I've seen how the girls look at you at practice. You're the bomb." Todd picked up a pack of pencils from Jericho's desk and tossed it from one hand to the other.

Jericho grabbed the boy and tousled his curly hair. "Kid, you are the coolest, flyest twelve-year-old in Batman pajamas that I've ever met. You're going to have to install a special computer program just to sort through the girls who want to go with you to that dance!"

"You really think so?" Todd slipped out of Jericho's grasp and sat on the bed.

"I know so. And I think you've got the wrong idea about my popularity. My girl dumped me last semester, and I been flying solo ever since."

"What about Olivia? Most days when I came to watch you practice, I noticed you took her home."

"Olivia is cool people, but she's just a friend. And at your age, that's all you need to worry about—having girls as friends. You're way too young to even think about anything else."

"There was a girl in my class who got pregnant last year," Todd said, grimacing. "Yuck!"

"In the sixth grade? That's messed up." Jericho gave Todd a devilish smile. "You're not the daddy, are you?"

Todd threw several pillows at Jericho. "Ooh, nasty!" the boy cried. Jericho pounced on his stepbrother, tickling him, while Todd screeched with glee. Rory heard all the commotion and joined in, the three boys wrestling and laughing and knocking things over until Geneva came in and put a stop to it.

JUST BEFORE HE FELL ASLEEP, JERICHO'S cell phone rang. He stumbled over to his desk, lifted it off the charger, and said groggily, "Hello."

"Hi, Jericho." Arielle's voice, coming across the phone line like a soft echo, startled him fully awake. He almost fell off the bed.

"Uh, what's up, Arielle?" he managed to say. He wasn't sure if he was glad to hear from her or not.

"I was just thinking about school starting next week, deciding what to wear and stuff, and I got to thinking about you."

"Me? Why?" His heart was beating fast. He wanted to hang up. But he didn't.

"We had a good thing going for a while there, Jericho. Something special."

He couldn't believe how her voice was melting him like soft butter. He hated himself for being so weak. "Yeah, we did. But you were the one who ended it, Arielle, not me," he said as harshly as he could.

"I know, but there was so much trauma drama going on. I couldn't cope with the stress. Josh was dead, the Warriors looked like they were going to jail, and everybody associated with them seemed to be in trouble." She sounded as if she was sniffling.

"If I remember, *I* was the one who was stressed. Josh was my cousin, my very best friend. I needed you and you weren't there!" he said angrily.

"I'm so sorry, Jericho. Can you forgive me?"

"You gotta be kidding!" He couldn't believe what he was hearing.

"I miss you, Jericho." Her voice was like candy.

"You're asking quite a bit, Arielle." He could feel himself weakening.

"I'm a better person now," she said. "I'm willing to start over if you are."

"What about Logan?" Jericho asked bluntly. Just saying Logan's name made him furious—not just because Arielle had gone out with him, but because of what he'd done to those kids.

"Logan's in jail and won't get out till he's twenty-one—at the earliest," she replied dismissively.

"But you wrapped yourself around him like he was the 'king of all that,'" said Jericho accusingly.

"I admit that was my bad. I made a mistake," she said sweetly. "Haven't you ever made an error in judgment? Haven't you ever hated yourself for something terrible you'd done and you wish you could erase it?"

How does she know how to stab me right where I'm weakest? he thought as he stared at the moonlight outside his window. "Yeah, maybe," he admitted.

"You were the best thing that ever happened to me, Jericho."

Her voice was pleading, almost plaintive, like one of his trumpet solos. He found himself sweating.

"Did you know Logan was dealin' drugs to little kids?" Jericho demanded.

"No, I swear I didn't," she proclaimed. "If I had known I would have turned him in. Honest. You gotta believe me."

"One of those kids could have died, you know."

"Yeah, but nobody did. That's all that matters."

"You really believe that?"

"You know what I mean, Jericho." Changing the subject, she asked, "How are your little stepbrothers?"

"They're cool. They think big brother Jericho is a football star."

"Well, you are," Arielle said, her voice sounding silky and smooth. "All the girls on the cheerleading squad say you be lookin' bomb diggety out there!"

"They do?" Jericho was amazed.

"Yeah, sometimes after our practice in the gym, we went over to the football field and watched you guys work out."

"I didn't even know you were a cheerleader," he told her.

"It seemed like the right thing to do for my senior year. It's fun, plus it will look good on my college résumé."

"So, uh, the cheerleaders go to every game?" Jericho hated to sound dumb, but he'd never paid much attention to the cheerleaders when he was in the band. They were just a bunch of girls with pom-poms who giggled on the bus and wiggled on the field.

"Ooh, yes! I'm really charged about the game with Excelsior! I hear their cheerleaders wear uniforms that glow in the dark!"

Everything was starting to sink in. "So you'll be going with us to Cleveland for that game?"

"Absolutely. I'm going to cheer for the team, but mostly I'll be there to support you, Jericho."

He honestly didn't know what to say. "Why?"

"Because I gave up a diamond in the rough, and I'm ready to show him how to shine like a jewel."

"Girl, you talkin' a bunch of mess."

She laughed. "Just give me a chance, okay? No strings. No promises. I'll see you at school Monday."

She hung up and Jericho sat there on the edge of his bed for several moments, looking at the phone screen, which glowed for a short while, then dulled as the line went dead. He finally went and put the phone back on the charger, but he didn't go back to bed right away. He stared at the late summer moon outside. Everything looked shimmery and unusually bright. The white lawn furniture in the backyard, reflecting the moonlight, seemed to glow like something out of an old science fiction movie. He knew it wasn't real. He wondered if he could trust anything anymore.

NOVEMBER SAT IN HER MOTHER'S CAR IN the school parking lot, her hand on the door. Students getting off buses and out of cars streamed past them, laughing and calling to one another in first-day enthusiasm. None of the girls, dressed in the latest short skirts, tight jeans, and funky tops, noticed the trembling teenager sitting in the battered Ford.

"I can't go in there, Mom."

"We've talked about this all summer, November. You could have chosen to go to Rafiki, you know."

"A special school full of pregnant girls who sleep around? That's not me, Mom. I'm not like them. I really *am* a good girl." Her eyes filled with tears.

"You're just as pregnant as they are," Mrs. Nelson said gently.

"I know, I know. I just didn't think it would be this hard to go in there." She wore a loose yellow T-shirt and a pair of jeans that were two sizes larger than she usually wore. At seven months, November had gained over twenty-five pounds already—way too much, Dr. Holland had told her—and she still had trouble with the swelling of her legs, ankles, and wrists. She felt like an elephant.

"Do you want to go back home?" her mother asked. "There's still time to enroll you in Rafiki. You'll only make it through first quarter, anyway. Then you'll probably be out until at least after Christmas."

"Do you think I can still graduate on time?" asked November bleakly.

"Your guidance counselor seems to think you can make up what you miss in summer school and still get your diploma this year. And you can still plan for college, you know, if . . ."

"If I sell my baby to the Prescotts," November finished for her, fire in her voice.

"Quit saying that! It would be a legal adoption. You can't keep putting off this decision, you know. Time is running out."

"I don't want to talk about it! Get off my case!" November's back was aching, and she really had to go to the bathroom. "Hey, I see Olivia, Dana, and Kofi walking this way. I'm going in with them."

Mrs. Nelson let the subject drop for the moment. "Okay, okay! But this isn't going away. I'll pick you up at three after my school gets out. Have a good day."

"Bye, Mom. I'm sorry. It seems like my feelings are like clothes tumbling in a dryer. Everything comes out upside down." Her mom gave her a quick hug, and she got out of the car reluctantly.

She called to Dana, who was dressed in soft, light blue Ultrasuede jeans and a jacket that seemed to hug her body as she walked. Her shoes, her purse, even her nail polish were color-coordinated in various shades of silvery blue. November noticed that boys stopped in their tracks and turned completely around just to gawk at Dana, but she pretended to be unaware of them. Kofi noticed, however. He glared at any male whose eyes lingered too long, until they gave him the head nod and moved on.

Olivia, who looked like she had lost a few pounds, wore a crisp white and red Douglass T-shirt, khaki slacks, and the new pair of Nikes she'd bought when they'd all gone shopping. Her hair had been freshly braided in a really attractive style, with short, curly extensions that complemented her high cheekbones and almond-shaped eyes. She waved happily at November.

As her mom drove off, November looked once again with dismay at the imposing face of the school. She was really glad to have friends to walk with.

"So what's up, little mama?" Dana asked as they headed across the parking lot. Kofi had to set up the computers in the lab, so he had hurried into the building before the doors opened.

"Big mama is more like it. I'm feeling pretty huge these days."

"You make *me* look good," Olivia teased. "Seriously, are you feeling okay?"

"Not really. But I'll make it." They walked up the worn stone steps and stood near the front door, waiting for the bell to ring. November couldn't help but overhear the comments of some of the girls standing nearby, who made no effort to stifle their words.

"Ooh, girl, she big as a house!"

"You just be hatin'."

"That's a messed-up way to start senior year."

"Don't make no difference. I had my baby and was back in two weeks," said a girl named Chiquita, whose fingernails, painted red and black, were so long they curled.

"She'll be back in shape by prom time."

"Probably get pregnant again by then."

"Not by Josh Prescott!" They had the nerve to laugh.

"Josh her baby's daddy?"

"That's what they say." Chiquita adjusted the earphones on her iPod.

November looked down at the ground and walked faster. But Dana, who had been watching the girls with increasing fury, was not so willing to pretend they didn't hear them. She marched over to where Chiquita stood, ripped the earphones out of the girl's ears, and shouted, "I heard you don't even know your baby daddy's name!" she said angrily.

"Don't be gettin' salty with me, girlfriend," Chiquita warned. But she didn't seem willing to fight.

"You just learn how to keep your mouth shut about stuff you know nothing about!" Dana said, stepping closer as Chiquita stepped back. Olivia stood right behind her, eyes narrowed with menace.

"I got business to tend to," said Chiquita. "Get out of my way." She and her friends hurried down the steps and around to the back door.

November breathed a sigh of relief. "You didn't have to

do that, but thanks, Dana. And I didn't know you had it in you, Olivia."

"Me neither," Olivia admitted with a grin. "But I had your back, Dana. I was ready to go at it with you if she tried anything. All I had to do was sit on her!"

Dana laughed. "I knew there wouldn't be a fight. Girls like that are all mouth, no guts. Besides, you think I'd get in a fight and mess up this outfit? You know how much my mama paid for this stuff?"

The bell rang and the three girls filed into the noisy confusion of the first day of school. Teachers stood in the hall, directing the new ninth graders and answering questions. Everyone seemed to be talking at once— greeting old friends, laughing too loudly, showing off new threads and kicks.

Nobody seemed to pay any attention at all to the framed picture of Josh that still hung in the hallway, November noticed.

The seniors were especially vocal. About twenty senior boys, Jericho and Kofi and Eric Bell in his wheelchair among them, stood in the middle of the main hall, blocking traffic and shouting as loudly as they could, "PANTHER PRIDE! SENIORS RULE! PANTHER PRIDE! SENIORS RULE!" Jack Krazinski, who had positioned himself right next to them, exploded his cymbals after every cheer. The noise was deafening.

A couple of the teachers, used to this kind of first-day foolishness, shushed them all and shooed them out of the hall. The boys good-naturedly broke up their impromptu pep rally.

Jack gave his cymbals one last clashing gong as he passed by, bowing to Olivia and giving Dana and November a polite nod.

"That boy really is crazy!" said Dana, shaking her head.

"Maybe not. You know what he calls it each time he clangs those two things together?" Olivia asked.

"What?"

"'A short splash of color in a dark gray world,'" Olivia told them. "Little kids use crayons. Jack uses sound."

"And high schools use the public address system. Is it just me, or is everything really loud and annoying today?" November asked.

Every few minutes the principal blurted out new announcements through the PA at the highest possible volume, so his broadcasts were always accompanied by the screech and hiss of distortion.

"*All ninth graders without a schedule are to report to the gym.*"

"*If anyone has found the purple binder with the locker assignments, please bring it to room 201.*"

"*Attendance forms can be found in the main office. Make sure they are filled out in triplicate.*"

"*Tickets for the football game with Excelsior Academy are on sale in the athletic office. If you plan to ride with us on the school bus, you must bring your permission slip by Wednesday.*"

November, for the first time since kindergarten, felt overwhelmed. Ordinarily she loved the smell of the first day of school—the freshly waxed hall floors, the newly painted walls (at least in the main hall where visitors entered), even the smell of food emanating from the cafeteria. But today was different.

Everything looked as if it had been prepared for everyone else except for her. She glanced at the notices on the bulletin board.

TRY OUT FOR THE SWIM TEAM TODAY!
SIGN UP FOR THE FUN RUN AND HELP THE HOMELESS SHELTER!
WANT TO LEARN GYMNASTICS? COME TO ROOM 444 AFTER SCHOOL.

Nothing applied to her any longer. *I can't run or jump or tumble or swim*, she thought miserably. *And all these activities seem so, I don't know, kinda childish. All of a sudden all the kids around me seem to be immature, with no real sense of responsibility or worry. Like kids. I guess they are.* She shook the thought away.

To Dana she asked, "So what's your first class? I got English."

Dana checked her schedule. "Yep, Senior English. Oh, no, it's Ms. Hathaway," she moaned. "That woman is a real dinosaur."

"What about you, Olivia?"

"Me too. English Lit. Piece of cake!"

"That's because you spent the summer working at the downtown library, reading," November said.

"Hey, the rest of the time I was sweatin' out there with the marching band, don't forget."

"Oh, yeah, that's right. I spent the summer watching the wallpaper peel and my waistline disappear. Boring." November shifted her book bag. "I talked to Jericho last night, and he told me he had Hathaway too."

Olivia looked up, interested.

"He's got her in the afternoon, though. He's not in the morning class with us," November explained. She glanced over at Olivia, who began digging intently in her book bag.

"So what's up with you and Jericho?" Dana asked Olivia with a smile. "Somebody told me he gave you a ride home a lot this summer."

Olivia blushed furiously, her coffee brown face suddenly a ruddy cinnamon. "It's no big deal. My house was on the way and he offered me a ride. I even paid him for his gas," she added.

"You're not acting like it's no big deal," teased November gently.

"There's no way a cool dude like Jericho would think about a girl like me," Olivia said as she stooped down to brush some dirt off her new shoes. "He's got a reputation to think of. I'm not even on his radar screen."

"You've got to stop coming down on yourself," said Dana. "Jericho picks his friends for who they are on the inside, not superficial stuff. He's deep."

"You think?"

"I know."

Olivia looked unsure. "Well, there's the warning bell." The crowds in the halls had begun to thin and the halls regained a bit of their echo.

Just as the three of them headed up the stairs to English, they heard a girl's artificial giggle—that laugh that women save for when they're with a man they want to impress—followed by a deep male laugh, hearty and pleased. All three girls turned to see who it was.

Walking up the steps, his eyes focused on the girl beside him, was Jericho. Arielle, dressed in a skirt short enough and tight enough to make stair-climbing not a very good idea, walked beside him, holding his hand possessively and looking up at him as if he were the last chocolate doughnut in the box.

OLIVIA, HER FACE A MASK OF HUMILIATION, covered her mouth with her hand and ran up the rest of the stairs, leaving November and Dana behind.

Jericho saw the coming confrontation, made what was obviously an instant decision, and said quickly, "I'm late—I gotta get to class. I'll check you all out later. I'll call you tonight, Arielle." He hurried back down the stairs and disappeared.

November paused on the landing, glad for an excuse to rest, and waited for Arielle to catch up with them. Dana looked as if she wasn't sure whether to follow Olivia and check on her, or confront Arielle instead. She chose to stay.

"What's up, Arielle?" Dana said coolly.

"Oh, hey, Dana. Nice hookup," Arielle commented. "You got it goin' on with that Ultrasuede."

"I wish I could say the same for you," replied Dana. "Could that shirt and skirt be any tighter?"

"You just jealous 'cause I got a killer body, and you look like a telephone pole in your clothes." She laughed and checked her fingernails. The late bell had rung, and the halls were empty. The three girls stood alone in the stairwell. "I suppose I should say that you look nice too, November," Arielle added weakly. "You sure got big quick!"

Ignoring her comment, November said, "I didn't know you and Jericho were back together."

"We're just friends—for now," said Arielle as she adjusted her big gold belt. "Since I'm a cheerleader, and he's on the football team, it just makes sense, don't you think?"

"To you, maybe. What do you do—find the flavor of the month to go out with, Arielle?" November asked.

"At least I can get a dude," Arielle shot back. "You look like a whale."

November wanted to smack her, but she just clenched her fists and her jaw tightly. "What does he see in you?" she asked, almost to herself.

"Opportunity!" replied Arielle with a toss of her curls.

"I haven't forgotten what you did to Olivia," Dana said, her voice low with warning.

"Oh, the fat girl?" She rolled her eyes. "Forget about that duck. People like that aren't worth worrying about."

"That girl is a friend of mine, and I'm warning you—you better worry. Payback is coming."

"Like I care!" Arielle smoothed her tiny, tight skirt and headed on up the steps. "Don't be tryin' to get between me and Jericho," she warned as she left. "I plan to take good care of him."

November and Dana, both bristling with irritation, shook their heads and headed on up the stairs, quite late, to class.

NOVEMBER DREADED THE CLASS THEY HURRIED to. Most of their teachers were pretty cool—they understood the silliness of teenagers and were willing to bend the rules a little. But Ms. Hathaway had a long reputation of never budging an inch. Josh used to say she had a steel rod stuck up her backside.

"How long has Hathaway been at Douglass?" November asked Dana.

"Longer than recorded time," Dana answered. "I hear she gives homework every single day of the year, including weekends, and detentions for being late—even on the first day."

"Well, as long as we're gonna get in trouble, let's make it worth it. I gotta go to the bathroom," said November.

"Remember last year when it snowed so bad, and they canceled the buses?" Dana asked as they headed to the restroom.

"Yeah! They didn't cancel school that day, just the buses. Teachers were supposed to come in, but most of them couldn't get out of their driveways. Even the principal stayed home. And hardly any kids showed up—it was like a free day. Me and Josh spent the day building a snowman," November said, remembering.

"Well, Hathaway showed up that day."

"For real?"

"Not only did she show up, but she gave a failing grade for the day to every kid who stayed home—more than ninety percent of her students." Dana looked at herself in the mirror and dabbed a bit of mascara on each eyelash.

"How can she get away with stuff like that?" November asked as she washed her hands.

"They can't fire her. They just keep hoping she'll retire, but she never does."

"I hear she's a really good teacher if you follow all her rules. Did you remember to get the red notebook? It can't be pink or purple—must be bright red."

"Yeah, I got one. The woman's got issues!" Dana touched up her lipstick next.

"Why does she stick around? It's obvious she hates kids." November looked at herself in the mirror and shook her head. She looked awful. *Not even mascara and lipstick will help this*, she thought as her swollen face looked back at her.

"Maybe she has nothing to go home to. She never got married, never had kids, probably has no friends—this is all she has."

"What are you tryin' to do, make me feel sorry for her?"

"No way. You'll get over that real quick anyway when you get in there. I just gotta warn you. I heard she's really hard on the pregnant girls," Dana said carefully.

"That's all I need," said November as she held up her hands. "So far, this day has not been great, and it's still early."

"Poor Olivia. I didn't know she was so into Jericho," Dana remarked sadly.

"I don't think she even realized it until she saw him with Arielle—that witch."

"How can boys be so stupid? Can't he see Arielle for what she really is?" Dana asked in frustration.

"Jericho is just looking at the good parts," November stated as she picked up her book bag.

"And we told Olivia he was deep."

"So much for deep dudes."

The two girls marched down the hall and into the classroom a full twenty minutes after class had started. The class was quiet, everyone busily writing in their red notebooks, but they all looked up expectantly when Dana and November walked in.

"And the reason for your tardiness, young ladies?" Ms. Hathaway said harshly. She was a tall woman, angular and gaunt. She wore no makeup, not even lipstick, so every line and wrinkle showed clearly on her pale face. Her gray-white hair was cut short, but without much style, November thought. She wore a red-flowered, long-sleeved dress, even though it was late August, but oddly, instead of the ugly black "old lady" shoes that one might expect, she wore comfortable-looking red sandals. *We need to get her*

217

a subscription to Vogue magazine, November thought with a giggle as she and Dana stopped by her perfectly ordered desk.

"We got lost," Dana said with a grin. She looked over at Olivia, who was already seated in the back of the room, and tried to make her smile, but Olivia just looked away.

Ms. Hathaway did not seem to be amused. "Miss Wolfe, your assignment is on the board, and you have less than fifteen minutes to complete it. I suggest you cease the banter and begin. Your assigned seat is the third seat in the fourth row. Your detention begins at three o'clock sharp. Do not dare to be late."

"Yes, ma'am," said Dana, but made a face when Ms. Hathaway turned her back. No one had the nerve to laugh. November noticed that Dana looked really pleased when she saw that her seat was right next to Kofi's.

"And you, Miss Nelson," the teacher continued, "I will see you out in the hall. Now. The rest of you continue working on your essays. Silently."

November glanced at Dana, shrugged, and followed the teacher. As soon as the door had clicked shut, Ms. Hathaway turned to November and demanded, "Why are you here, Miss Nelson?" She spoke quietly, but every word seemed to stab at November.

"Excuse me?"

"Don't they have that Rafiki program for girls like you?" Her deep-set black eyes never left November's face.

How dare she talk to me like that! "I chose not to go there, ma'am." November refused to let this woman see her cry. "I wanted to be with my friends here at Douglass."

"This school is not a social club. Our purpose here is academic." She paused and seemed to peer down the empty hallway. "You had so much potential, Miss Nelson. I must say I'm really disappointed in you."

"A lot of people seem to feel that way," November answered, lowering her head. She looked down at her swollen ankles and noticed that even Ms. Hathaway had nicer legs than she did.

Ms. Hathaway continued, "I've observed you since you were a freshman—poised, intelligent, articulate— always willing to volunteer for a good cause. You must feel awful."

November, surprised that the woman knew enough about her to make such a statement, replied angrily, "You have no idea how I feel!" The baby shifted and moved within her, but she gave no indication to the teacher.

"Actually, I do," Ms. Hathaway replied quietly.

"Huh?" November was stunned.

"I had a child once."

November gasped. Not this straight up hater! She couldn't even come close to imagining her as young, or in love, or pregnant. "Yes, ma'am," was the only phrase her mouth would form.

"They took her from me. And then she died."

November couldn't believe Ms. Hathaway was telling her this. "I'm sorry, ma'am. Really, I am."

The teacher shook her head, as if to clear her mind. All business once again, she said, "We must get back to the classroom. I will expect you to keep up with every scrap of homework so that you do not fall behind during your absence. If you do decide to go to college later on, I will not allow my class to be the one that prevents that from happening."

"Thank you, ma'am. I promise to work real hard. I like English, and I'm a pretty good writer."

"We'll see about that. In fact, I want you to write me a personal essay about your pregnancy—your thoughts, emotions, fears, everything. It will help you sort through your feelings, and give me something to grade you on while you are out of class. When are you due?"

"November second."

Ms. Hathaway nodded. "Until that time, you are aware I have strict attendance and behavior policies in my classroom?"

"Yes, ma'am. I will do my best not to miss a day, except for, except for, uh, medical reasons."

As they walked back into the classroom, the chatter suddenly ceased and everyone returned to their writing as if they had been doing it the whole time. "Your seat is here in the front row, Miss Nelson. I will see you at detention." November had already forgotten about the DT.

She was relieved when Ms. Hathaway turned her attention to another unfortunate student—Jack Krazinski—who had come to class without a pen or pencil.

"You were aware this was the first day of school, Mr. Krazinski?"

"Yes, ma'am."

"And you received my letter in the mail two weeks ago about my classroom requirements?"

"Yes, ma'am."

"You are a senior in high school—about to graduate and become one of the decision makers of our society?"

"Yes, ma'am."

"And yet you chose to appear before me without supplies?"

"I forgot!" A few class members giggled, but stopped when they saw the fire in the teacher's eyes.

"It takes talent to make a failing grade on the first day of school. Congratulations, Mr. Krazinski. I hope you perform better in the marching band."

"How'd you know I played in the band?" Jack asked, scratching his head.

"Small children in the next *county* huddle in fear from the noise of your cymbals, Mr. Krazinski!" The slightest hint of a smile touched her lips. The class allowed themselves a small laugh, then went back to work.

November, who had been standing at her seat, watching the scene with amusement, finally decided to sit down. The desk, made of wood and full of pencil scratches and carved doodles from years past, was one of those that looked like a chair but had a lapboard to set books and papers on. November tried for several moments to find a solution, but no matter how she tried to adjust her body, she could not fit in the desk. She finally gave up in frustration and sat in a chair at the front table, right next to Eric Bell, who had to sit there because he was in a wheelchair.

IT WAS JUST BEFORE DISMISSAL, AND November, Dana, and Olivia sat together at a table in the back of the library. November, who couldn't believe how hungry she was, was sneaking potato chips into her mouth when the librarian wasn't looking. Olivia flipped through a magazine, but she had refused to talk about Arielle and Jericho.

Finally, in order to break the tension, November asked, "You excited about the Excelsior game, Olivia?"

She shrugged. "It's just another football game. Sweaty boys. Simple girls who think cheerleading is an academic activity."

"Don't forget about the band," Dana reminded her gently. "The band always rocks."

"We're going to look stupid—and dirt-poor. This is one of the richest schools in the country. I bet they laugh at us." Olivia opened another periodical—one of those fashion magazines where all the models were incredibly thin and beautiful. She snorted and tossed it aside.

November glanced through it and for the first time understood why Olivia would toss it away. Seeing the skinny girls in there made her feel like a blimp now.

She didn't know how to make Olivia feel better. "A whole busload of Douglass kids are going up to support the team and the band. We'll scream and holler and cheer our guts out," she said, trying to sound encouraging. "Plus a lot of people are driving up. Jericho told me his dad and stepmom, as well as Todd and Rory, are driving up Saturday afternoon."

"Are you going?" Olivia asked in surprise.

"Yeah. I wouldn't miss it," November replied. She figured she could use the distraction, plus she'd promised Jericho she'd come watch.

"You know who rides up on the band bus," said Olivia, her voice flat.

"The cheerleaders," November said sympathetically. She really felt for Olivia.

"How am I going to put up with five hours of her skinny behind?" Olivia moaned. "She'll be up and down the aisles, showing off, talking stuff, and making sure she's in my face with all of it."

"You're so much better than she is," Dana stated.

"Bigger, maybe," Olivia said. "Look, I'll be fine. This is the story of my life. I should be used to it now. Just keep my mouth shut, do my homework, and play my instrument. And don't expect anything more."

November and Dana were silent, helpless to offer a

solution. Finally Dana said, "We'll be there to support you, Olivia."

Olivia looked up at them. "You know, you guys are great. I never really had close friends before. It makes all this mess a little easier to deal with."

"We got your back, girlfriend," November said with a smile.

"Me and Kofi are driving up to the game on Saturday morning, November. You think your mother will let you go with us instead of on the bus?"

"Probably. She worries about everything, though—gets on my nerves. You have to agree to stop every hour so I can use the bathroom, though."

Dana laughed. "No problem. Anything to make the little mama comfortable." Then, her voice suddenly serious, she asked, "Have you heard from the Prescotts lately?"

"I have another appointment with them and their lawyer on September twenty-first. I need to make my decision by then."

"But why?" Olivia and Dana asked at the same time.

"So when the baby comes, everything will be set. Either I will take her home forever, or the Prescotts will."

"You sound so sad. Are you sure you'll be ready to make such a big decision?" asked Olivia, concern in her voice.

"I'm not sure of anything."

"Are they still putting heavy pressure on you?" Dana wanted to know.

"Josh's mom calls once a week—trying to be nice, I guess. She offers to take me shopping for maternity clothes, or drive me to my doctor appointments. I guess they figure being nice to me is a better way to make me decide in their favor."

"Is it working?" Olivia asked.

November shrugged. "Not really. But Jericho told me that as soon as they heard the baby would be a girl, they decorated one of the rooms in the house as a full nursery—done up in pink bunny rabbits."

"They must feel awfully confident about winning!" Olivia commented.

"Pink rabbits? Give me a break," said Dana.

"Have you bought any baby stuff, November?" Olivia asked gently.

November looked dreamy. "Not yet. . . . I just can't yet. . . . But if I did, it would be yellow. When I think of her as a real person—a baby, a toddler, a child—I call her Sunshine."

"What a glorious name," whispered Olivia.

"In my mind I see her crooked little smile—just like Josh's. I see her talking and walking and running in the park on a sunny day—with me," November continued.

"I was waiting for this to hit you," said Dana quietly.

"What do you mean?" November asked.

"For your heart to catch up with your head."

November looked at Dana and Olivia, relief plain on her face. "You know what?" she said, the hesitation in her voice turning to confidence.

"What, girl?"

"I don't think I can do it."

"Do what? What do you mean?" Dana asked, touching November's hand.

"Give up my Sunshine."

THE TEAM ARRIVED AT THE RITZ-CARLTON Hotel in downtown Cleveland about seven o'clock on Friday night. After five hours on a Greyhound bus, Jericho was glad to stretch his legs. He walked around the lobby of the swanky hotel, trying not to gawk at the marble floors and huge chandeliers above.

Coach had made them all wear suits, with a white shirt and red tie, and he had to admit they looked pretty good as they checked in, even though they were a little rumpled. "Dinner in a half hour, men. We'll eat at the restaurant here in the hotel. Suits and ties required. We've ordered steak Diane, potatoes au gratin, and steamed broccoli for everyone. Dinner is provided for us by the Excelsior Alumni Association Boosters, as are your rooms and everything else this weekend."

"Can I order me a deuce at dinner, Coach?" Roscoe asked with a grin. "Or maybe a forty!" The other boys held back laughs as they waited to see if the coach would go off on Roscoe.

Coach Barnes seemed to be unfazed. "In the first place, a four-star hotel like this doesn't even sell that cheap malt liquor your gangsta friends like to drink. And in the second place, if I *ever* catch you with so much as a *whisper* of alcohol on your breath, you're off this team until you're twenty-one—the age you'll probably be when you get enough credits to graduate!"

"Ooh, he got you, man," Cleveland hooted. The rest of the team doubled over with laughter.

Their voices echoed loudly in the tall lobby, and several of the other guests looked at the group of teenagers nervously. One old lady, Jericho noticed, clutched her purse tightly and scurried over to the elevators.

Roscoe smirked and took it in stride. "You want me to take a lap around the lobby, Coach?"

"Hey, I'm considering it!" Mr. Barnes said. "Get on up to your rooms now and get freshened up. I'll see you down here in thirty. Remember, we're acting like gentlemen and champions tonight."

"I'm starved!" Jericho said. "How much does a champion need to eat?"

"Enough to help us win tomorrow. I want you strong and quick tomorrow, Jericho. Our defense is going to need you. Are you ready?"

"Ready as I'll ever be, Coach." Jericho boarded the elevator with the others. "Hey, do they have apple pie in that restaurant?"

"You can have three slices—with ice cream!"

"Gotcha. I'll be back down in five minutes."

When Jericho and Roscoe reached the room they were going to share, they slid the keycard into the lock, opened the door, and just stood there for a moment, gaping at the two full-size beds, the thick, plush-looking comforters that had been turned down by the housekeeping staff, and the huge window that overlooked Lake Erie. Soft classical music played on the radio.

"Man, this is the business!" Jericho said as he stretched his six-foot-three-inch body on the bed. "I could get used to this kind of lifestyle."

"Look, man!" Roscoe cried out. "Bathrobes! They got bathrobes in the closets! Only high-class places do that. I'm taking this home to give to my mama!"

"Look, you little scatback. You better leave that here. You get charged for it, you know," warned Jericho.

"Am I payin' for the room?" Roscoe had put the robe on over his suit, but it still engulfed him.

"No, but the robes are for you while you're here, man. Don't be rippin' the folks off." He laughed. "Besides, you look like you got on your daddy's clothes!" Roscoe was only five foot eight, but he was tough and wiry.

"My mama would *love* this," Roscoe replied, rubbing the silky fabric, but he hung it back up in the closet. "Well, let's go eat as much of these folks' food as we can. They brought us up here to slaughter us, so I'm gonna eat well before they cook us like marshmallows over a fire."

"Coach don't want you talkin' like that," Jericho warned as they headed for the elevator.

"Coach lives in a dreamworld. There is no way in heaven or hell we can beat Excelsior."

"But we've practiced all summer. Luis is a dynamite quarterback. Even you can be pretty fast if somebody sticks a lightning bolt up your behind!" Jericho said, faking a punch. "You think all those plays, drills, and skills he taught us won't work?"

Roscoe laughed. "Remember when we saw that movie in history last year—the one where the Romans put the Christians in the arena with the hungry lions so the people could watch it like we watch HBO?"

Jericho nodded.

"Those poor folks in that arena thought they had skills too. But they got ate up, man. Gobbled."

Jericho looked at his buddy. Was that what the fancy digs were all about?

The elevator door opened to the lobby. Jericho and Roscoe joined Luis and the rest of the team as they headed to the restaurant. The meal was delicious, and Jericho really did eat three pieces of pie—two raspberry and one chocolate cream. The raspberry, which was tart but sweet, for some reason reminded him of Arielle. That second pie was *really* good.

When he finally collapsed on the incredibly soft bed a couple of hours later, Jericho dreamed of lions and footballs and Josh standing helplessly, waiting to be gobbled.

THE NEXT MORNING, AFTER A BREAKFAST of maple-saturated waffles and scrambled eggs, the team, dressed in their white dress shirts and dark suit pants, waited expectantly in the lobby. Their bags of gear were stacked neatly in a corner of the lobby, shirt jackets and red ties draped over each one, ready to be loaded on the bus. Jericho felt nervous, partly because of the game that loomed before them, and also because he knew that Arielle would arrive at any minute. Mr. Tambori had called Coach Barnes to say that the band bus was in the area.

"Don't get used to this kind of treatment," Coach Barnes announced as he took attendance. "For most away games we get there on the big yellow school bus, we eat at McDonald's, and we stay at a Motel 6. Got it?"

"Just like your mama does!" Roscoe whispered to Jericho. "You're gonna get iced before the game even starts if you talk about my mother one more time," Jericho warned. His voice carried a tone that was both friendly and threatening. "At least I didn't steal a bathrobe for my mama."

"Back off, man!" Roscoe said genially. "I got one for your mother as well! Chill out! The day is young and we ain't been beat up yet!"

Coach Barnes continued, "Let me give you the rundown for the rest of the day. The Excelsior Alumni Association Boosters, in addition to our accommodations, transportation, and meals, have provided each of you, as well as the members of the band and the cheerleaders, tickets to visit the Rock and Roll Hall of Fame. They have been unbelievably generous."

The boys hooted and cheered until he quieted them with his hand.

"You'll have until noon to tour the museum, then we'll have a buffet lunch at Pier W, a seafood restaurant right on Lake Erie. By then it will be time to head for the stadium to prepare for the game. Luis, is there anything you want to say?"

Luis stepped to the front and stood with the coach. "I just want to say I'm honored you chose me to be your captain, and I'm proud to be quarterback of this team. Together, we're going to make a miracle happen tonight!"

He stepped back with the others, who once again burst into noisy exultation, breaking into the song that schools all over the country chanted before every big game:

We are the Panthers—the mighty, mighty Panthers
Everywhere we go-oh, people want to know-oh

Who we are-r, so we tell them—
We are the Panthers—the mighty, mighty Panthers
Everywhere we go-oh, people want to know-oh
Who we are-r, so we tell them . . .

Their voices reverberated in the cavernous lobby, so the coach quieted them once more. "Let's save that for outside, men. Are there any questions about tonight?"

Roscoe raised his hand. "What's the weather supposed to be like, Coach?"

"Cloudy. Good chance of rain. Perfect football weather for real men!" Then he added, "Oh, and Roscoe?"

"Yeah, Coach?"

"You know those bathrobes that you took out of your room? Unless you plan to wear them on the field tonight instead of a uniform, I suggest you put them back!"

Everybody on the team rolled with laughter as Roscoe muttered about the coach's psychic powers and went to find his bag.

Just then the bus with the band members and cheerleaders rolled up in front of the hotel. In just a few minutes the lobby resounded with raucous laughter, noisy confusion, and dozens more teenagers. Crazy Jack came in with his cymbals and crashed them together while standing in front of the fountain, singing "God Bless America." Mr. Tambori went bananas, screeching about decorum and behavior, but chaos seemed to be winning for the moment.

As soon as she spotted him, Arielle, dressed in a dazzling outfit—tight red jeans and a slinky silver belly top—

waltzed directly over to Jericho. He had to admit he was thrilled.

"You ready for tonight?" she whispered in his ear.

"You mean the game?" he asked her.

"Yeah, that too," she said suggestively.

"Cut that out, woman! You're gonna mess up my concentration!"

She laughed, gave him the briefest kiss on his cheek, and went back to giggle with her cheerleader friends, all carbon copies of herself—cute, sexy, and petite.

Jericho couldn't stop beaming. Then he spotted Olivia standing near the door of the hotel alone. She looked more like an observer of the high school hubbub than a part of it. He felt his heart tug as he saw her sad expression.

He headed over to speak to her, but at that moment Coach Barnes called the football team over to him.

"I know all of you were up early, and I know you need to let off a little steam, but this is not the time or place. Let's not embarrass ourselves here, okay, Douglass?" the coach reprimanded the entire group.

Mr. Tambori apologized to the hotel staff, and quickly the two of them, plus a couple of parents who had come along as chaperones, escorted everyone outside. Jericho lost sight of Olivia.

The whole group—Jericho figured there were about a hundred of them—walked leisurely down the block to the Hall of Fame. Some folks in cars gave friendly waves; others frowned and made fists or other rude hand gestures, especially when the kids blocked an entire intersection as they crossed the street.

All the way down the street they chanted, over and over again:

We are the Panthers—the mighty, mighty Panthers . . .

Inside the museum the kids split up, visiting various areas of interest. Arielle and her friends, Jericho noticed, hovered around the fashion area, marveling at the dresses once worn by famous singers. Jericho was pleased to find himself alone to browse for a few minutes, and he marveled at some of the items: Junior Walker's saxophone; one of John Lennon's report cards; a guitar that belonged to Jimi Hendrix; a red satin tuxedo once worn by James Brown, the lapels covered with rhinestones.

"I kinda thought he was bigger than that," a voice behind him said.

"Hey, Olivia," Jericho said with genuine warmth as he turned around. "You're right. James Brown was such a big star I guess you'd expect him to be ten feet tall."

"I know. A lot of things are like that—not exactly what you expect them to be." She looked at him without smiling. "Before you leave, check out the section on Louis Armstrong. I know you admire him and his trumpet. Good luck in the game tonight." She walked away from him then and didn't look back.

Jericho watched her go, a strange look on his face. He wasn't sure, but somehow he felt like he'd lost something really important.

AFTER LUNCH, THE FOOTBALL TEAM, dressed once more in their dark suits and red ties, boarded the Greyhound and headed to the academy's stadium on the outskirts of town. The yellow bus that transported the band and cheerleaders would follow later, along with the bus they were calling the Fan Van, full of energetic Douglass supporters, all dressed in red and white.

Even the parking lot of the high school stadium was huge, with a blacktop so smooth and black it looked as if it had been painted. Looming ahead of them was the Excelsior Stadium, which people around here called the X.

As he stepped off the bus, Jericho was overcome by a feeling of smallness—as if the world had grown to hold giants, and he had shrunk to the size of a bird. No one spoke much, not even Roscoe, as the team walked slowly and almost reverently into the stadium, looking up at the rows and rows of seats that surrounded them.

The grass grew long and thick, like a bright green carpet. Each of the end zones had been painted with diagonal blue and gold stripes, and in the middle of the field, on the fifty-yard line, a huge blue and gold Excelsior wildcat had been painted.

"This is awesome," said Jericho. "There must be a million rows of seats."

"It looks professional," Coach Barnes admitted.

"They got glass-enclosed press boxes—one on each side!" Luis said. "And not one, but two scoreboards—the electronic kind that light up with strobes."

"Here comes one of the academy people," the coach told the boys. "Wipe those looks of awe and admiration off your faces. Don't give them that satisfaction."

"Welcome to Excelsior," the gray-haired, nimble-looking man said as he approached Coach Barnes. "I'm Bob Rubicon, president of the Excelsior Alumni Association Boosters. I trust your stay thus far has been satisfactory?" He wore a navy blue wool blazer with a large gold Excelsior insignia on the pocket, beige pants, and highly polished brown loafers.

"Yes, thank you. You and your organization have been more than kind," Coach Barnes replied.

"All of us here at Excelsior are looking forward to the game tonight," Mr. Rubicon said.

"As are we. We've prepared all summer," said Coach Barnes, looking proudly at his team.

"Isn't that nice." Mr. Rubicon looked at his watch. "We have a little time. Would you and your boys like a tour of the campus before you get dressed for the game?"

"Yes, we would. And I refer to them as young men."

Mr. Rubicon chose to ignore the coach's statement, turning quickly and heading back to the parking lot. "I think the quickest way to do this is if we get back on the Greyhound, and I'll narrate what we're seeing from the bus microphone. Sound like a winner?"

The coach and the team climbed back on the bus, and Mr. Rubicon directed the driver up a long drive flanked by weeping willows. "In front of us you'll see the main campus of Excelsior," Mr. Rubicon said. "That's our arts building to the right and the science building on the left. As we pull around to the back here, you can see our athletic complex—tennis courts, the polo fields, and our outdoor swimming pool. Our indoor swimming facility is Olympic-size. We've had several athletes win gold in the high school championships," he said proudly.

"What do you need a barn for?" Roscoe asked as he pointed to the wooden structure they drove by next.

"Oh, those are our stables. That's where we keep the polo ponies, as well as the horses we use for students involved in various equestrian competitions."

"Man!" Roscoe muttered.

As the bus completed the circle of the campus, Mr. Rubicon pointed to an area under construction and added, "One of our alumni recently donated a million dollars, so we're building a radio and television studio for our communications majors. It should be finished by next year."

"Is this a high school or a college?" Jericho whispered to Roscoe.

"Are you convinced now that there's no way we can beat these dudes?" Roscoe whispered back. Jericho looked at the neatly manicured hedges that lined the campus roads and shook his head.

"We'd like to thank you, boys, for gracing our campus," Mr. Rubicon said as the bus pulled up in front of the guest locker rooms. "I'll leave you now to prepare for the game." He climbed off the bus and waved good-bye, then Jericho watched him climb into a navy blue Jaguar.

Coach Barnes looked really ticked, Jericho thought, as the team piled out of the bus, got their gear, and walked into the changing area. It was, like the rest of the campus, elaborate, clean, and perfect. The lockers—brightly painted, of course, in blue and gold—were wide enough to hold shoulder pads and equipment, unlike the ordinary school lockers in their equipment room back at school. Smooth benches of light-colored wood were conveniently placed in a circle. On one wall hung a huge poster listing the schools that had competed in recent state championships, and the scores of those games. Jericho looked closely. Excelsior had won in eight of the last ten years.

"Gather round, men. And I do mean *men*," Coach Barnes said clearly. He stood in the center of the group. "I've had just about enough of their showing off. If I saw one more fancy building or pretty tree, I was gonna barf!"

The boys laughed and seemed to relax a little.

"Yeah, they have a lot of stuff, but that's all it is—stuff. The reason that Rubicon dude showed us around the campus was to intimidate us, to weaken us. But we are tougher than that. A man is not measured by what he owns, but by what he's made of inside." He pounded his fist on his chest for effect. "And we are made of steel."

"Yeah!" the boys repeated. "Steel!"

"It's not the size of the cat in the fight; it's the size of the fight in the cat. And we have a real catfight ahead of us tonight. Panthers against Wildcats. But our Panthers will emerge victorious! WE WILL WIN!"

"WE WILL WIN! WE WILL WIN! WE WILL WIN!" Jericho began to believe again.

"All right, specialty players and ball handlers get taped and dressed and get out on the field for warm-ups. The rest of you take your time, but start getting into your uniforms."

Jericho looked at his uniform with a little awe and trepidation. Everyone seemed to take it for granted that he knew what he was doing, but this was actually his first time in a varsity football game. Summer practices and scrimmages meant nothing. This was the real thing. *Why did I wait so long to start playing ball?* he berated himself. *Everybody else has been playing for years and knows what to expect. I feel like a seventh grader on the first day of school. I don't belong here!* He was starting to panic when Coach Barnes walked over and sat next to him on the bench.

"I'm really proud of your progress, Jericho," he said. "You got heart, and that's all a coach can ask for. You're one of the biggest guys we have out there, and you might not believe this, but you're one of our best. Even though you're new at this, you're a natural. I believe in you, and in the power of this team to prevail."

"Wow. Thanks, Coach. I needed that."

"Just go out there and do your best." Coach Barnes left

and went to sit next to another player who was adjusting his shoulder pads.

Twenty minutes later, the specialty players came back in, glowing with sweat, eyes bright with excitement. "What's it like out there?" Roscoe asked as he put on his shoulder pads. "Is it dark yet?"

"Almost—it looks like it's going to rain," Luis told them. "But it's a good field—even if it's wet, we'll do great."

"The stands are filling up—must be thousands of people out there," the kicker reported, "all wearing the Excelsior colors."

"Did the bus with the kids from Douglass get here?" asked Jericho.

Luis nodded his head. "It was hard to see with all the lights, but I could hear their weak little cries coming from one side. They were trying, but their cheers sounded like nothin' out there!"

"Where's your positive outlook, men?" the coach asked them as he signaled the rest of the team to gather around him.

"Out there on that grass someplace!" the kicker quipped in response.

The rest of the team had finally finished dressing, taken what the coach called a "nervous pee," and gathered around the coach once more. Jericho looked around the room. He had to admit they looked really good. The uniforms—bright white with shiny red markings—smelled fresh and new, but carried an odd chemical odor.

"Everybody up," Coach Barnes said. "In these new uniforms we look like champions—let's go out and play like that! We've prepared and practiced and we're ready to go. Now it's crunch time. Yes, it's up to us as a team, but that team is made up of individuals—and each man must do his part. Do you have the heart, men?"

"Yes, sir!"

"Do you have the desire to win, men?"

"Yes, sir!"

"Let me share something with you. Three years ago today—this very day—my father died. He loved this team and never missed a game. He *believed* in this team, and he knew we were champions! He'd be so proud to see you here today." The coach stopped and bowed his head. "Let's win this one for Daddy Barnes," he said, his voice taut.

Luis stepped to the center. "For Daddy Barnes, men! We got this won already!"

The players, full of adrenaline and emotion, grabbed hold of the phrase and rallied with it. "For Daddy Barnes! For Daddy Barnes! We're gonna win this one for the coach's dad!"

Jericho had never met the coach's father, so he thought of Josh instead. *I'm going out there for you, Josh.* He couldn't believe how charged he felt.

The coach led them in a brief prayer and it was time. "Strap up those helmets and let's take it to them!" Coach Barnes shouted. They headed out of the locker room, pumped and ready, chanting, "Go! Go! Go! Go! Go!" The only other sound was the clicking of dozens of cleats on the concrete.

AS THEY RAN THROUGH THE TUNNEL AND
out onto the field, Jericho could hear the
noise out there reach a crescendo. He could
hear cheers, predominantly from the Excelsior side, he estimated, and he could barely
make out the sounds of the Douglass band,
striving to be heard above the din. He thought
briefly of Olivia puffing on her sousaphone, but
soon the world became, as Crazy Jack had said,
an uncontrollable splash of color and noise.

The first people he saw when they reached the
field were the Douglass cheerleaders, who screamed
and jumped as if they were possessed when the team
was announced. Arielle blew him a kiss, but it barely
registered.

The Douglass players trotted over to their bench and
waited for the Excelsior team to emerge onto the field.
The lights around the stadium were bright and glaring, like
small suns, and their new uniforms looked iridescent under

their glow. Beyond the delicious odor of hot dogs and popcorn, which wafted by from time to time, it seemed to Jericho that the air smelled like rain was coming.

The appearance of the home team onto the field was truly a spectacle. The Excelsior band, almost one hundred strong and dressed in blue uniforms that seemed to shimmer under the lights, began to play. The drummers started first—pounding a beat until the rumble of the drums became a roar. Then the brass section took up the sound, the music boldly working the crowd into a frenzy. Finally the announcer spoke, with the excitement of a true fan: "Ladies and gentlemen! It is my great pleasure to introduce to you, the Eeeeeeex-ceeeeelllll-siiiiiiiii-ooooooooorrr Wildcats!"

The crowd erupted with frenzied screams. Their band danced and played wildly. The team, in blue uniforms with gold trim, burst through a massive paper hoop held by their cheerleaders. Then a cannon exploded from the top of the stands. Jericho and the rest of the team jumped, then stared at one another.

"What the hell was that?" Roscoe asked.

As if the announcer had heard, he said then, "Ladies and gentlemen. For those of you who are not familiar with our traditions, every time Excelsior scores a touchdown, our Wildcat cannon will be set off in jubilation! Keep it ready, Willie!"

The crowd cheered again and the Excelsior players continued to file onto the field. It seemed as if they'd never stop coming. They filled up the players' benches on the field, plus several other blue-and-gold-painted benches behind them.

"Who *are* all those guys, Coach? They can't have that many boys on a team, can they?" Jericho asked.

"They dress their ninth-grade team, and, I suspect, their junior high boys as well. Those kids don't play—they just sit there in all that blue and gold, trying to impress us with volume. It's simply more intimidation. Ignore it."

But their sheer numbers were hard to ignore. Jericho knew that Todd and Rory were out there somewhere, cheering and stomping like crazy, and his dad and Geneva, too. He hoped that Kofi and Dana and November were out there as well, but it was amazing how focused he had become. After a while, the band, the crowd, the cheers—everything began to fade as game time approached.

"Captains to the middle for the coin toss," the coach commanded. He swatted Luis on the butt as he ran out.

"We got the ball, Coach," Luis cried out after the flip of the coin gave them the advantage.

"Okay, here we go. Receiving team on the field," ordered the coach. "Roscoe, when you get out there, back up. This boy can really kick. Don't do anything fancy—just catch the ball. Got it?"

Roscoe nodded and hurried to the backfield, his face tense with expectation. Jericho and the others trotted onto the grass and got into position, facing their Excelsior opponents, waiting for the kickoff.

There was a brief flurry of activity from the other side, and suddenly the ball soared in a high arc, a swirling disk heading directly toward Roscoe. As it spiraled through the air, Excelsior thundered on the ground, heading directly for the Douglass team and that ball.

"I got it! Fair catch!" Roscoe yelled, as he signaled that he had the ball. Jericho knew Roscoe was somewhere behind the twenty-yard line, and the ball was now out of play.

But suddenly, someone from the other team cried, "Fumble! He fumbled the ball!" The football had slipped from Roscoe's grasp, and it was back in play.

That Roscoe! Jericho thought as he ran toward the ball. *Always acting silly, and now he's dropped the ball on the very first play of the game. Coach is gonna kill him!*

Everyone converged in that direction, trying to get their hands on the free ball. Whoever picked it up would have possession. Coach Barnes was yelling at Roscoe, "Pick up the ball, Roscoe! Pick up the ball and run with it! Run, boy, run!"

Out of the corner of his eye, almost as if in slow motion, Jericho saw Roscoe scoop up the ball, tuck it in the crook of his elbow, and take off with it. Roscoe glanced around and saw that the field was thick with Excelsior boys to his right, so he pivoted and headed toward the left side of the field, where, incredibly, no Excelsior players waited.

He streaked down the left side line, no one between him and the far goal line except for one Excelsior lineman wearing the number 88. Jericho saw what was happening and leaped into action. He sprinted across the field as fast as he could to cut off the other guy's angle of pursuit. Breathing heavily, but running as if he were made of sound instead of substance, Jericho flanked and shielded Roscoe from the lineman who was desperately trying to stop him.

The crowd, at first stunned into silence by Roscoe's unbelievable run, began to cheer for him. "Go! Go! Go!" Jericho kept up with him the entire length of the field.

When Roscoe reached the end zone and scored the touchdown, the small crowd from Douglass went wild. No cannon exploded for them, but they didn't need it. "Roscoe! Jericho! Roscoe! Jericho!" Finally even some of the Excelsior fans joined in the cheers.

The announcer reported, in a voice thick with disbelief and disappointment, "And the first touchdown of the game is scored by Cincinnati's Frederick Douglass High School!"

In vibrant colors the scoreboard displayed what most of the crowd thought would be impossible: Excelsior: 0. Visitors: 6.

Jericho and Roscoe, covered in sweat and trying to catch their breath, jogged back to the sidelines, where the rest of the team raced toward them, slapping them on their helmets and cheering.

"I didn't know you could run that fast, Jericho!" Luis exclaimed. "You kept up with Roscoe step for step, and he's a little squirrel!"

"You're the man, Roscoe!" said Coach Barnes. "An eighty-five-yard touchdown run! I knew you could do it."

"I think I'm starting to believe in your magic, Coach," Roscoe replied with a grin.

The coach turned to Jericho, his face a huge grin. "Way to go, man! Roscoe's personal escort the whole run. Dynamite!"

"We bad! We bad!" Roscoe said, jumping up on the bench.

The coach brought him back to reality. "No time to kiss yourself, Roscoe. Extra point team—listen up. They think we're going to kick for the one point, but let's go for the two-point conversion instead."

"You mean we're gonna *run* it?" Jericho said in disbelief.

"Why not? They won't expect it because they think we're weak. But we've got power, men. Power and speed. Let's do it—man for man. Our best against their best."

Jericho, Roscoe, and the others ran back out onto the field. The Excelsior players looked angry. They lined up in tight formation. Number 88, who probably outweighed Jericho by fifty pounds, placed himself directly in front of him. His face was a snarl.

The ball was snapped, and the quarterback grabbed it, faked a move to his left, then deftly handed off the ball to Roscoe. Jericho, lunging straight ahead, put the force of his whole body into the meatball who was number 88 and bulldozed him straight back. Roscoe darted through the opening and into the end zone, scoring the two extra points.

The crowd went wild.

"Impossible!"

"Incredible!"

"Unbelievable!"

The Douglass cheerleaders screamed and screamed. Jericho heard his name and Roscoe's coming from their area, where the small Douglass crowd was in a frenzy. He thought he might have heard Arielle screaming his name, but he couldn't be sure—and surely had no time to think about it as his team exulted for the moment in their success.

But Coach Barnes wouldn't let them gloat, because every play required focus and concentration, and the game continued relentlessly.

After a while it all became a blur to Jericho. The grass, which grew muddier as the game progressed. The white lines on the field—indicators of first downs and progress—which gradually smeared. The distant sound of the bands and roar of the crowd in the bleachers. The distinct smell of impending rain, then the cool relief of heavy raindrops on sweaty bodies. Tackles. Hits. Runs. Blocks. But no more scores. Jericho could barely believe it when he glanced up at the scoreboard—still, amazingly, reading Excelsior: 0, Visitors: 8. It was almost halftime, and the supposedly magnificent Excelsior team had been unable to score against Douglass. Their cannon had remained silent.

The rain, which had begun like a pleasant shower, quickly turned into a storm. No thunder or lightning, but it was as if the heavens had decided to open the clouds and simply drown the football field with a flood of water. Jericho was dimly aware of umbrellas and blankets being raised in the stands as fans huddled to stay dry, but no one seemed to want to leave as this incredible game rushed to halftime.

On the field, both sides, dripping with sweat as well as rain, moved into position for the very last play. Three seconds remained on the clock. The grass, muddy and slippery, squished under Jericho's feet as he took his place on the line.

Excelsior was in scoring position, and Jericho could tell from the looks he got as they lined up that they wanted this bad. *How dare this lowly little poor school from nowhere dare to challenge the mighty ones?* he imagined them thinking. Number 88, directly in front of Jericho once more, mouthed a curse at him. Jericho narrowed his eyes and stared him down.

The ball was snapped, their quarterback caught it, but it was wet and slick with mud. He dropped the ball. The entire Excelsior cheering section—almost twenty thousand of them—gasped. The clock ran out, the buzzer sounded, and the first half was complete.

AS THEY RAN OFF THE FIELD, THE DOUGLASS team couldn't contain their joy. They started cheering even as they ran, echoing the cries of the cheerleaders on the sidelines, "Panthers! Panthers! Panthers!"

Once they got back into the locker room, the coach let them jump on the benches for a few minutes, scream and yell, and beat on the lockers in exultation.

"Hoo-ha! Hoo-ha!"

"Sweet success!"

"I need me a cheerleader to kiss! Ooh, them girls looked fine in them little bitty skirts!" Roscoe yelled.

"You still talkin' to Arielle, Jericho? That girl knows how to shake it!"

"I thought you're s'posed to be watching the game, not my girl!" Jericho said with a laugh.

"I know how to multitask, my man!" replied Roscoe.

Strains of music from the half-time show filtered into the

locker room, adding to the feeling of celebration. Jericho thought briefly of the band, which was marching in tight lines on the muddy grass, of the trumpet player who had taken his position, of Olivia and her giant sousaphone, then turned his attention back to his teammates.

"We held 'em, Coach!" Roscoe cried as he ripped off his helmet. "You were right! You were right! We're gonna beat these suckers!"

The whole backfield stood on a bench then, arms around one another's shoulders, yelling, "We bad! We bad! We bad!"

"All right. Settle down, men," the coach said. The team, wet, muddy, and clammy, gathered around in a circle. "I am so proud of you I want to pop. You did so well—truly an extraordinary job out there, but we have another half to play. Don't plan the celebration party yet."

A little more subdued, the players, gulping now from water bottles, looked at the coach expectantly. But Jericho's heart was still beating fast as he thought about what they had just accomplished. He couldn't wait to face number 88 again. He began wiping the mud off the front of his uniform so his own number would show. He glanced down at his uniform then and frowned.

"Hey, Coach!" he called out. "What's up with this?" The huge satin 75 on the front of Jericho's uniform was dripping with bright red dye. The same thing was happening to the numbers on the fronts and backs, the names, even the decorative stripes on the uniform of every guy in the locker room.

Red ink stained the hands of every player. Red ink blended with the water that had puddled on the floor, making the whole scene look as though a massacre had taken place.

The rest of the team looked around in horror. Their uniforms were turning a messy, wet, bubble-gum pink.

"We look like we're bleeding, man!" shouted Cleveland. "Oh, no! What are we gonna do?"

Even the ever-calm Luis looked alarmed. "Coach, we're pink!" he said, his face aghast.

"We can't go out there lookin' like this, man! They'll laugh at us!" Roscoe cried. "Where'd you get these cheap things?"

"Did we bring the old uniforms?" asked Jericho, although he knew the answer.

Coach Barnes shook his head and looked more distraught than Jericho had ever seen him. "I know we got the uniforms cheap—now I understand why. Heads will roll when I call the distributor who sold them to us. But first we have to deal with right now. Let's not let this get us rattled, men."

"Too late! We look like a commercial for Pepto-Bismol!" Cleveland groaned with dismay.

The coach squared his shoulders. "Stop this! It is not what a man looks like on the outside that counts. It's the strength of the man on the inside!"

"But we're *pink*, Coach. We look like a bunch of girls!" Roscoe shook his head. The other boys refused to look the coach in the face.

Coach Barnes slammed a locker. "We are the same powerful team that kicked their butts in the first half, and we are going to go out there, heads held high, and do it again the second half. Are you with me, men? Where is your power? Where is your Panther Pride?"

"It melted," mumbled Roscoe.

"I refuse to let this stop us. And I won't let you go out there thinking like losers. I want you to look at that chart of all the past state championships on the wall. What does it tell you?"

"That Excelsior won the state title eight of the last ten years," Jericho said glumly.

"What it tells *me* is that Excelsior *lost* that game twice. Two of those years they were defeated by a team that was tougher, stronger, hungrier. A team like us!"

"Didn't we stomp them the first half?" Luis said, trying to rally the team along with the coach.

"Yeah, we did. We made 'em cry!" Jericho agreed.

"It's almost time to go back out there, men. We can't afford to lose our concentration," the coach began. "Do *not* let this little problem become a distraction."

"But Coach—," Roscoe began.

"No more negativity! We have to fight this battle on several levels. We must be fierce and dominant, and we have to believe we can win. If we focus on what we have to do, and eliminate the mental mistakes, we *will* be victorious! Are you with me, men?"

"Yeah!" the boys cried, but without their earlier enthusiasm.

"Let's go out there and win this!" cried Luis, trying to sound positive.

"Panther Pride!" several of the boys yelled out.

"Let me hear it!" the coach implored his team.

"Panther Pride!" they called back.

Finally Luis began to chant softly, and the rest of the team joined him, getting increasingly louder as they repeated it several times. But regardless, the feeling of power seemed to be gone.

We are the Panthers—the mighty, mighty Panthers
Everywhere we go-oh, people want to know-oh
Who we are-r, so we tell them—
We are the Panthers—the mighty, mighty Panthers
Everywhere we go-oh, people want to know-oh
Who we are-r, so we tell them . . .

Jericho jogged out with the team for the second half, wondering what would happen when everyone saw their unfortunate transformation. The rain had stopped and the huge mercury vapor lights, which had earlier made their uniforms glow, shone harshly on the wet and muddy field. The Douglass boys ran over to their bench. This time the glaring reflection of the overly bright lights made the ruined uniforms look a dazzling rosy pink.

The crowd, who at first clapped and yelled politely for the team who had been victorious in the first half of the game, stopped, almost in mid-cheer.

"Look at that!" someone called out.

"What happened to their uniforms?" another voice said.

"They're pink!"

"That's the funniest thing I've ever seen in my life!"

"Pink, man! Pink! Pink punks!"

Then the laughter began, slowly at first, then swelling as

every single eye focused on the mottled pink uniforms. It was deep, rippling, contagious laughter, which grew loud and uncontrollable as the Excelsior crowd pointed and hooted at the hapless Douglass team.

"And they call themselves the mighty Panthers!"

"They look more like the pink Panthers to me!"

That started another wave of laughter. "The pink Panthers! Ha! The pink Panthers," the crowd roared.

To add to the insult, the Excelsior band began to play the unmistakable theme from the movie *The Pink Panther*. Quietly at first, then louder. "Dah-DUM, dah-DUM, dah-DUM-dee-Dum-da-Dum, dah-dum-de-DUM, de-diddle-dum." The people in the crowd joined in, laughing and humming along with the song, over and over again, as the Douglass boys waited, stone-faced.

Finally the Excelsior team returned to the field, their uniforms still blue and impressive-looking, to the cheers of their adoring fans. The second half began, but the magic was gone. Excelsior turned on their power and scored twice in the first ten minutes. The smell of gunpowder filled the air as their cannon exploded victoriously—not once, but twice, then twice more before it was all over. The Douglass team, although they tried to rally, merely survived to the end of the game—pink, muddy, and defeated. The final score was 28–8.

CHAPTER 43
NOVEMBER
SATURDAY, SEPTEMBER 4

NOVEMBER SAT CURLED UP IN THE BACK-seat of Dana's car as they rolled down I-71, heading home from the game, and tried to make herself more comfortable. She had balled up a sweatshirt and stuffed it behind her head as a pillow, but the car, a small Ford, just wasn't very roomy, and she couldn't lie down like she wanted to.

Kofi drove, while Dana popped in a new CD every fifteen minutes or so. At least November had the backseat to herself, and she stretched her legs out as much as she could. She was really glad she hadn't decided to ride on the yellow school bus with the rest of the Douglass fans. Five hours on a cramped, poorly cushioned school bus seat was not her idea of luxury transportation. Besides, she'd been feeling pretty rotten most of the day.

"You okay back there, November?" Dana asked, looking behind her. They were a little more than halfway home.

"I'm just so tired, and my back is killing me, but I'll be okay." November placed her hands on her belly and grimaced as the whole lower half of her body seemed to tense up and tighten, just as it had been doing, off and on, all day. *It's my own fault*, she thought. *I got up early this morning to leave for the game, sat in this backseat for way too long, endured a rain-soaked football game, and now I'm back in this car. It's no wonder I'm pooped!* Even though they had already made two stops, November felt like she might have to go to the bathroom again soon.

"Any music you want to hear? I got my whole CD case."

"You got any blues?" November asked. "I know. I know. I can't believe I've started groovin' to my mother's blues music either. But it's weird—it's got this strange calming effect."

"Sorry, no blues. Unless you count Alicia Keys."

"That'll work, I guess." November grimaced again and grabbed her stomach. *I definitely shouldn't have eaten that second hot dog*, she chided herself.

"Why don't you close your eyes and try to sleep a little?" Kofi suggested.

"Who can sleep after a game like that?" replied November. "Jericho and his macho football boys will never live this one down."

Kofi shook his head. "The Pink Panthers! It was just plain embarrassing! You got that song in your pile of CDs, Dana?" he asked, teasing.

"Not my kind of music!" she retorted, laughing. "The football team are the ones who need to listen to the blues all the way home! Public humiliation requires serious music!"

"Poor Jericho," November said as she shifted her hips, trying to ease all her various discomforts.

"The first half was dynamite, though!" Dana reminded them. "I couldn't believe how cool that was! Jericho ran down that field like he had on ballet slippers instead of cleats!"

"Ha! Jericho in a tutu. Now *that's* an image I want to forget!" Kofi turned the music down.

"Those rich kids didn't know what hit 'em! For a while there, we were a freight train full of bricks on a mission to destroy!" Dana added.

November felt another twinge. This time it actually hurt. She hated to admit it, but her mother had been right when she said she probably shouldn't make this trip. *I'm gonna sleep all day tomorrow!* she decided.

"Too bad the train ran off the track—it's a shame they couldn't keep up the momentum," Kofi said as he switched lanes. "The rain just messed everything up."

"Yeah, those pink uniforms just broke their concentration. Hard to focus when you got a stadium full of people laughing at you."

"That was too cold."

"Hey, November, did you check out Arielle during half time?" Dana asked, just as she turned the music back up.

"Yeah, I saw her. That girl is a piece of work! Besides the fact that she had rolled her skirt up so short that you could see her underwear, she was flouncing around, all up in the face of Brandon Merriweather, the dude on the track team who got the BMW for his eighteenth birthday."

"It's a real nice car," said Kofi, nodding appreciatively. He adjusted the volume of the music to a softer level once again.

Dana turned it back up. "So that's a good reason for her to creep on Jericho like that?" she asked, her voice rising.

"I just like the dude's car. I don't care what Arielle does!" Kofi shot back at her, turning the music back down.

"Jericho deserves better," Dana stated, her voice softer, but the music got louder.

"My man Brandon probably does too," Kofi said with a chuckle. "I bet he has no idea what he's about to step into!" Quieter music.

"For real. Arielle gets around, just like good old Cleopatra," November said, thinking back to her mother's crossword puzzles. Her abdomen constricted sharply once again. She felt a little nauseous.

"Do you think we should say something to Jericho on Monday?" Dana asked November. She turned the volume up real loud.

"About Arielle?"

"Yeah. He's got a right to know, doesn't he?"

"Maybe not. As soon as she acted like she wanted him back, Jericho jumped so quick you could feel the breeze!" November said. "He should have known she was a snake from the last time she bit him."

"And he hurt Olivia something awful," said Dana sadly.

"I don't think Jericho ever even noticed how Olivia felt," November commented.

Kofi adjusted the volume once more. "Yeah, I gotta admit—dudes can be a bit dense sometimes."

"Duh! You think?" Dana said with a smirk as she reached for the volume control.

"Will you two quit playing with the CD player?" November

finally said in exasperation. "It's making me dizzy!"

"What are you talking about?" Dana and Kofi said at the same time. Dana turned to November and looked genuinely baffled.

"It's loud, then quiet, then loud, then soft again. What's up with you two?"

They looked at each other and laughed. "We do it so much when we're in the car together we never even notice," Kofi admitted. "But I guess you're right. Sorry if it bothers you."

November just waved a hand as if to dismiss it. She envied the closeness that Dana and Kofi had, weaving in and out of each other so seamlessly that they didn't even notice the pattern.

For several miles the rhythm of the music and the movement of the car lulled them all into silence. But November was feeling increasingly sick—unlike any illness she'd ever had before. She was hot, then cold, then she felt like she couldn't breathe. And the cramps. Such odd, painful cramps. *Something's not right*, November suddenly realized. *I haven't felt the baby kick all day. And these weird gut-squeezes I keep getting. I'm going to have to call Dr. Holland first thing Monday morning. I might even take the day off from school to go see her.* She rolled the window down and gulped in the cool night air.

"Rest area up ahead," Kofi announced. "You need to make a pit stop, November?"

She grabbed her belly, in fear this time, as it once again tightened and hardened like an overinflated basketball. "Yeah, I think I better," she replied weakly. "I don't feel so good. Not good at all."

Kofi pulled into the rest area and turned off the motor. "What's wrong, girl?" Dana asked, turning on the overhead light. "Oh, November. You look really sick—your eyes are sunk in, and you're sweating like crazy. Tell me what's wrong! What should I do?"

"I think I might be in labor, Dana. But I can't be! It's too soon!" November grabbed her stomach as another contraction washed over her.

DANA LAUNCHED INTO ACTION. SHE GRABBED her cell phone from the holder on her waist and pulled Kofi's phone out of his shirt pocket at the same time. She handed Kofi his phone and told him, "I'm calling the state and local police. You call somebody, anybody with a cell phone who's on the Douglass Fan Van. Tell them what rest stop we're at and that we have an emergency. Then contact the band bus and tell them the same thing. There are lots of chaperones on each one—they'll know what to do." She ran her fingers through her hair. "Finally, see if you can catch Jericho on the football bus. I think all three loads of kids are still behind us. We left pretty early." Dana hopped out of the car and started punching at her phone.

November could hear Dana barking orders and taking charge, and she smiled in spite of the waves of pain. *Couldn't wish for anybody better to have my back!*

"Yes, we are at the rest area just after the Jeffersonville exit—about sixty-five miles from Cincinnati," November heard her saying. "Please hurry. My friend is about to have a baby! How old? Uh, she's sixteen."

November grimaced once more as another pain assaulted her. It felt like a volcano exploding in her guts. *I had no idea it would HURT so bad!* she thought as she waited for the pain to pass.

November started shaking uncontrollably, so Kofi tore off his jacket and covered her with it. *The baby can't come NOW,* she thought frantically. *I'm not ready! The baby's not ready either. It's too soon!* As another contraction hit her, she thought, *What if it comes out messed up like Gus?* She knew her brother's condition was genetic rather than circumstantial, but that didn't make her worry any less. The pain was making her irrational.

Dana poked her head in the back window. "How you holdin' up, little mama?"

"Not so good, Dana. I'm scared. Can you call my mother?"

"I'm on it," Dana assured her.

"It's amazing how much mothers get on our nerves until we get in trouble," November told Dana tearfully. "I really want my mom."

"I know, kid. Let me try her cell phone again," said Dana as she frantically pressed buttons on the phone. "Still no answer," she reported after a minute, "but I've left about five messages. We'll hook up with her soon."

November knew that Dana was trying to sound soothing and reassuring, but she could hear the fear in her voice. "Are you scared, Dana?" she asked.

November's face was beaded with sweat. Dana took a tissue out of her pocket and wiped November's forehead. "I do this every Saturday night after a football game. Don't you?"

November's grin turned into a cringe as another pain hit her. She tried not to cry out, but it hurt so bad. "Hey, Dana?" November called when the pain had subsided.

"Yeah?"

"Josh should be here."

"Yeah." Dana's voice was somber.

"You know what I'd do if he opened the back door of this car?" November said to Dana through the open window.

"Hug him?"

November winced through a smaller contraction. "No, I'd kick him in the nuts for doing this to me!"

Dana cracked up. "At least you haven't lost your sense of humor! Hey, two of our buses just pulled in to the rest stop, and here comes the ambulance. Relax, now. Everything is going to be fine."

All November could really see from her nest in the backseat was the twirling and blinking of the ambulance's red lights. One technician, a woman with a huge, wind-blown Afro, opened one of the car doors, while another paramedic opened the other one. Each one quickly did an assessment of the half of her that could be reached.

Who wears an Afro these days? November thought irrationally.

"My name is Alma," the woman at her feet said gently. "We're gonna take care of you, okay? So just relax. When is your due date, hon?" she asked as she jotted down November's blood pressure and temperature.

"November second," she replied.

Alma's face frowned in concern. "Are you sure? That would make you a full two months early."

"I know!" November wailed. "Is my baby gonna die?" Her heart thudded.

"Babies survive born earlier than this, sweetie. Now, let Alma see what we have here." She lifted November's shirt and put a stethoscope to her abdomen.

"Hey, there. I'm Ralph," the other paramedic said. He had a booming bass voice, but November couldn't see him. "How often are your contractions?"

"I don't know exactly." November was breathing rapidly. "But they're coming fast and hard. Something's wrong, isn't it? It's not supposed to be like this!" She tried to sit up, but the paramedic at her head gently laid her back down.

"Relax now. Let me finish examining you. You're gonna be fine."

November was trying not to cry anymore, but another wave of pain assaulted her. She bit her lip. "It *hurts*!" she exclaimed.

"I know, hon," Alma said gently. "Babies aren't Pop-Tarts. They come out the oven the hard way."

"Am I going to have the baby right here at a rest stop?" November asked, panting.

"We certainly don't want that!" Ralph replied pleasantly. He deftly tightened a rubber tube around her arm and quickly inserted a needle.

"Ouch!"

"If that's all the pain you feel tonight, I'll let you complain about that little pinprick," he said as he connected a bag of clear liquid. His voice had a soothing quality that helped calm November a little.

"Alma here has called this in to the doctors down at Good Samaritan," Ralph explained. "They've instructed us to give you a tocolytic to try to slow the contractions, so you should feel a little relief soon, okay?" He turned away and began speaking into his walkie-talkie.

November looked up at the IV doubtfully. "That medicine he gave me isn't gonna hurt my baby, is it?" she asked Alma.

"Not at all," Alma told her. "If anything, it will help to keep that little muffin cooking just a while longer." November thought the paramedic was overdoing it with the cooking references, but she was in no position to complain.

Alma carefully slipped off November's jeans and underwear, making sure she was shielded from any curious onlookers.

"Why are you doing that?" November asked, alarmed.

"Well, hon," Alma replied with a smile as she covered November with a warmed blanket, "we want to see how far you're dilated, and check your baby's heart rate." Alma placed a fetal monitor on November's belly and recorded the data on the clipboard.

November shivered. "I'm cold."

"Well, let's just snuggle you a little more, hon," Alma said, piling another blanket on.

Ralph returned then and told November, "We've called for Air Care to come and pick you up; I want you at an ICU unit in case the tocolytic doesn't stop the contractions."

"What hospital?" asked November, although she didn't really care. She just wanted the pain to stop.

"The helicopter is going to take you to Cincinnati's Good Samaritan Hospital; it has the best neonatal facilities in the state," Alma explained.

"A helicopter?" November asked incredulously. "Is that safe?"

Alma smiled. "It's a whole lot safer and cleaner than the backseat of a Ford! What's going on tonight, anyway? I see a parking lot full of high school kids—must be three buses out here. Are they all here for you?"

"Sort of. We had a big football game," November answered weakly. "We played Excelsior in Cleveland." She groaned as another pain hit her.

"Excelsior! I hear they're a powerhouse team. Did you win?" asked Ralph.

"Almost," November told him, breathing hard. "Almost." She could hear the *whup-whup-whup* of the rotors of the helicopter as it got closer.

Almost as loud was the sound of Jericho's worried voice yelling at someone who seemed to be trying to keep people away from the car. "But I'm her cousin!" he roared, stretching the truth. His large smiling face appeared in the car window the next minute.

"Hey, Cuz," November said with a small smile.

"Well, you would have been if you had married Josh! Are you okay?"

"I'm feeling a little better, but I am *sooo* embarrassed," November admitted.

Jericho made a face. "Look girl, let me tell you about

public humiliation. Are you wearing pink in front of twenty thousand folks?"

She grinned and shook her head.

"Well, get over it. All you've done is go into labor on the side of the road, tie up about ten police cars, two ambulances, and three busloads of kids, stop all traffic on both sides of I-71, and have a helicopter land in the middle of the highway!"

"Call me a drama queen! I'm just making sure I'm the center of attention," she quipped weakly.

"Let me talk to her!" November heard then. It was Olivia. "Is she going to be okay? What about the baby?"

"Hey, Olivia. I know she'll be glad to see you," Jericho said as he stepped back.

"Why didn't you just say you didn't want to ride home in the backseat of a Ford?" Olivia's cheerful, booming voice filled the whole car.

"I like to make a scene," November told her with a laugh, although she grimaced as another contraction hit.

"You scared?" asked Olivia quietly.

"Terrified," November admitted.

"You're at twenty-eight weeks—maybe twenty-nine if we stretch it. The baby could still be okay," Olivia said.

"But it's so early!" November answered weakly. "I'm so scared about the baby, Olivia."

"Well, I heard that if a baby is three months early, things can get really scary. But you're way past that," Olivia said, her voice full of confidence. But as she leaned in to the backseat, November saw fear in her eyes.

Dana stuck her head in the window on the other side

then. "Here come the EMTs from the helicopter, November. I finally reached your mom, and she'll meet you at Good Sam."

"Good," November replied with relief.

The EMTs carefully helped her from the car and strapped her to a gurney. As they rolled her across the parking lot and out to the highway where the helicopter waited, November glanced around at what she could see from her perch on the stretcher. "Wait!" Jericho's voice bellowed. November turned her head toward his frantic voice. "I gotta go with you! I promised I'd be there! I promised!"

"You can't go with her on the helicopter, son," Alma told him. "She needs medical help, not friends right now."

November reached out and touched Jericho's arm. "I have a feeling I'll be a little busy for a while. Come to the hospital as soon as you can—I'll see you then."

Jericho clenched his fists in frustration, but he nodded as they rolled November to the helicopter. Several groups of kids from Douglass huddled together, whispering and pointing as she was rolled by. Some waved. "Good luck!" several kids shouted. November smiled as she heard Crazy Jack's cymbals.

Dozens of cars were parked all over the grass because the emergency vehicles, and even vans from local news stations, seemed to be blocking the parking area. Almost everyone she saw had a cell phone out, calling home, calling friends, passing along this juicy bit of news.

The last thing she heard as they lifted her into the helicopter was Olivia's voice. "Don't be afraid, November—you've got Sunshine!"

CHAPTER 45
SATURDAY, SEPTEMBER 4

THE FLIGHT IN THE HELICOPTER SEEMED like something out of a movie. It didn't seem real—not the blinking lights on the instruments, not the latex-gloved hands of the technicians, not the whirring sound of the blades above them. She couldn't even sense any real movement, although she knew they were speeding through the air toward Cincinnati. She lay flat on her back, looking up at the smooth fiberglass interior of the aircraft.

"Too bad I can't enjoy this—it's my first helicopter ride," said November faintly as one of the attendants wrapped a blood pressure cuff around her arm.

"It's dark outside—you wouldn't be able to see much anyway," the attendant replied with a smile. "What's your name, dear?"

"November Nelson." She grimaced as another pain surged through her.

"My name is Joy. How are you feeling?"

"A little better. The pain stops and starts. But I'm pretty freaked out."

"That's perfectly understandable," Joy told her. "But you're in good hands. We're going to get you and your baby safely to the hospital."

"I hardly think about her as a baby. I figured I still had a couple more months to get used to that idea. She's just like this 'presence' who's been sharing my space. You get what I'm saying?"

"Yes. I think I do."

"Could you call my doctor?" November suddenly thought to ask. "Her name is Dr. Holland—Obioma Holland."

"I'll be glad to," replied Joy. "But I don't want you to worry—we have doctors on staff who will take good care of you until your doctor arrives. Okay?" Joy told the other attendant, "Call the dispatcher and have him contact Dr. Obioma Holland in Cincinnati. Let her know her patient, November Nelson, is in labor, and to meet us at Good Samaritan Hospital A-S-A-P." The EMT nodded and proceeded to call.

"Thanks," said November, then lowered her voice to a whisper. "Babies born too soon can be pretty messed up, right?"

"It's possible—complications can arise," Joy replied carefully.

November started to cry.

"Relax, dear," Joy said. "I've seen miracles on this job. Did you say it was a girl?"

November smiled. "Yeah. Her name is Sunshine."

"Lovely."

They flew for several minutes in silence. November tried to relax between the increasingly intense bouts of pain. She hadn't felt the baby move in several hours, which terrified her, but she was afraid to say anything.

Finally Joy glanced out the window of the copter. "We're here, November. We'll be landing on the roof, then the hospital staff will take over as soon as the rotors let them approach. They'll take you downstairs to labor and delivery, where you'll be in the hands of experts."

"I won't see you again?" November said in alarm.

"My job is over," Joy replied kindly. "You'll be fine. And dispatch just told me that your mother is downstairs waiting. I'm sure she's worried."

"My mom can be a pain, but there's nobody else I'd rather be with right now." She could feel the helicopter land with a surprisingly gentle thud.

"I've got a mom too!" Joy said with a smile. "And soon you'll be a mom as well. Lots of things fall into place when that happens."

November grabbed Joy's hand and squeezed it as she left the helicopter. "Thanks!" was all she had time to say before she was whisked into the hospital corridor and onto an elevator. Another huge contraction washed over her and she cried out.

"We'd better hurry," she heard someone say. "I don't think this baby is going to wait much longer."

In the examination room, November was aware of only the edges of what was happening around her. Increasingly frequent horrible cramping spasms overwhelmed everything else. *I can't take this! My guts are going to explode! I'm going to die! I'm sure I'm going to die!*

A calming voice broke through her wild thoughts. "November. Focus on me for a minute. There, that's good. My name is Ling Yee. I'm your nurse, and I'm going to be with you every step of the way."

November nodded. "I'm scared. It hurts."

"I know, but you'll be just fine. Let's get the rest of you undressed, sweetie," Nurse Yee said. "I think you'll be more comfortable in a hospital gown."

"What about my clothes?" November asked frantically as the nurse helped her peel off the sweaty Douglass sweatshirt she'd been wearing. She felt like she was losing control of everything.

"I'm putting all your things into this bag labeled with your name—even your football game program."

"I didn't leave that in the car?" November asked in confusion.

"You had it squeezed pretty tightly in your hand when you got here," the nurse said with a chuckle as she put November's shoes and socks into the bag. "Was it a good game?"

"It wasn't like anything we expected," November murmured with a small smile. The smile disappeared as another contraction pulsed through her. She gasped at its intensity.

"Let's roll, honey," said the nurse. "You and this baby have important business to take care of tonight!" She popped a pillow under November's head, pulled up the sides of the bed, and rolled her down the hall and into what November surmised was the room where babies were born.

All November could see were ceiling tiles and ductwork above her. She felt like she was in a movie with the camera floating someplace just beyond her vision. When she got into the next room, she looked at the masked faces above her and panicked. "I gotta get out of here!" she cried, trying to sit up. But when she tried, deep, concentrated pain enveloped her, and she fell back onto the pillow.

"Take it easy, now." It was Nurse Yee's soft, soothing voice. "Let's see how dilated you are."

November nodded, but tears trickled down her cheeks. She'd never been so terrified in her life. *Where is my mom?*

November could see only the circle of the light they had placed above her. Her body, and what the doctors were doing, seemed to be separate from her, as if all this activity was happening to someone else. Monitors were strapped to her belly, which undulated like she'd seen in those movies about aliens that take over a human body.

She felt a needle briefly sticking her arm as another IV was started, and noticed that everybody seemed to have cold hands, even under the latex gloves they wore. Cold fingers prodded her rectum and vagina to check on the progress of the baby.

She listened with increasing alarm to the faceless voices—clipped, serious, businesslike.

"Mother's heart rate rapid and thready."

"She's fully dilated, doctor."

"Uh, what does that mean?" November asked fearfully.

"That means your baby is ready to be born," Nurse Yee told her.

"But I'm not ready for a baby yet!"

"Babies don't care, sweetie. They rule!" Then, turning her attention back to the monitors, she said, "Blood pressure dangerously high, doctor."

"The mother or the fetus?"

"Both."

November heard another voice, even more urgent, say, "Fetal monitor indicates the baby is in distress."

"I can't find a heartbeat for the baby!" Nurse Lee cried.

November wanted to shout out and ask them what exactly was happening, but all she could think was, *Is my baby going to die? What's going on? Oh, please don't let my baby die!*

Finally one of the doctors said, "When you feel the next contraction, I want you to give me one huge push, okay?"

November nodded, her eyes shut tight in pain. She was drenched in sweat. *Where is my mother? I can't have this baby now! I don't know what to do! I'm not ready! Ooh, my guts are going to explode!* She felt like she was going to throw up out of one end of her body and have a bowel movement out of the other.

As the next contracting wave rolled over her, the doctor shouted, "Push! Push!" November pushed and pushed and pushed. She knew she had lost control of everything— her life, her body, even her thoughts. She could not stop screaming.

And suddenly the baby was out.

"It's a girl," November heard a voice say clearly. It might have been Nurse Yee.

"But she's not breathing! Suction!" another voice said.

November wanted to lift her head and see what was going on, but she had no strength.

"Come on, little lady, breathe for me!" another voice implored. *Aren't babies supposed to cry when they're born?* November thought fearfully. *Why isn't she crying?*

"I have a heartbeat—but it's weak."

"Page Dr. Massey immediately."

November looked pleadingly from face to face. *What's wrong? Please tell me what's wrong! Where's my mom!*

Tears in her eyes, she tried to speak, but she couldn't seem to remember how to talk. She found she had nothing left—not even the strength for a word or a prayer. She passed out.

JERICHO HAD NOT SLEPT SINCE HE'D stretched out in that comfortable bed at the Ritz-Carlton Hotel the night before the game. Riding in the back of Dana's car, he felt awkward because her car was so small, and overwhelmed with the recent presence of November. The whole car smelled of blood and sweat, even though they kept the windows open the whole time. No one said much. Kofi drummed his fingers on the steering wheel as he drove. Jericho could count his own heartbeats. He was afraid if he spoke, he'd lose it.

They pulled into the hospital parking lot around three a.m. "I should be with her!" Jericho muttered, jumping out of the car. "I hope we're not too late."

"Relax, man," Kofi said, placing his hand on Jericho's shoulder. "She's got a million smart doctors takin' care of her right about now. One large, nervous football player would really get in their way."

"Yeah, maybe." Jericho blinked at the artificially bright lights of the hospital lobby as the three of them walked in together. He was surprised to find his entire family sitting on one of the plastic sofas. Todd and Rory, quiet and sleepy, sipped on juice boxes.

His dad stood and gave his son a big hug. "I'm proud of you, boy—all three of you," he said as he stood back and acknowledged Dana and Kofi. "You kids probably saved November's life—and maybe the life of the baby as well."

"We didn't do nothin', sir," Kofi said with a shrug.

"We weren't really sure *what* to do," Dana added. Her voice sounded strained.

"Have you heard anything?" Jericho asked his father. "I need to find her. I told her I'd hold her hand—or something." Jericho looked frantic. His hair was still matted from his football helmet and his eyes were bloodshot from worry and lack of sleep.

"She's already had the baby, Jericho," his father began. "I doubt if they would have let you in the delivery room anyway. She . . . uh . . ."

Jericho interrupted him, almost babbling with excitement. "Wow. Already? What did she have? Is everything okay?"

Geneva walked over and took Jericho's hand. "I called upstairs to my friend Ling Yee, who's a nurse on the delivery floor, and she told me the baby had been delivered, but it seemed to be having some difficulties," Geneva explained, her voice serious. "She didn't give me any details."

"What does that mean—difficulties?" Jericho asked, unable to swallow.

"The baby is in critical condition," Jericho's father told

him. "It's two months early. That can't be good."

Jericho groaned. "What about November?"

"According to Ling, she's stable. That's all I know," Geneva said softly.

"I gotta go find her!" Jericho said, pulling away from his family and friends.

"Chill, Jericho," Kofi said, "at least for now. Nobody is lettin' you see her just yet. She's in good hands. Have a little faith, my man."

Jericho breathed heavily. "I know she's scared, man."

"Look at all the kids who are here supporting November," Dana said, nudging Jericho.

He glanced around the lobby, noticing for the first time all the students who huddled together or had curled up on the couches in the lobby. Most of them also looked as if they'd had no sleep. Some dozed, some whispered quietly, same sat with their iPods or cell phones. Among them were Olivia, Luis Morales, and Crazy Jack—without his cymbals for once.

Jericho was amazed that so many of the kids who had been on the busses had beat them to the hospital. "How'd you get here so fast?" Jericho asked Olivia as he walked over to where she sat. She was the only student who sat alone on a lobby sofa.

"While you and Kofi and Dana were answering questions from the medical techs and the police, our busses took off. One bus dropped kids off at school, but the band bus came directly to the hospital. Mr. T contacted the parents. We've only been here a few minutes."

"Have you heard anything?" Jericho asked.

"Mostly just rumors by way of text messages. People who don't know what's going on sometimes make stuff up." She shifted in her seat and looked uncomfortable as she talked to Jericho.

"I'm gonna find out. I'll get back to you," Jericho promised as he looked at the signs on the wall, trying to figure out which elevator might lead to the place where November had been taken.

Then he noticed a couple of teachers as well—Coach Barnes, Mr. Tambori, and incredibly, the English teacher, Ms. Hathaway, who sat away from the others on the far side of the lobby.

Mr. Tambori and Coach Barnes walked over to Jericho and shook his hand warmly. "I just wanted to let November's family know that my prayers are with them," the music teacher said. "Somehow I feel responsible—maybe just because I was one of the adults on the trip."

"Me too," said the coach. "You know, Jericho, incidents like this put everything into perspective. Football games. Band concerts. Even homework. They're all meaningless when it comes to human life." He wrung his hands.

"Thanks, Mr. T, Coach B," Jericho said earnestly. "This really means a lot. I'll be sure to tell them. And it's nobody's fault. Stuff just happens," he said with a shrug.

Jericho walked, with a little trepidation, to where the English teacher sat. She was reading a book.

"Uh, hello, Ms. Hathaway."

"Good morning, Mr. Prescott," she said. Her voice had lost some of the shrill qualities that seemed to permeate her classroom.

"It's awfully nice of you to come down here." Jericho wasn't sure what to say to her. He hated to admit it, but she was pretty intimidating in class, and he was a little afraid of her.

"I saw the news on television. Miss Nelson is an excellent student. Somehow I just felt I should be here to offer my support."

"Wow. That's really cool, I mean, uh, considerate, that you would come." He stumbled over his words.

"You don't have to pull out the vocabulary book, Mr. Prescott. It's Sunday. Even English teachers take a day off," she said with a smile.

Jericho couldn't believe she was acting like such a human. "Are you going upstairs to see November?" he asked.

"She might think I've come to collect homework!" the teacher said. "But will you tell her I stopped by, and that I understand?"

"Understand?"

"She'll know what I mean."

"Okay, I'll be glad to do that. I better get back to my family now. Thanks for coming. For real."

Ms. Hathaway nodded and returned to reading her book. She made no move to leave the lobby. Jericho left her sitting there as he shook his head with wonder.

Coach Barnes and Mr. Tambori were heading to the parking lot as Jericho returned. "Get some sleep, Mr. T," Jericho said. "Listen to some good music."

"Good idea. You know, you should do the same."

"I will, Mr. T. I promise. And Coach?"

"Yeah?"

"Burn those pink uniforms!"

The coach laughed. "Maybe we'll have a bonfire after our next practice. You'll be there?"

Jericho looked at the football coach, and at his music teacher. Both stared at him with expectation.

"I'll be at practice, Coach," he said finally. "We've got a team that can be a winner—should have been a winner yesterday. I'm not going to let you down and quit because of a rainstorm."

The coach gave him a thumbs up sign. The music teacher turned to leave. "But Mr. T?" Jericho called out to him.

"Yes, Jericho?"

"I'm dusting off my trumpet. I need my music. When football season is over, I'm coming back to music class. If that's okay with you," he added.

Mr. Tambori grinned broadly. "I think that's a great idea, Jericho."

The two teachers walked out of the hospital together.

DANA HAD GONE WITH OLIVIA TO GET A cup of coffee from the machine in the lobby. "This tastes like glue!" Dana muttered after the first sip.

"You drink glue very often?" Kofi teased her.

"Good thing I got the hot chocolate," Olivia said to Dana. "It's not bad." Jericho noticed that Olivia would not look directly at him, but he didn't think about it long. He had too much other stuff on his mind.

"Is that Ms. Hathaway sitting over there?" Dana asked Jericho.

"Amazing, isn't it? She came because she's concerned about November."

"Who woulda thought she even cared?" said Dana.

"Lots of people are deeper than you think," Olivia remarked quietly.

"Let's go upstairs before she sees me. I owe her an assignment!" Kofi said.

"Have you heard anything new?" Dana asked Jericho.

"Just that the baby is in pretty bad condition," he answered.

"Oh no!" Olivia said in anguish. "What about November?"

"I think they said she's gonna be okay." Jericho glanced at Olivia and thought he saw tears in her eyes.

"You think we can go see her?" Dana wondered.

Jericho's dad had just returned from the information desk. "I have her room number. Let's go up, but I don't think we should crowd her."

Geneva said, "Then I'll wait here in the lobby with Todd and Rory. I'll see her later."

Upstairs in the maternity ward, Jericho felt uncomfortable, but surprisingly in control. He whispered to Kofi, "Don't let this medical stuff freak you out. Don't let on to November that we're worried."

"Gotcha!" Kofi whispered back. When they got to her room, they saw November lying curled under a pile of blankets. Her hair was a mess. Her mother sat in a chair next to her bed, rubbing her back.

"What's up, little mama?" Dana asked gently. "How you feeling?"

November started to cry. "You keep calling me that, but I'm not much of a mama. I couldn't even figure out how to have a baby correctly! Women from the olden times used to go out in the fields, have the kid, and then go back to work the same day. I couldn't even keep her in long enough for her to be safe and healthy."

"Babies are tough. She's gonna be fine. And you were outstanding! Did you know you're in this morning's paper?" Olivia told her.

"Really?"

"Yeah, girl. You're all that and a bag of chips!" Dana said, maybe a little too cheerfully. November smiled.

"Have you seen the baby yet?" asked Jericho. Kofi had stayed in the hall.

"*I* have," Mrs. Nelson replied. "She weighs three pounds. She's no bigger than a child's doll. . . ." She paused. "And she's . . . she's just beautiful!" She glanced away.

Jericho was starting to feel overwhelmed. Girls. Babies. Labor and delivery. He didn't think he could take much more of this. But he'd made a promise to November, even to Josh's memory. He inhaled and gave November a broad, fake smile. "Whassup, November? You really know how to make a scene!"

November sniffed and managed a weak grin. "Hey, Cuz."

"They wouldn't let me come with you on the 'copter, you know. I was so pissed! I tried, November—I really tried."

November reached over and touched Jericho. Her hand was wrapped in gauze and an IV line protruded from it. "It was a very small helicopter, Jericho. It wouldn't have worked anyway. But it makes me glad to know you made the effort. And you're here now—that's what counts."

Jericho wanted to ask her about the delivery, the baby, the complications—but he couldn't find the words. *This is way out of my zone,* he thought. So instead he just mumbled, "I hope everything gets straight real soon."

"It's okay, Jericho. I know this place is makin' you sweat. Go get some air. I'm fine."

"I'll be back in a few," he said gratefully. Jericho jetted

out of the room and inhaled deeply when he got into the hall.

"I knew better," Kofi told him as he casually leaned against a far wall.

"I hate hospitals, man! First Josh. Now this. Enough is enough!"

"I feel ya. What time is it?"

Jericho glanced at his watch. "It's five thirty in the morning, man. The next time I pull an all-nighter, it's gonna be for a party!"

"You got that right. Let's kick rocks."

"Naw, man," Jericho said resolutely. "I'm gonna stick around awhile. I gotta see this through."

They stood in front of the elevator. When the door slid open, Brock and Marlene Prescott, along with a man dressed all in beige, stepped out. Kofi got in, but Jericho waved him on and let the elevator leave without him.

"What's up, Uncle Brock?" he asked.

"We've come to check on the baby, Jericho." Brock's unshaven face looked gaunt in the florescent hospital lighting.

"How did you find out so soon?" Jericho asked, glancing at the man in beige.

"Several people who were on the busses called us. It's the kind of news that spreads quickly. Besides, all four local channels have been scrolling the story all night long."

"That's messed up," Jericho said, shaking his head.

"Reporters are having a field day—'Teenage Girl Gives Birth After Football Game! Trauma and Drama on the Side of the Highway'!" Brock explained.

"I had no idea," Jericho said. "So what are you two gonna do, Aunt Marlene?" He noticed that her eyes looked much clearer than the last time he'd seen her.

"I came to see my granddaughter, of course."

Jericho nearly had to jog to keep up with them as they marched purposefully down the hall toward November's room. *They sure didn't waste any time*, he thought.

"Uh, did November ever sign the papers?"

"We had scheduled a meeting with November and her mother for the twenty-first. We had not anticipated that the baby would be premature," said the beige man, who Jericho assumed was the lawyer November had been so upset by.

Jericho knew that November did not need to be dealing with his aunt and uncle today. She had enough to worry about. He thought a moment, then said, "Hey! Have you even seen the baby yet? Why don't you do that first?"

The lawyer turned abruptly. "Excellent idea, young man."

"Where can we find the Nelson baby?" Marlene asked a nurse at the desk. "We're the grandparents," she added proudly. Her fuzziness had long since disappeared now that she had a purpose, Jericho noticed.

"She's in the NICU," the nurse replied. "In critical condition."

"Nick-You?" Jericho asked, his heart thudding at the word "critical."

"That's the Neonatal Intensive Care Unit," the nurse explained. "Sorry, we toss around those acronyms without thinking sometimes."

"Oh, my!" Marlene said, stepping back in surprise. "We

knew the baby was premature, but we had no idea it was this serious."

"The news reports didn't give any of the details," Brock said in confusion.

The nurse gave them directions to the NICU, and they hurried off down the hall, beige lawyer trotting behind them. Even though he really wanted to go outside and breathe fresh air, to get as far away from that antiseptic hospital smell as he could, Jericho went with them.

The nurse at the door wouldn't let them enter the NICU—parents only—but as Brock protested that they were the grandparents, she told them to go over to the glass wall and she'd point out the Nelson baby from inside. Jericho was immensely relieved that they weren't going in.

Each infant lay in what looked like a very complicated plastic box that had wires and tubes and monitors feeding in and out of it. Two round circles had been cut in its sides, and Jericho could see nurses wearing special gloves reaching in to tend to the babies.

He'd never seen so many tiny, helpless creatures. Baby humans. All in distress.

The nurse pointed to the incubator closest to the window. A wrinkled, red baby girl, small enough to fit into the palm of his hand, jerked her legs spasmodically. Her hands were covered with gauze, as were her eyes. A tube, which was taped to her little cheek, had been inserted into her nose. A knitted cap, so tiny it could fit on the end of a cell phone, covered her head. Someone had pasted a pink bow on it. A pink sign, taped to the side of the incubator, said BABY GIRL NELSON.

Marlene gasped. "Oh, my! She's so impossibly tiny!" she whispered.

"She's a very sick child, Marlene," said her husband gently.

"She just needs to get bigger and stronger, right? This is Josh's child—of course she'll be perfect," Marlene replied, hope in her voice.

"It's possible," the lawyer interjected. "But preemies can have a whole host of serious complications."

"I want to talk to a doctor," Brock said, looking up and down the hall.

As they stood gaping at the infants, the door to the unit opened, and, as if he'd heard Brock, a red-haired doctor came out into the hall. He wore light green scrubs, and his face wore a look of compassion. Jericho figured he'd dealt with a lot of worried parents and grandparents, a lot of tears and tragedy.

"May I ask you a couple of questions, Doctor?" Brock said in the deep, authoritative voice that Jericho had grown up with. "We have a new little one in there—our grand-daughter." He smiled at the doctor and shook his hand.

"Sure. I'm Dr. Mitchell. How can I help you?"

"The Nelson baby. I know it's early, but can you tell us her chances?"

"Oh, she just came in here a few hours ago. Her chances of survival? Pretty good. We're very good at keeping them alive." He paused. "I know this is difficult, but I'll be honest with you. Preemies can be amazingly resilient, but there are often complications. Many are fairly minor. Others"—he cleared his throat—"can be much more serious."

Marlene's eyes welled with tears as she pressed herself against the glass that separated her from the baby. Jericho thought his aunt faded a little at that moment, back to that place she had escaped to when Josh died. The lawyer scribbled something on a notepad.

"I'm sorry to be so harsh, but sometimes it helps to understand the risks and possibilities. You can be a great support to the mother, who will need you as she deals with the complications this child may have."

Fat chance of that happening! Jericho thought.

"Can you elaborate, Dr. Mitchell?" asked Brock.

"Well, I hope I'm wrong. I can't see the future, and I've seen things here that could be called miracles, but a premature baby is not merely a small baby—it is an underdeveloped baby. It is not ready to live outside its mother. The younger it is, the more problems it will have."

"Why?" Jericho asked. He felt a stone in his stomach. "She was born in the hospital, not the car. Shouldn't she be okay?"

"Let me explain, son. Are you the father of the child?"

"Me? No way! It was my cousin, Josh," Jericho said quickly. Even the thought of being a father made him start to sweat. He knew he had to get out of that hospital soon. Still, he had to ask, "What kind of problems?"

"Well, let's see. The brain, intestines, and lungs of your little cousin over there are not finished growing. She can't breathe on her own. She can't digest food, or even eat yet, for that matter. Her immune system isn't working, so she is very prone to infections."

"Can't she grow out of all that stuff?" Jericho asked. He felt sick.

"Some of it, perhaps. But this little one didn't breathe when she was born. It was several minutes before she took a breath on her own."

"So what does that mean?" Jericho asked.

"You look like you're an athlete, am I right?"

"Yeah. Football."

"You keep scores in sports, and we do the same for newborns. It's called an Apgar score. It's a little like a grade on a test."

"The kid is just born and already you're giving her tests? That sucks!" said Jericho, trying to lighten the mood a little.

"No spelling tests yet, but we do check things like heart rate and breathing and muscle tone."

"I follow you," Jericho said, his heart beating fast. Marlene, Brock, and the lawyer all leaned forward.

"Well, we take this measurement at one minute after birth, and again at five minutes after the baby is born. A perfectly healthy baby is given a ten, but an eight or nine is acceptable."

"So what did the Nelson baby score?" the lawyer asked.

"At birth her score was one-half. At five minutes it was a one."

Marlene inhaled sharply. No one else spoke. Jericho felt weak.

The doctor continued. "When the brain is deprived of oxygen, those cells that determine intelligence and thought, and even walking and talking, well, they simply die. Although we can't be certain, there's a chance the child may have suffered some significant brain damage."

Jericho bolted down the hall and disappeared.

JERICHO COULDN'T WAIT FOR THE ELEVATOR.
He found the door that indicated the stairs, and he leaped down the cement steps two at a time, his footsteps echoing against the bare gray concrete walls. He didn't even know he was crying until he emerged into the lobby.

Todd ran up to him. "What's wrong, Jericho? Why are you crying?"

"I'm fine, little dude. Give me a minute." Jericho pushed into the closest bathroom, locked himself in a stall, and allowed himself to feel real. Months of anger, sorrow, and tension finally exploded in deep, body-racking sobs. He let it all go. Finally he took a deep breath, blew his nose, and opened the door of the stall. He ran some cold water on his face, squared his shoulders, and went out to face whatever would happen next. This time he felt like he could handle it.

Todd stood by the bathroom door, waiting for him. "I got your back, Jericho. You okay?"

Afraid he'd lose it again, Jericho made a funny face, sniffed, and slapped the boy gently on his back. "You got a little bitty back!" he teased.

"I'll grow," the boy said wisely. "Hey, Jericho, can I ask you something?"

"Yeah, kid, anything."

"Do you think I'm too young to learn how to play the trumpet? Could you teach me? I miss hearing you play."

"As soon as football season is over, let's do that." Jericho put an invisible trumpet to his lips. Todd did the same, and the two brothers grinned at each other as they fingered a silent tune. But Jericho's smile faded as he looked up and saw who was getting out of a car and heading into the lobby. Somehow, Arielle just didn't seem to fit into this picture.

She ran right over to him and hugged him. "Oh, Jericho, this has been so horrible for all of us. How are you handling everything?"

He gave her a strange look, then took her arms from around him. "I'm okay, Arielle. Really. It's November and the baby that we're all worried about."

"I heard the baby might die. Or it might be retarded. Is that true?"

"The baby is pretty sick, but we think she'll pull through." He spoke stiffly.

"How awful to have one of those messed-up kids to deal with the rest of your life. If I was November, I'd just put it in a home and get on with my life."

Jericho looked at Arielle as if he was seeing her for the first time. "Well, I guess it's a good thing you're not November," he said quietly.

"Why are you acting so cold, Jericho?" she asked, a petulant smile on her face. "I want to make up for last time, and show you how supportive I can be in a crisis." She reached for him, but again, he gently pushed her away.

"You're just getting here?" he asked her. "Lots of kids from school have been hanging out in the lobby most of the night—just to be here for her, you know."

"Well, I had to go home and freshen up a bit—you know, do my hair and change clothes." She twirled around so he could see her outfit—tight blue jeans; a gold-stitched, V-neck embroidered sweater that was cut deep enough to show everything beneath it; a low-slung shiny gold belt; and black leather boots.

"You look really nice," he conceded.

She gave him another big hug. "I knew you'd notice!"

Before he could push her away the elevator doors opened, and Dana and Olivia stepped off.

When Jericho saw the pain and disappointment on Olivia's face, his stomach churned and knotted up, and his fists clenched with the need to protect her. She just stood there, staring at Jericho and Arielle, her face so sad he couldn't bear it.

Dana whispered to Olivia, "Let's go out to the parking lot."

Olivia shook her head. "No. I have just as much right to be in this lobby as anybody," she said clearly.

"You sure take up more space than anybody!" Arielle

scoffed as she released Jericho and put her hands on her hips. She turned to look at Olivia directly.

"A solid mass always beats the emptiness of air," Olivia responded, her arms wrapped tightly in front of her chest.

"You're solid, all right. I could fit five pairs of my jeans into one of yours! Not that it matters, though. I'm here for Jericho, who happens to *like* my tight, size two jeans and the cute butt that sits in them!"

"Wait just a minute, Arielle," Jericho interrupted angrily. "Who do you think you are?"

"I'm your girl, Jericho," she said in that voice he usually found so irresistible.

"No. You were never my girl. Everything you ever did was for you, not for me."

"That's not fair!" she said, tossing her curls. "I joined the cheerleaders just so we could spend more time together."

"So I guess you'll be joining the track team next so you can get rides home from practice in Brandon Merri-weather's new BMW!" he said harshly. "Did you think I wouldn't find out?"

By this time a crowd of students had circled around them, and they collectively cried, "Ooh!"

"Brandon's just a friend—he means nothing to me," she retorted, looking directly at Jericho, her eyes imploring. "Can we go outside and talk about this, Jericho? I want to apologize properly." She reached for his hand.

He jerked his hand back. "No, we can't, Arielle. I'm with somebody."

"Who? Dana? She's Kofi's girl. I don't see anybody else

you could possibly be interested in. Certainly not the elephant woman here!" She laughed.

Jericho reached back and grabbed Olivia's hand and
pulled her next to him. He glanced at her and smiled. For
a moment she looked stunned, and then she squeezed his
hand.

"Olivia is more woman than you will ever be, you little
piece of gutter fluff!" Jericho told Arielle, eyeing her
calmly, and suddenly absolutely certain of his feelings.

"Well, you're right about one thing—that's a whole lotta
woman you got there!" She was about to laugh again when
Olivia reached out with her free hand. Arielle tensed.

It looked as if Olivia were about to slap Arielle, but
instead, she took her thumb and middle finger and flicked
Arielle soundly on the nose, as if she was flicking away an
annoying insect. "Bip!" Olivia said lightly. The students
who had watched the whole thing like a television soap
opera cracked up in laughter.

"How *dare* you touch me!" Arielle screamed, seemingly
more embarrassed than hurt.

"I told you I never forget anything," Olivia said quietly.
"Maybe it's a good time for you to go home now."

Arielle looked around, saw no support from anyone in
the lobby, and ran out to the parking lot. No one followed
her.

NOVEMBER PUSHED AWAY THE TRAY OF hospital food. She was sitting up in bed and feeling a little better, but every time she moved another pain assaulted her. *Nobody tells you how bad it HURTS afterward—even just trying to pee!* she thought. *My guts feel like scrambled eggs.* Her mother had brushed her hair and helped her to wash up. November had been touched at the tender way her mom had squeezed the warm washcloth into the basin and gently wiped away the tension from her daughter's face. It was a mother's touch. Would she ever learn that?

"This is worse than school lunch food, Mom," she said as she nibbled on a piece of dry toast.

"For sure this isn't the Ritz," her mother replied.

"The Labor Day fireworks show on the river is tonight," November commented. "I guess I'll miss it."

"They show it on television," her mother offered.

"It's not the same. You gotta be there."

November noticed that once again she and her mother had fallen back into the old habit of not talking about the thing that was screaming loudly in each of their minds. But she couldn't play the game this time. She needed to talk. However, the question she most wanted to ask just wouldn't come out of her mouth. She cleared her throat, opened her mouth, closed it again. But she knew she had to ask.

"Will the baby die, Mom?" she asked finally.

Mrs. Nelson blinked back tears and looked directly at her daughter. "I think she'll live, November. When I talked to the doctors earlier, they seemed to think she'll pull through. She's a tough little cookie."

"I want to see her. All the other mothers on this floor have their babies with them. I've got to see my baby!" She looked among the wrinkled sheets for the nurse call button, but before she could find it, a plump, cheerful-looking nurse wearing an outlandish blond wig bumped through the door pushing a wheelchair.

"Would you like to take a little trip down to the preemie ward to see your daughter?" she said in a booming voice. After all the silence and whispering, this boisterous woman was a pleasant change.

"Oh, yes! It's not going to feel real until I can see her and hold her."

"Well, you can't sit down and hold her in your lap—not just yet at least—but you can touch her. Is that okay?"

November nodded vigorously and eased herself into the wheelchair. Wow! Did it hurt to sit down! She was surprised at how weak and dizzy she still felt. When they got to the neonatal intensive care ward, November was buzzed into the unit. Her mother waited in the hall.

The nurse, whose voice had lowered to a whisper, rolled November over to the baby's incubator. November gasped, not really prepared for the sight. But even though the miniature baby was surrounded by tubes and wires and equipment, November knew she had never seen anything more beautiful.

The baby looked delicate, as if she was made of rosy crinkled paper. Her skin was nearly translucent—November could almost see the little blood vessels beneath it.

"If you put on this gown and these gloves, you can slip your arms through those openings and touch her," the nurse said softly. "Her skin is very thin—that's why she looks so red—but she's tougher than she looks."

November trembled. She could barely get the gloves on. She pulled at them, trying to get two fingers out of the pinky hole. *It looks so easy on those TV medical shows*, she thought. Finally they were on. She took a deep breath, then put her arms into the incubator. As she gently placed her fingertip on the baby's leg, the infant jerked in response. November pulled her hand back in alarm. "Did I hurt her?" she yelped.

"No, honey. She was responding to you. Babies know their mamas."

"Really?" November began to stroke the tiny infant's legs, which kicked vigorously, and her arms, which were no thicker than pencils. As November continued to stroke her, the baby's movements slowed, as if in response to her mother's touch.

This is a real little human person, November thought with reverence. *She was in me, and now she's not. And I'm her mother.* It was almost too much to comprehend.

"Have you named her yet?" the nurse asked, interrupting November's musings. "We like to call the preemies by their names. It helps us to connect with them, and I think even these little ones respond better."

"Her name is Sunshine," said November with tears in her eyes. She couldn't stop touching the child.

Just then, a doctor with a thick head of curly red hair entered the unit and walked over to November. "Hi," he said cordially as he pulled up a chair and sat down next to November. "I'm Dr. Mitchell, chief resident for the NICU ward. You must be the mom of our newest guest here."

"Hi. I'm November Nelson, and I'm not feeling very much like a mom right now," November answered honestly, keeping her hand on the baby.

"You're doing exactly the right thing," said the doctor. "A mother's touch is sometimes the best medicine we have around here." He paused and looked at the baby's chart. November noticed that even his eyelashes and the hair on his arms were pale red.

"How sick is she?" November finally asked bluntly.

"Well, we think you had something called toxemia, also known as pre-eclampsia."

"Huh? Is that contagious? Did I give it to my baby?" November felt frantic.

"No, not at all. It is a dangerous condition that occurs in about five percent of all pregnancies and is characterized by high blood pressure, swelling, headaches, and other symptoms. The elevated blood pressure can reduce the supply of blood to many of your organs, including the placenta, and that can deprive your baby of essential oxygen and nutrients."

"So this is something *I* did?" November felt overwhelmed with guilt. "Maybe I shoulda eaten more oranges like my doctor said. I didn't exercise like she told me to. I ate a few french fries, even after she told me to quit!"

"This is not about a few fries or the lack of an orange. Sometimes, even though we try our best, problems arise in a pregnancy. We cannot control them or prevent them, and I do *not* want you to waste time with what-ifs. Are you hearing me?"

November, trying not to cry, nodded. Then she looked up at the doctor. "Please tell me everything."

"Now you're sounding like a mom," the doctor said encouragingly. Then he continued, "We think your baby, either in the womb or just after delivery, suffered a lack of oxygen. Oxygen is what keeps brain cells alive and thriving, so that is a serious problem, and your little girl might face some challenges in the future because of this."

"Like what?"

"She might have developmental delays, meaning that when other children are learning to walk, she won't be ready yet, and she might have some learning disabilities."

His voice was gentle, but it was cutting November like a razor. Her head, reeling from the list of horrible possibilities, throbbed. "Could you be wrong?" she asked, desperation in her voice.

"Absolutely," Dr. Mitchell said. "As doctors we hate to be wrong, but in your case, I hope I'm way off base and you'll come back in a year and visit me with your fat and healthy little girl giggling and laughing as she runs up and down these halls."

"I gotta believe that's possible," November said quietly.

He put his hand on November's shoulder. "I'm a practitioner of medicine, but I still allow myself to believe in miracles, November. We have no way of knowing what brain cells, if any, were affected. I've seen seriously ill babies in the very space your daughter now lies and been amazed by their remarkable recoveries."

"Thanks for being honest with me," November told him.

He stood up. "For now, let's just get this little one strong enough to go home with you. We've got to get her eating and breathing on her own. What's her name?"

"Sunshine."

"Well, I'll be checking on little Miss Sunshine every hour. If you need to call me at any time, have them page me." He gave November his card as he adjusted some of the dials and monitors on the baby's isolette.

November sat there for a few minutes, absorbing all the doctor had said. As she touched the paper-thin arm of this person who was her daughter, she could not help but think of Josh. *Oh, Josh. Look what we have done.* He seemed so very far away.

The nurse came over then and insisted that November go back to her room and get some rest but promised to let her return later in the day. November reluctantly agreed, but asked, "Can my mom come in now? She's tried for months not to love this baby, but I know she does."

"I understand," the nurse said. As the two of them went out into the hallway, November was shocked to see the Prescotts and Henderson Grant, the lawyer, in deep discussion with her mother. No one looked happy.

"What's going on?" November asked from her wheelchair.

"You're not going to believe this, November," her mother said. "I'll let them tell you."

Mr. Grant spoke first. "I hope you're recuperating well, Miss Nelson," he said, walking over to shake her hand.

"I'm doing okay," November mumbled.

"We've been here all morning, talking to the doctors and trying to assess the condition of the baby," explained the lawyer.

"Why? And what business is it of yours anyway?" November asked bluntly, although she knew exactly what they were up to.

"Well, in light of our previous discussions, we originally came here today with the papers for you to sign so that the Prescotts could take custody of the child when she is released from the hospital." He shifted his weight from one foot to the other. The Prescotts, holding hands and standing near the far wall, were silent.

"So what has changed?" November crossed her arms across her chest, a look of challenge on her face.

"Well, ah, because of the premature birth, and the associated physical problems that can occur with such births, my clients are concerned that, ah . . ." He stopped.

"That the baby will be messed up? Brain damaged? Retarded?" November asked harshly.

"We certainly wouldn't use those, ah, words, but, ah, it seems as if perhaps this decision should be put on hold for a few months until developments become more clear." He wiped his forehead with a beige silk handkerchief.

"So you're telling me that you want to wait a few months to see if the baby will have physical or mental problems, then, if she's perfectly normal, they still want to take the baby from me, but if the baby is messed up, I get to keep her. Am I reading you right?"

"I wouldn't phrase it quite like that. The Prescotts need time to consider how a disabled child would affect their lives." The lawyer looked embarrassed. The Prescotts refused to look at November at all. "You still have the opportunity for a college scholarship and a sizable check, don't forget. If everything works out," he added.

November glanced at her mother, who seemed to know what her daughter was thinking. Both of them smiled.

"Can I see those papers, Mr. Grant?" November asked, reaching out a hand.

"Sure, but it's all just legal talk. You don't need to bother yourself with them right now."

"Yes, I do. Just let me take a look at one thing."

Reluctantly, the lawyer handed her a thin sheaf of papers.

November took the papers and, without glancing at them, ripped the pile in half, and then in half once more. She tossed them on the floor. "Let me tell you something, Mr. Grant. And you, too, Mr. and Mrs. Prescott." Josh's dad put his arm around his wife's shoulder.

"You can't do that!" the lawyer said in dismay as he picked up the papers.

"There's a trash can behind you," November stated. "I will not play games with my daughter's future. I had already decided not to take your money or your scholarship, but now that I see how shallow you really are, there is no way in heaven or hell that I would sign anything that gives custody to people who only want her if she's perfect!"

"We just wanted to make sure," said Josh's mother weakly.

"Life doesn't come with guarantees," November declared, her voice strong. To the lawyer she said, "And if you ever so much as *whisper* the words 'unfit mother' in my presence, I swear I'll turn into one of those mother bears you see on television and tear you to pieces!"

"I consider this matter finished," the lawyer said to November dismissively. He turned to pick up his briefcase.

As he and the Prescotts walked away, Josh's mother turned around and said, "I'm so sorry. Take good care of her." She was crying.

NOVEMBER CURLED UP IN HER FAVORITE chair in her mother's living room, sleepily thumbing through a book on infant care. She had clicked off the television because nothing on those shows—the soap operas, the game shows, the old movies—could match the reality of life. The house, for the moment, was pleasantly peaceful. Her mother wouldn't be home from work for another hour, and Sunshine was finally asleep in the next room.

Today would have been my due date, she thought ruefully. *A nine-month, fully developed, plump, healthy baby. Well, maybe. Instead, Sunshine is already two months old—still delicate and fragile, but alive.*

She switched on the satellite radio, found the blues station, and let the sounds surround her. Heart-thumping rhythms. Soul-grabbing refrains. Melodies of sorrow and joy. If she'd had a box of crayons, only the shades of blue would have worked to visualize what she heard.

She hated to admit it, but her mother had been right about the high cost of everything. Formula, diapers, bottles, the cost of Sunshine's pediatrician—all of it was stretching their budget to the max. And this was just the beginning. November knew she would have to get a job when the baby got a little stronger.

Sunshine had been released from the hospital just two weeks before, so November was still getting used to the new routine. Instead of going to the hospital every day, as she had for the past six weeks, spending hours in the intensive care ward with little Sunshine, November finally had her at home.

But it wasn't easy. Sunshine usually slept only an hour at a time before waking fretful and irritable. She cried most of the night, every night. November, dizzy from lack of sleep, woke every hour to feed the wailing child, and then tried to get her back to sleep. The only thing that worked was to walk with her—up and down the short hallway, into the living room and kitchen, then back to the hall. Every hour. Every night. It usually took about thirty minutes to get her quiet and back to sleep, then November would fall, exhausted, onto her bed, not even bothering to get under the covers. An hour later Sunshine would be up crying once more. The nurse had warned her this would happen—Sunshine's stomach was so tiny she could only take in a small amount of formula at each feeding, so she got hungry again really quickly.

It wasn't like this in the hospital, November thought as she patted the wailing baby on the back one black morning at three a.m. It seemed as though Sunshine had slept more when she was there. But then November realized that she had never seen the baby's night routine. *Maybe this is what the night nurses went through. I gotta send them a card or something! How do they do it?*

November also had to bring Sunshine to see the doctor once a week. Yesterday's visit had been a nightmare. November was still reeling. Sunshine, instead of acting like her name, had performed like a true thunderstorm. She didn't just cry, she screamed—from the moment they arrived at the doctor's office through the entire examination. Other mothers looked at November with obvious disapproval on their faces as November tried in vain to quell the baby's tantrum.

"Is something hurting her, Mom?" November asked helplessly, walking the baby in the small waiting room. "I don't think she's hungry, and she's not wet," November added, as she slipped her finger under Sunshine's diaper.

"Maybe she has a tummy ache. Let me have her." Mrs. Nelson took the baby and hugged her closely while she rocked and hummed, but Sunshine, her face red and blotchy from exertion, continued to wail.

"Sunshine Nelson," the nurse called finally. November gently took the screaming baby from her mother and hurried to the examining room in the back, avoiding eye contact with the other mothers, whose babies gurgled and played quietly while they waited to be called.

Sunshine screamed while they waited for the doctor, screamed while she was being undressed, screamed while the doctor weighed and examined her, and continued without stopping while November got her dressed again. November had developed a pounding headache.

"Well, it's clear her lungs are working fine," Dr. Emory said.

"Why won't she calm down?" November asked. "Am I doing something wrong?"

"I don't think she likes me," said Dr. Emory with a smile. "Seriously, this is probably a good thing. Your daughter has strong opinions and does not like to be out of her comfort zone. This is a strange place, and we poke her and prod her and stick her. I don't really blame her," she said over the baby's continued protesting yells.

"She cries a lot at home, too," November admitted. "She doesn't sleep much."

"She's so tiny she needs to eat often, so I'm not concerned about her frequent waking right now. Does she go back to sleep after you feed her?"

"Eventually. But sometimes it takes a long time."

"I bet you could use about eight hours' uninterrupted deep sleep, right?" the doctor asked as she looked in the baby's ears.

November exhaled. "My mom says I don't get that for the next eighteen years!"

"Your mom is very wise." The doctor scribbled notes on Sunshine's chart, which was already thick from all her hospital data.

"How is Sunshine doing?" November asked.

"Physically, I'm very pleased. She's gained seven ounces since last week and her heartbeat and respiration are right on track. Her stitches from where we removed the feeding tube have healed nicely. Her muscle tone is still a little weak, however, and her sucking reflex is not what I'd like it to be, but we're taking one day at a time, and today looks good. I'll see the both of you next Wednesday."

As soon as November and her mother placed the baby back in the car seat, which had been a gift from Jericho, Sunshine took a deep breath, burped, and promptly fell fast asleep.

The phone rang, breaking the silence. November snatched it up on the first ring. She didn't want to wake the sleeping baby. It was Dana.

"How's it going, little mama?" Dana asked.

"Better every day. The doctors took the feeding tube out last week, and she's doing pretty good at learning how to suck from a bottle."

"Babies have to learn that?"

"Sunshine does. She has a special little bottle that helps her—like training wheels on a bike, only this is a specially designed bottle. And she only needs the oxygen at night, just as a precaution."

"And you do it all yourself? The medicine, learning how to work a feeding tube and a breathing machine?"

"I guess it's just like a new job. You learn the equipment and do the best you can."

"What's the hardest part?" Dana asked.

"Not sleeping. You know how I *love* cuddling in my bed with six pillows and staying there for twelve hours. Well, I used to." November laughed. "But she needs to be fed every hour and a half, and when she's not asleep, she cries. She doesn't just cry—she screams."

"Really? Is she in pain or something?"

"No. The doctor told me it was just irritability and she'd

grow out of it. But she cries and cries and cries. Sometimes I want to scream!"

"I don't blame you! When you feed her, does that help?"

"Yeah, for a minute. Then she sleeps for maybe half an hour. But she wakes up and starts crying again. Sometimes she cries for a solid hour. You should have seen her at the doctor yesterday. It was embarrassing! I rock her and walk with her and even sing to her. Nothing helps. Eventually she gets tired and falls asleep, but by then she's hungry and the whole cycle starts again." November rubbed her eyes and stretched. "I'm *so* tired."

"That's really rough, girl. Do you feel like a mom?" Dana asked curiously.

"I haven't really thought about it. I just kinda do what she needs—I even know what she's gonna need ahead of time. I guess that's what a mom does. What's going on at school?"

"Not much. Hathaway forgot she was human and assigned us a forty-page research paper."

"I'll never catch up!" November groaned. She hadn't been back to school since Sunshine had been born. Since the baby had such serious complications, she'd had no choice but to stay home and care for her. She worried that she might lose her entire senior year. Graduation looked unlikely. She shook the thought away. "So tell me more about school. I can't believe I miss it!" she told Dana.

"Well, Eric Bell—you know, the kid in the wheelchair? He's trying out for the school play. He thinks he should have the lead in *Macbeth*, in spite of his disability."

"Good for him. I hope he gets the part. What about Arielle? Wasn't she the superstar of the drama club last year? The part of Lady Macbeth, the killer queen, really fits her!" November laughed.

"I don't know if she's trying out or not. But our Miss Arielle has had big troubles lately. Brandon Merriweather broke up with her. She got kicked off the cheerleading squad for not showing up to practice. And she just plain got dissed in the main hall before class. I almost felt sorry for her. Almost."

"What happened?" November asked as she got up, walked over to her mother's bedroom door, and peeked at the sleeping baby, who was surrounded by a circle of sofa pillows on her mother's bed.

"Girl, it was too funny! It was first thing in the morning. You know how crowded the main hall is before the bell rings."

"Yeah," November said, remembering with a pang the noisy confusion. "So what did she do?"

"Well, she had gone to the bathroom when she first got to school, and I guess she left out of there too quickly." Dana started to laugh.

"What?" November couldn't imagine.

"From what I could figure out, she must have been in a hurry. She rushed out of the bathroom in her cute little outfit, and dragging behind her, tucked in the waistband of her new leather jeans, was a long, slightly soiled length of toilet paper! It looked like a long, white tail."

"Girl, shut up!" November couldn't help but giggle.

"She was flouncing around like she always does, flirting with everybody else's boyfriend, making sure everybody saw her new jeans, when people started to laugh. It got louder and louder, with everybody in the whole main hall,

mostly seniors, cracking up and pointing. She couldn't figure out what was going on."

"You're kidding!"

"I'm straight up! Finally somebody told her to turn
around, and she saw the toilet paper. She screamed and
ran back into the bathroom. People were laughing so hard
they were rollin' on the floor."

"That's really cold." November was still chuckling.

"I think if it had been anybody else, a friend or somebody would have taken her aside and told her quietly."

"I guess what goes around comes around," said November.

"When she got to physics class the next day, somebody
had placed an unopened four-pack of toilet paper on her
desk."

"Oh, no! What did she do?"

"She tried to act like it didn't bother her. She just put it
under her seat and pretended it wasn't there. But kids still
giggled behind her back. The teacher asked what was so
funny—you know how teachers get that clueless look. But
nobody would tell."

"That's the best story I've heard in a long time,"
November said, still laughing. Then she heard the doorbell
ring. "Hey, I gotta go. Somebody's at my door. Will you call
me back tonight?"

"Sure. I got rehearsal for the debate team anyway, and
me and Kofi are on the committee to plan the Christmas
Dance. But I'll catch you later."

November thought longingly of all the school activities she
was missing, but there was nothing to be done about it now.
She hung up and went to answer the door, then grinned when

she saw who it was. Jericho stood there, stomping his feet on the porch, and Olivia, wearing a puffy down jacket, stood behind him. She carried a plastic bag from Target.

"You tryin' to freeze somebody out here?" Jericho joked as he walked in the door. "It feels like winter already." He was carrying a small foil-covered bowl and a leather case.

"Hi, November," Olivia said quietly as she walked in with him. She took off her coat and laid it carefully on a chair. "How's Miss Sunshine? She could warm up any day."

"She's growing, and eating, but still crying a lot. More than normal, I think."

"That's what babies do, right?"

"Not like this. But guess what?" November said as she took their coats.

"What?"

"Yesterday she smiled at me for the first time!" November almost danced as she told her. Olivia hugged her.

"That's a good sign," Jericho said. "Real good."

"How's football?" November asked Jericho.

"We won the last two games! And I heard a couple of college scouts have been taking a look at me."

"That's great. No more pink games?"

Jericho laughed. "No. The company replaced those funky uniforms, so none of our games have been quite so colorful."

"You didn't tell November that a recruiter from Juilliard has also talked to you," Olivia reminded Jericho, her voice full of pride.

"Yeah, well. I guess I got lotsa options!" He grinned and pretended to swagger around the room. "And he hasn't even heard me play yet! Mr. T put in a good word for me, so I guess I better get it together before the audition next month."

"That's great news, Jericho," November told him enthusiastically. "What about the band, Olivia? How's that going?"

"It's not as much fun marching when it gets cold, but the season is almost over." She looked at Jericho shyly and added, "But after the games sometimes me and Jericho go get pizza. That's pretty cool." She looked pleased and embarrassed all at the same time.

Then she switched gears and asked about the baby again. "Is she awake? I brought her another outfit." She handed November the Target bag.

"Girl, that child has more clothes than I do, thanks to you. You don't know how much it meant when you brought all those baby gifts that you collected from the kids at school."

"No sweat," Olivia said, brushing off the compliment. "So where's my girl?"

"She should be up soon."

"Hey, Geneva sent you some of her homemade chili. It's delicious," Jericho told her as he placed the bowl on the kitchen table. "Why do women think they have to send food all the time?"

"She probably figured if she didn't give it away you'd eat it all!" November joked. The three of them laughed.

"Probably so." Jericho sat on the sofa, exhaling deeply as he sank down. Olivia went and sat next to him—not touching, but close. She looked ridiculously happy.

"That's some nice music you've got playing," Olivia said as she relaxed into the sofa cushions. "I like the blues." She closed her eyes.

November nodded. "I used to think it was dumb, old-timey music. Maybe you gotta deal with some stuff before you can really feel the blues." She looked at Olivia, and the two girls exchanged knowing glances.

"Mellow," Jericho said as the harmonies surrounded them.

"I see you brought your trumpet," November observed, pointing to the leather case Jericho had in his hand.

He rubbed his hand across the dull sheen of the leather. "I polished it up last night. The case and the horn," he added.

"I'm glad you got it out again," Olivia told him.

"Yeah, I been hiding from the music for way too long." Jericho slowly pulled the gleaming instrument out of its case. "Do you think it would bother the baby if I play?" he asked November.

"I think she likes music," November replied. "I bought her a couple of those classical CDs and she seems to quiet down when they're on. Music is one of the few things that stops her crying."

Just then the baby whimpered. November jumped up and ran to the next room, picking up her daughter carefully. After changing her diaper and wrapping her in a soft yellow blanket, November came back into the living room, the tiny infant's head barely peeking out of the blanket.

"Hey, Miss Sunshine," Olivia said softly. "You look pretty in yellow."

"Looks like she's grown since we saw her last," said Jericho.

"She's a full five pounds, one ounce now," November stated proudly.

"What's the latest from the doctors?" Olivia asked.

"We won't really know if she'll have any problems for a while, at least. Her hearing and eyesight seem to be fine, so there's at least that to be thankful for. Her doctor told me that if she doesn't roll over, or try to sit up, or try to grab for things in the next few months, then she'll be a little concerned. But right now we have hope."

November warmed a tiny bottle of milk and fed Sunshine while the three friends sat in the living room, listening to the soft blues music. The baby gave a soft burp and smiled at November as she rocked her. No one said much. The baby did not cry.

Jericho got up off the sofa, looked at November to see if she minded, and turned off the radio. He put his trumpet to his lips, then brought it down. "This song is for Sunshine," he told them.

He picked up his horn, inserted the mute, and, ever so smoothly, began to play. Bright sweet notes flowed from the instrument, clear and pure. He played his own kind of blues—a soulful version of a song they'd all learned in grade school, "You Are My Sunshine."

November hummed along as she rocked her baby girl, her baby girl with the shaky future.

You are my sunshine,
My only sunshine.
You make me happy
When skies are gray.
You'll never know, dear,
How much I love you.
Please don't take my sunshine away.